RESTLESS SPIRITS

OTHER BOOKS FROM JORDAN L. HAWK:

Hainted

Whyborne & Griffin:
Widdershins
Threshold
Stormhaven
Necropolis
Bloodline

SPECTR
Hunter of Demons
Master of Ghouls
Reaper of Souls
Eater of Lives
Destroyer of Worlds
Summoner of Storms

Short stories:
Heart of the Dragon
After the Fall (in the *Allegories of the Tarot* anthology)
Eidolon (A Whyborne & Griffin short story)
Remnant, written with KJ Charles (A Whyborne & Griffin / Secret Casebook of Simon Feximal story)
Carousel (A Whyborne & Griffin short story) in the *Another Place in Time* anthology

RESTLESS SPIRITS

Spirits Book 1

JORDAN L. HAWK

JLH

ISBN: 978-1505557107

This book is a work of fiction. Names, characters, places, and incidents are products of the author's imagination or are used fictitiously. Any resemblance to actual events or locales or persons, living or dead, is entirely coincidental.

Edited by Annetta Ribken

PROLOGUE

THE COLD bit deeper than any Vincent had ever endured, beyond a night spent out in the snow or the sting of wind through a threadbare jacket. This was the cold of the grave, of something buried a thousand years in permafrost or shut away in a tomb untouched by the sun for centuries.

His eyes felt as though they'd been gummed shut; it took effort to peel them open. Broken glass glistened beside him on a polished wooden floor. Rain blew in through the shattered window, soaking his skin and clothes. The flavor in his mouth was beyond horrible: river slime and rot, blood and wet bone. But the taste already faded, shifting from reality to lingering memory, the presence which had caused it now departed.

Every muscle, every fiber, ached as if he'd been beaten. Had he? Recollection fluttered at the edge of his cold-numbed mind, but he couldn't quite grasp it. Did he drink too much gin or let some stranger talk him into going back to a room in an attempt to get out of the weather, even at the risk of his life?

No. Those days were long over. Gone. He remembered now.

Where was he?

The taste—there'd been a spirit present. Had he channeled it during a séance?

Vincent tried to sit up, to take stock of his surroundings, but his body refused to obey. Exhaustion hollowed out his bones, the vital spark of his existence drained almost to the point of flickering out. His tired heart labored as panic crept in—what had happened to him?

"Lizzie?" he tried to ask, but his tongue was too sluggish to form the words.

No, wait. She hadn't been with them. He'd come here, wherever *here* was, with Dunne. To remove a poltergeist. Or what they'd thought was a poltergeist.

Memory offered up an icy laugh and a patch of darkness, of shadow cast independent of any light source. A touch, gelid and glutinous, not on skin but on his very soul. The flavor of slime and decay.

What had happened? Where was Dunne?

His mentor wouldn't have left him. Wouldn't have abandoned either Vincent or Lizzie. But the room around him was quiet, except for the tap of rain and the sigh of the wind.

Vincent managed to turn his head. Broken furniture, shattered glass, bedding hauled off a frame and ripped to shreds, its down stuffing covering the sodden floor like unseasonable snow.

Why was he so cold?

Dunne would know. Vincent just had to find him.

With a monumental effort, he gathered what little strength he had left and rolled onto his side, away from the window.

Dunne's face lay inches from his. Glassy eyes stared at the ceiling, and a congealed line of blood leaked from his nose.

Dead.

Vincent opened his mouth to scream, but no sound came out.

CHAPTER 1

"How are the readings?" Jo asked. The Wimshurst machine whirred merrily as she cranked it, arcs of electricity cracking and snapping along its metal brushes. "Are we getting close? Because my arm is going to drop off if this takes much longer."

Henry Strauss pushed his spectacles higher on his nose and checked the galvanometer. "Don't stop yet. We must make certain the air is sufficiently charged for a spirit to manifest." Exactly what voltage might achieve such a result, he wasn't entirely certain, not having a spirit to actually test the device on. But he wasn't about to admit it to Jo. Ever since she'd found the error in his calculations last month, she'd been even more insufferable than usual—and, given her age of sixteen, she was quite insufferable enough already.

The scent of ozone competed with the workshop's reek of grease and machine oil. Henry let the needle creep up the dial just a bit more. "There—keep cranking! If there were a spirit about, it would have enough energy to manifest, even without the presence of a medium."

"Then why can't I stop?"

Did she have to question everything? If he'd known what he was getting into when she showed up on his doorstep…

Well, he still would have taken her in. But he might have stocked up on scotch ahead of time.

"Because if the Electro-Séance is to work properly, we must be able to dismiss any troublesome spirits as necessary. Altering the conductivity of the air to prevent them from gathering the energy to manifest is one means of doing so. Without a ghost, the charge from the Wimshurst machine will have to substitute."

"I'll have to get a job with a sideshow," Jo complained. "See the woman whose cousin made her work until her arm fell off."

"You're not a woman, you're a girl," Henry corrected absently. "And it would have to be the no-armed woman, because I'll just have you crank with the other one."

"Such familial love."

Henry checked the misting machine a final time. Everything was in place: the Leyden jar battery, the piezoelectric crystal, the bowl of water. Holding his breath, he attached the battery to the wire running to the crystal. Within moments, a fine mist began to rise from the dispeller as the vibrations from the crystal vaporized the water.

"Look at the fog—the dispeller is working!" The note of excitement in Jo's voice made Henry grin. Despite her complaints, she had all the makings of a first-rate scientist or inventor. Assuming the twin barriers of her gender and race would allow such a thing.

Henry put aside the familiar twinge of worry for Jo's future. "Let's not get ahead of ourselves," he cautioned. "It's operational, but not 'working' unless it removes the electrical charge from the air."

His eyes remained fixed on the galvanometer as the atmosphere grew increasingly humid. The dial twitched, dipped—and began to fall steadily. "Yes! Stop cranking!"

"At last!"

Henry ignored her. The galvanometer continued to show a decrease, soon reaching normal readings. Everything had worked just as he predicted. "It's done, Jo. With these devices, we'll be able to summon and dismiss a spirit through science alone. The Electro-Séance is complete!"

"Wonderful!" Jo clapped her hands in delight. Her tightly curled hair—inherited from her mother, who had also gifted her with caramel skin and dark brown eyes—had come half out of its bun. Sweat dampened her blouse despite the winter chill of the workshop. "And just in time. Will you present your findings to the Psychical Society tonight?"

"Yes." He scooped up his notes and diagrams from the table, sorting them into some semblance of order. "They may have scoffed at my proposals during previous meetings, but they can't ignore today's success. And once I have their backing, I can attract investors." Perhaps even buy a shop in a better part of Baltimore, one with a sound roof and walls that didn't let in the winter wind. Or even a small house, so they no longer had to live out of the rooms in the back.

Buoyed up by his dreams of the future, he turned to her with a grin. "Mark my words, my girl, soon you and I will be sipping champagne with the best minds on the East Coast!"

"Sorry, old chum," Arthur Burwell said a few hours later. He downed his whiskey in one swallow and signaled the bartender for more. "The society is nothing but a bunch of dunderheads."

Henry sighed and stared at his own glass of whiskey. They sat in a small saloon, not far from the house where the Psychical Society held its monthly meetings. At least the whiskey served here wouldn't eat a hole in his stomach, as opposed to the cheap rotgut that was all he could normally afford. "I know. But it's hard not to be discouraged. I was certain they couldn't ignore me this time."

Arthur clapped him on the shoulder. "I know you, Henry. Nothing keeps you down for long."

Henry didn't speak to the obvious lie in the statement. *Down* was the direction Henry had been going for a long time. He and Arthur had been boyhood friends, raised in neighboring houses, their parents fast friends.

Arthur's world had remained intact. His suit was of good quality, tailored nicely to his figure. The pocket watch he checked every few minutes was new, not purchased from a secondhand shop. He'd recently married a woman of slightly higher social standing, though not so much as to make the match scandalous, and they expected their first child before winter's end.

When everyone else had abandoned Henry, Arthur had remained his friend. He'd even paid for Henry's membership to the Psychical Society, a fee out of Henry's reach even before Jo appeared on his doorstep.

"It's just…I know I have something to offer the world," Henry said. He picked up his whiskey and swirled it around the glass. "Something to make people's lives better. But the world doesn't seem to care."

"They just don't see the advantage," Arthur said. "Why worry about wires and batteries when any decent medium can do the same with half the fuss?"

Henry glared at his drink. "Don't speak to me of mediums. Ninety-nine out of a hundred are frauds, bilking the desperate. Society looks the other way at their licentious behavior, which only gives them further power to take advantage—" He caught himself before his voice rose too sharply. "Machines are dependable. Consistent. Just as the imperfect weaver has been replaced by the textile mill, the Electro-Séance will replace mediums."

"I'm sure it will," Arthur said. Always the friend. "Perhaps you should look elsewhere. Wasn't some preacher denouncing spiritualism in the papers again last week, accusing mediums of promoting fornication and sodomy? Surely his sort would prefer to see them replaced by wires and batteries."

"His sort would prefer to see them replaced by nothing at all," Henry said gloomily. "They deny ghosts exist and claim any spirit visitation is a trick of the mind or Satan. But that isn't true. The dead do return. I know what I saw."

"Of course," Arthur said soothingly. "I never doubted it, you know that. Is there anything more I can do?"

"No." Henry stared at the shelves behind the bar, lined with bottles, the liquids inside glowing a soft gold or brown in the gaslight. "All I need is a genuine haunting to test the apparatus. It would not only prove my theories, but the measurements on the spirit would give me an idea of what needs to be done to conduct an ordinary séance."

"I'm afraid the only spirits I have for you are at the bottom of this glass," Arthur said with a grin. He clinked his glass against Henry's. "Don't give up. The society will come around eventually."

Henry tossed back his whiskey. It burned going down, like golden fire. "The Psychical Society can go to the devil, if he'll have them. I don't need their support. I'll manage on my own if I must."

"Of course you will," Arthur said, but the look on his face was one of pity. "Good night, Henry. I'll call on you soon."

The cold had deepened in the brief time they'd spent inside the saloon. Henry hunched his shoulders and huddled into his overcoat, wishing his gloves were a bit thicker and better insulated. Still, he was far better off than some of the wretches he'd seen near the waterfront. He had his repair shop, and clothes and food for himself and Jo.

Maybe he should leave off his researches into the spirit world. Concern himself with other avenues of invention less likely to be met with such a wall of skepticism and disdain. But how could he, when he was so close?

He needed something to settle his mind tonight. There were men with whom he might find…well, not companionship, but release. A few quick moments in an alley with another man's hand on his prick would clear away the disappointment of the evening.

Or result in a different sort of disappointment. His last few such encounters had left him feeling more depressed than relaxed.

Perhaps it came from seeing Arthur married and happy. What would it be like to have such companionship? Someone who cared about him, who wanted more than an anonymous hand or mouth in an alley?

Henry tipped his head back as he walked. The stars shone in all their glory, cold and sharp as they always seemed in winter. Sunday would mark the beginning of a new year.

A new year. A new start. Surely something would happen, something would change, and he could finally reclaim his place in the world. Be the man he would have become if things had happened differently.

Something would change. It had to.

Vincent squinted in the early light reflecting from the waters of the East River. The amulet he'd worn every instant for the last six months trembled against his chest, like a medal for failure rather than bravery. He wasn't due in the shop yet. He could put this off, come back in a few hours. Delay the inevitable.

"Morning, Sitting Bull!" the grocer called from across the street.

Vincent ground his teeth together but pasted on a smile before turning to the grocer. The "joke" hadn't been funny the first time, but it was better than the old routine of asking him if he'd scalped anyone yet today.

"Good morning, sir," he said as pleasantly as possible before unlocking the shop. The sign, still bearing the legend *Dunne & Apprentices, Occult Emporium*, creaked in the morning wind as if laughing at him.

He slipped inside, leaving the placard turned to "closed." He peered through the dark storefront, the windows shrouded in velvet draperies. "Lizzie?" he called, feeling his way across the room. Despite having worked at the shop for years, in the dimness he managed to bark his shin against the table where Lizzie wrote the messages she received from spirits.

He bit back a curse—Lizzie disapproved of swearing—and groped his way to the book displays. "Lizzie?" he shouted again. "Are you awake?"

The steps leading up to the apartment above creaked. "If I hadn't been, I certainly would be now, Mr. Night."

They'd known one another since they were fifteen. Lizzie addressing him as "Mr. Night" was the precise opposite of a good sign. He waited until she came into view, just a shadow on the steps, dressed in flowing draperies.

"Happy New Year?" he tried.

The gas lamp at the foot of the stairs flared to life, leaving him squinting yet again. "It's January second," she said icily.

"Oh, is it?"

He tried to avoid the glare of her green eyes, a task made more difficult since they were on a level with his own. "Yes. It is. We had an appointment on the first. Last night."

His heart beat harder. "It must have slipped my mind."

Her glare deepened, and for a moment he almost thought she might strike him. He even half hoped she would, because he'd damned well known exactly where he was supposed to be last night.

And he'd tried. God, he'd tried. He'd walked halfway to the house. *"An easy job,"* Lizzie had said. A simple séance, meant to contact the spirit of a small girl who had drowned on the same day last year.

It was always easier for spirits to return on the anniversary of their death—something about it strengthened their connection to this side of the veil. Meaning less energy needed to be drawn from the medium. It wasn't a hard job at all, the sort of thing he'd been able to do within six months of becoming Dunne's apprentice.

A gentle young spirit, innocent, who'd doubtless want to give comfort to her family. Surely he could manage *that* much at least.

But it still meant allowing the spirit to use him as a channel between worlds. To let it control him, however briefly. And he'd found himself standing on the street, shaking too hard to take another step. The memory of Dunne's unmoving body, of the taste of rot and slime, flooded his mind and blotted out everything else.

He'd run all the way back to his little apartment, salted the door and windows, and spent the rest of the night clutching the thin protection of the amulet meant to keep any spirit from possessing him.

Now Lizzie took another step toward him. "I don't think you understand what you've done." She bit out each word as if chewing them in her rage.

He stared at the occult journals for sale in the corner. Half of them were rubbish, but clients loved them. "I'm sorry I forgot. Did you do a bit of spirit writing for them?"

"Yes, but it wasn't what they wanted." Lizzie stepped closer yet again, the hem of her skirt brushing against his boots. "It wasn't what they paid for. They won't be coming back, and they'll tell their friends to avoid us as well. Do you *want* to end up on the streets again?"

"Lizzie—"

"Don't you 'Lizzie' me!" She jabbed a finger into his chest hard enough to make him wince. "I've tried to be patient. I have. But this business can't survive if I'm the only one doing any work."

"I work," he objected.

"Sweeping the floors? Straightening the displays? Posting flyers around town?" She turned from him in disgust. "I can hire any urchin off the street to do the same thing at a fraction of the price."

He took a deep breath, but couldn't argue with her. "Maybe you should."

"We might have made something of this store. Made Dunne proud." Lizzie sank into the chair at her reading table, staring into the crystal ball perched on its brass stand. "Instead, we've let everything he built fall apart."

Vincent wanted to close his eyes, but if he did, he'd only see Dunne's lifeless face. Instead he sat across from Lizzie, in the client's chair. "Not we. Me. I'm the one to blame."

"We're going to lose the shop—*his* shop—if something doesn't change."

"I know. I'm sorry."

"I don't want you to be sorry—I want you to be the way you were! Vincent Night, medium extraordinaire. Able to sense a spirit even when it didn't want to communicate. The best conduit we'd ever seen." She sighed and gave him a sad look. "I know this is hard, Vincent. But you can't just pretend you're not a medium any more."

He resisted the urge to touch his amulet through his shirt, if only to reassure himself it was still there. "I'm not."

She rose to her feet. He started to stand as well, but she signaled for him to stay put. Going to the counter, she shuffled some papers, then returned and laid a single sheet of paper on the table. "This came on Saturday. Read it."

Now deeply confused, he picked up the letter. The paper was of good quality, heavy and thick, and bore a crest at the top.

Dear Miss Devereaux,

Allow me to introduce myself. I am Dominic Gladfield, of Syracuse, New York. My niece, Miss Wilma Prandle, recently visited your shop concerning the matter of a missing will.

Vincent vaguely recalled Miss Prandle. "She had part of the will, yes?

But a page had been lost?"

Lizzie nodded. "Correct." In addition to automatic writing, Lizzie had a talent for psychometry. Objects spoke to her of those who had once used them, allowing her to find the page easily enough.

I'm sure it will come as no surprise for you to learn that the missing page was in the precise location you named. Wilma is very impressed by your work and has championed you to me for a small experiment I wish to conduct.

"Experiment?" Vincent asked.

"Keep reading."

I find myself in possession of an older house in upstate New York. While uninhabited for some time, the building is sound and could profitably be converted into a luxury resort to rival those in Newport. There is, however, one small problem. The house is haunted.

I recently encountered a gentlemen who proposed the novel idea that science, specifically the branch concerned with electromagnetism, can replace the medium in the matter of spirit communication and the laying of troublesome ghosts. He assures me his Electro-Séance will transform your industry, if I may term it so.

Naturally such a challenge can only be met on the field. To that end, I have a proposal. If you are agreeable, you and any assistants will join me at the haunted property on January 9th. I will send train tickets and arrange for all transportation. The scientific gentleman and his assistants will do the same, and my niece, my valet, and I will join you. There we will pit machine against medium, science against spiritualism. Whichever of you is able to successfully exorcise the house will receive a reward of $500.00 and my continued patronage.

If this is agreeable to you, please wire as soon as you receive this letter, and I will set things in motion.

Yrs Truly,

Dominic Gladfield

CHAPTER 2

HENRY STARED at the letter he held in his trembling hands.

"Jo?" he said; his voice cracked slightly.

She looked up from the velocipede whose bearings she'd been greasing. A strand of hair flopped across her forehead, and she'd managed to get grease all over the front of her heavy canvas apron. "What? Is something wrong?"

He held out the letter. "Could you read this and make certain I'm not hallucinating?"

Frowning, she wiped her hands on a rag before taking the letter. Her brows drew together—then a joyful smile transformed her face as she reached the end.

"I can't believe it!" she squealed, flinging her arms around him. "Five hundred dollars! This is incredible!"

Henry returned her hug. Finally, someone had listened! He'd spoken briefly with Gladfield after the November meeting of the Psychical Society—if he recalled correctly, the man had been a visiting friend of the society president. But he'd had no idea Gladfield had truly considered Henry's project worthwhile.

"I'll wire him right away." Henry grabbed Jo's hands, and they danced around in a circle, both of them laughing like idiots. "We have only a week. We must start our preparations immediately." Some of their equipment was delicate and would need to be carefully packed. They'd have to arrange a wagon to haul it to the rail station. And of course he'd have to close up the shop—but what of it? When he returned, he'd have five hundred dollars in his pocket and a wealthy patron. "The Psychical Society will be sorry they ever scoffed at me, once Strauss's Electro-Séance is in every parlor in America!"

Jo sobered slightly. "What about the medium, though?"

"What of her?" Henry waved a dismissive hand. "She's sure to be a fraud. She can perform as many tricks as she likes, but won't be able to exorcise the ghost."

Jo bit her lip. "Are you sure? What if the medium is real? Or tricks Mr. Gladfield somehow?"

"Hmm." He regarded her thoughtfully. "You have an excellent point, Jo. Successful charlatans must be devious to hide their lies. Such duplicity would eventually be exposed, but it might take some time, depending on the nature of the haunting."

"And if she isn't a fraud?"

Henry snorted. "Oh, I don't deny there are some mediums who genuinely channel the spirits of the dead. But even then, their methods will never be as reliable as those offered by science. And the chances of this one being genuine are slim indeed, given the number of fakes drawn to the profession."

Jo pursed her mouth. "Why do you think that is? I mean, that there are so many charlatans."

"Easy money, swindled from the grieving at their most vulnerable," he replied. And of course the very nature of a séance—a group of persons sitting around in the dark, holding hands, legs brushing beneath the table—meant a certain relaxation in standards of behavior, which some found irresistible. But he wasn't about to mention that part to Jo.

She only nodded. "Right. Can you find out who she is?"

"I'll ask when I wire." He chewed on his lower lip in thought. "But unless she's famous, what will it tell me? A week isn't enough time to delve into anyone's past, especially if she doesn't live in Baltimore. Even if she does, we have our own preparations to make."

Jo's eyes shone. "Hire a detective!"

"Hire a—Jo." He regarded her sternly. "Have you been reading dime novels again?"

Her blush confirmed it. "They're exciting."

"A bit too exciting, I'd say," he muttered. "Besides, how would I afford a detective?"

Unless…would Arthur lend him the money? And for once it would be a loan, not a gift. As soon as Henry had the five hundred dollars in prize money, he'd pay Arthur back. And if he walked into the haunted house with proof of the medium's fraud already in his pocket, winning would be a certainty.

Henry hastened to the coat rack and pulled on his overcoat. "Lock up behind me, and don't answer the door," he said automatically. When Jo had first come to live with him, he'd tried leaving her to mind the shop while he ran errands. Unfortunately, he'd quickly come to realize callers would make propositions to Jo they would never have dreamed of making to a white girl. After thrashing one of the devils, and nearly ending up hauled in by the police for his trouble, he'd given up on keeping the shop open when he wasn't present. Jo's safety was far more important than any amount of lost commerce.

"Where are you going?" Jo asked as she followed him to the door.

"First to the telegraph office," he replied, scooping up his hat. "And second to call on an old friend."

"Oh." She regarded him uncertainly. "Maybe I shouldn't have hugged you. You have grease all over your clothes."

"Five hundred dollars," Lizzie said as Vincent lowered the letter slowly to the table. "Five. Hundred. Dollars."

He tried to read the words again, but his hands shook too badly. He dropped the paper between them. "It's…a lot of money."

Money which could make all of the difference. Save the shop. Dunne's shop.

But a haunted house…

"I can't even bring myself to channel the spirit of a harmless little girl." There. The words were out. "And you expect me to go to a haunted house?"

She leaned back in her chair and regarded him steadily until he looked away. "We don't know the circumstances of the haunting."

Vincent reflexively touched the amulet, the silver a hard disk beneath the soft cotton of his shirt. "We know it's bad enough the place is uninhabitable. I can't, Lizzie."

"You can." She remained silent until he turned his gaze back to her. She sat with her long fingers folded in front of her, an unyielding expression on her face. "Don't hide from your gifts, Vincent. It's the last thing Dunne would have wanted."

"I'm pretty sure the last thing he wanted was for me to stop strangling him," Vincent snapped. "He didn't get that wish, either."

Lizzie flinched as if he'd slapped her. But her implacable gaze remained pinned on him. "You didn't kill him. The ghost did."

"Wearing my skin." He rose to his feet, the chair clattering behind him. "What if it happens again? Dunne is *dead.* Do you think he'd want you to risk ending up the same?"

"Of course not." She finally looked away, shoulders slumping. "But he'd want you to learn from the experience, not lock yourself away from life."

"You don't know what he'd want." He went to the window and stared out at the street beyond, because it was easier than seeing her disappointment. "You haven't been able to contact him, have you?"

"I haven't tried."

Surprise caused him to glance over his shoulder at her. "You haven't? I would have thought…don't you want to hear from him? One last message?"

"Why would I?" There was sorrow in her eyes, but she met his gaze. "Dunne loved us. He wanted us to be happy, and he wanted us to use our ability to contact the spirit world to help people. He said those things often enough when he was alive. Why would he change his mind in death?"

Vincent turned back to the window, but he sensed her still watching him. "Using Dunne to bolster your argument? That's a low blow, Lizzie."

"You know I'm right."

"What if I say no?" He could just make out her reflection in the glass, her face a pale oval amidst the darkness of the room. He wished he couldn't. "If I refuse to get on the train, to take part in this madness? Will you forget about the contest?"

Her lips tightened. "No. I mean to accept Mr. Gladfield's offer whether you accompany me or not."

"Are you insane?" God, he needed a drink, and it wasn't even close to noon yet. "Your talents are psychometry and spirit writing. You can't exorcise a haunting."

She shrugged. "I have to try. I can't let go of the shop…of him… without making every effort possible. If the spirit only needs some prompting to move on, I'll be able to convince it to do so even if you aren't there."

He ran his hand over his face as if he could scrub away all his fears and misgivings. The amulet felt heavy around his neck. "Lizzie…"

"You have to make a decision," Lizzie said. "Who are you? Are you still a medium? Still Vincent Night? If not, then let this all go: the shop, the guilt, everything. And if you are, then come with me."

If only it were that simple. "You win. I'll go with you. But this is a terrible idea."

"You're probably right." Her shoulder lifted in an elegant shrug. "But it's the only one I have."

Henry huddled deeper into his coat, cursing the temperature, which was much lower in upstate New York than in Baltimore. Hopefully his winter things would be up to the task, as he hadn't been able to afford anything new.

"I can't believe we're here!" Jo exclaimed as they stepped onto the platform. Steam from the train's engine billowed around them, and a brisk breeze forced her to grab her hat to keep it from blowing away. Her brown eyes sparkled, and she smiled as if this were all some sort of grand adventure. No doubt it was to her.

Arthur had been kind enough to lend him the money to hire a detective to investigate the mediums he would be up against: Elizabeth Devereaux and Vincent Night. "Night" was certainly some sort of stage name, and heaven knew if Miss Devereaux used the name she was born with or not.

Unfortunately, Henry didn't know either. The blasted detective had failed to send any information before they'd boarded the train. Henry had left instructions to forward any findings to the train depot here, as he still didn't know what their final destination might be. But he didn't have very high hopes that the detective would deliver as promised. Once he returned to Baltimore, he'd warn Arthur against paying the wretch.

"Mr. Henry Strauss?" asked a pleasant voice.

Henry turned to find a man who appeared near his own age of twenty-six. Hazel eyes, a broad grin, and ruddy cheeks showed above a thick scarf and coat. Despite the layers of clothing, it was clear he had broad shoulders, and Henry imagined a fit form underneath.

Not that he should have been imagining anything. "Yes?"

The man gave him a neat bow. "Please, sir, permit me to introduce myself. I'm Connor Bamforth, Mr. Gladfield's man. I've come to take you to the house."

"Oh, excellent." Henry indicated Jo. "This is my cousin and assistant, Miss Jocelyn Strauss."

Bamforth looked surprised at the "cousin" part, but to his credit gave her a small bow as well. "A pleasure, Miss Strauss."

"If you'd be so kind to help us, we'll get our baggage loaded and be on our way. Is it far to the house?" Henry added with a casual air.

Bamforth laughed. "Mr. Gladfield said he hadn't told you where you'd be staying. He didn't want either party to be able to look into the history of the house and thus have an unfair advantage."

"Quite right." It had prevented Henry from learning anything, but with any luck it would limit the mediums' ability to plan their fakery ahead of time as well. "Your employer is a wise man."

"If you say so, sir," Bamforth said. "But to answer your question, the road hasn't been very well maintained over the last few decades. We have a bit over two hours' journey ahead of us."

Henry winced. Two hours wasn't long, but over an uneven road, with the instruments subjected to even more rattling than they already had been, he feared the chances of breakage were high. Still, it couldn't be helped.

"Very well," he said. "Let's load our things and be off."

The two hours proved to be some of the dreariest Henry had endured in quite some time. As soon as they left the small village and entered the low hills, their progress slowed to a crawl. The road had probably once been a fine one. Now, though, it was nothing more than a pair of ruts hemmed in by trees gone bare with winter. Branches scraped at the sides of the wagon and snatched at sleeves and hats. The overcast gray sky blended with the gray trees and the outcroppings of granite. Snow had fallen at some point in the last few days, the surface no longer pristine but pockmarked with raccoon tracks and fallen branches. The passage of the wagon had reduced the snow in the road to a brown slush, which splattered the flanks of the horses trudging stolidly through it.

"Can you tell us anything more about where we're going?" Henry asked eventually.

"Ordinarily I would," Bamforth replied. "But Mr. Gladfield wants to be the one to relate the details. He gave me strict orders to say nothing."

Blast. "But you've been there?"

Bamforth hesitated. "I suppose it won't hurt to tell you. Mr. Gladfield sent me ahead to prepare rooms for sleeping, cooking, and eating. I can't say as I liked the place, and I made sure I was back in town by sundown."

"Quite a long drive to make twice in a day," Henry observed.

"I'm not a coward, but Mr. Gladfield couldn't pay me enough to stay there alone after dark," Bamforth said flatly. "I hired some women from town to help with the cleaning, and every one of them quit by the end of the week."

"Why?" Jo asked, sounding more fascinated than afraid.

Bamforth cast her an uncertain glance. "I shouldn't say any more, begging your pardon, miss. Mr. Gladfield's orders. It's no place for a young lady, to my way of thinking—no place for any of us, really."

They fell silent on that pronouncement. Henry watched Bamforth from the corner of his eye. Was the man trying to scare them? Or had he —presumably with foreknowledge of the house's history—been frightened by his imagination? Or was the place truly haunted?

Certainly Gladfield believed it was. But part of their procedure would be to establish whether there truly was spectral activity in the house. If so, they would proceed. He'd use the Electro-Séance to call up the spirit, then send it to the otherworld where it belonged. And he'd do it all without the help of a medium, real or fake.

The clatter of hooves and creak of wheels formed a constant background, occasionally punctuated by the caw of a distant crow. Just as Henry began to slip into a light doze, Bamforth said, "Look—there it is."

Henry pushed his spectacles higher on his nose and peered through the net of branches. "I don't see anything."

"Just wait until we get around this bend here—you'll get a clear enough look." Bamforth's earlier cheer had slipped away, as if the prospect of returning troubled him.

The narrow road dipped sharply and looped around a boulder. The wagon rounded the other side—and the house lay before them.

Henry gasped at its sudden appearance, even though he knew it was nothing more than a trick of dense woods and winding road. Bamforth must have heard, though, because he smiled thinly and said, "Welcome to Reyhome Castle, Mr. Strauss."

CHAPTER 3

"REYHOME CASTLE," Henry murmured as if reciting a charm. And perhaps it was—this place would be the site of his vindication, after all. Of the triumph of science over fakery. But the first sight was rather daunting.

The Gothic Revival mansion's imposing walls of gray stone competed with the trees for height—three stories at least, with an attic space beneath the sharply peaked slate roof. Tall, narrow windows stared blankly out over the remains of formal gardens now barely distinguishable from the encroaching woods. A tower loomed immediately to the right of the covered porch. Lightning rods jutted from various points around the house, like the spines of some poisonous animal.

The portico extended over the drive, allowing visitors to disembark with a minimum of exposure during inclement weather. As the wagon rattled to a halt, the front door swung open, and Gladfield emerged. The tip of the cigar he smoked glowed bright in the shadow of the portico. He paused at the bottom of the steps, resting his hand lightly atop one of the stone lions guarding the balustrade. "Mr. Strauss, thank you for coming."

"Thank you for the opportunity, sir." Henry hastily scrambled from the uncomfortable wagon seat and shook the other man's hand. Gladfield's suit and overcoat were of a sober cut and color, but the tailoring and fabrics proclaimed them to be of the best quality. His brown hair had started to thin, but he compensated with a luxurious mustache.

Gladfield removed his cigar from his mouth and frowned in Jo's direction. "I thought you meant to bring your cousin with you?"

Henry sensed Jo stiffen, although she didn't say anything. "Allow me to present my cousin and assistant, Jocelyn Strauss," he said, struggling to keep his voice neutral. They needed Gladfield's money and approval, but he'd be damned if he'd treat Jo like the shameful family secret.

Gladfield looked clearly taken aback. "I see." Perhaps not knowing what else to do, he nodded politely to Jo. "Would you care to wait inside? My niece, Miss Prandle, would be grateful for the company, I'm sure."

"I need Jo's assistance to unload our equipment from the cart," Henry said.

Gladfield frowned. "Surely Bamforth can perform the task."

Heat crept up Henry's neck. He sounded like a brute, forcing a girl to help him lift and carry, but there was nothing for it. "No offense to Mr. Bamforth, but some of my equipment is very delicate. I determined before we left only Jo and I would handle it, to make certain of its safety."

"It's all right, Mr. Gladfield," Jo said cheerfully. "I helped load it on the train and off again. And it's nothing to hauling water for the cows on Aunt Emma's farm."

Gladfield blinked, clearly uncertain what to make of her statement. Or of Jo herself, perhaps. "I see. I'll leave you to it."

Bamforth removed their personal bags, while Henry and Jo pulled out the first of three crates. All of the instruments within nestled in straw, but one of the first orders of business would be to open the crates and make certain nothing had been damaged in transit.

"Ready, Jo?" he asked, gripping one side of the crate.

She nodded, and they lifted it from the back of the wagon and maneuvered it up the stairs. Bamforth hurried ahead and held the door open as they passed within.

The vestibule was surprisingly small given the huge size of the house. A pair of narrow glass panes to either side of the oak door let in some light, but the gas lamps burned despite the early hour. Slate tiles covered the floor, and dark paneling hung on the walls, making the space seem even tinier.

"Go to the left or the right—both lead into the grand hall," Bamforth advised. "I'll get your luggage in the meantime."

They carried the crate through the vestibule and into a narrow passage. Henry went to the right, noting a door that must open into the tower. Within a few feet, the passage came to an abrupt end, opening up into a huge hall. For the second time, he let out a gasp of amazement.

On the other side of the wall forming the passage, double staircases ran up to the second and third floors. The hall itself was open all the way to the rafters and had clearly been designed to mimic a medieval castle. An enormous fireplace dominated the western wall, and an iron chandelier fitted for gas hung from the crossbeams. Dusty heads of boar and elk decorated the walls alongside faded tapestries. A great bay window in the northern wall, directly across from the stairs, looked out onto a patio and what must have once been a formal garden. The rest of the windows were high and narrow; years of dirt covered them, adding to the general air of gloom. The scent of dust itched in Henry's nose.

A woman rose from a chair near the fireplace as they entered. No doubt this was Miss Devereaux, the medium, given she dressed in the flowing draperies beloved of aesthetes. A thick choker circled her neck, and her golden hair hung in ringlets. Henry didn't speak to her until he and Jo had the crate properly settled. When he straightened to greet her, he found her tall enough to look him directly in the eye.

"You must be Mr. Strauss," she said. She spoke softly, in a deep, throaty voice. "Permit me to introduce myself. I am Miss Elizabeth Devereaux."

He bowed over her hand only as much as required by politeness. Curse Gladfield for disappearing, leaving him no choice but to speak to the woman. "Mr. Henry Strauss. This is my cousin, Jocelyn Strauss."

"I'm Henry's assistant," Jo added. "May I say how lovely your dress is? I—"

"We have work to do," Henry interrupted.

Jo frowned, but Miss Devereaux only inclined her head. "Of course." She glanced toward a dark-skinned man who stood staring out the hall's bay window. "Please, let us know if we can offer any assistance."

Probably she wanted the chance to wreck his equipment. "Jo and I are sufficient." Still, no sense in making Bamforth suffer. "But if you'd have your boy help Bamforth with our luggage, I'd be grateful."

Miss Devereaux stiffened, and the man at the window turned. "Mr. Henry Strauss," Miss Devereaux said icily, "may I present to you my fellow medium, Mr. Vincent Night."

Heat suffused Henry's face—bad enough to have assumed the

fellow was a servant based on his skin, but to have done it in front of Jo was inexcusable. A second look showed Henry what he should have noticed from the first: namely that the man dressed more fashionably than he did.

A third look sent heat rushing through areas of his body other than his face.

Mr. Night was clearly a Red Indian, his skin bronze and his black hair thick and shining. Heavy brows hovered over eyes so dark it was difficult to tell where iris ended and pupil began. He had a wide nose, full lips, and high cheek bones. A bottle-green coat, buttoned only at the topmost button, showed off the watch, chain, and patterned vest beneath. The somewhat foppish attire did little to hide the trim form underneath.

Henry swallowed against the sudden dryness of his mouth. It really had been too long since his last fumble if he found himself drawn to a medium, no matter how good looking. Night's handsome face and form were no doubt tools he used to take advantage of those foolish enough to hire him.

Just as Isaac had done.

"Forgive me, Mr. Night," Henry said, half choking on the words. "I didn't mean to cause offense."

For a moment, Night merely regarded Henry's outstretched hand as if considering whether or not to shake it. The heat in Henry's face grew, and he wanted to sink through the floor.

"Of course," Night said at last, in a voice like honey drizzled over chocolate: rich and dark. He shook Henry's hand with long, soft fingers.

"Are you an Indian?" Jo asked as Night bowed over her hand.

"Jo!" Why on earth was she determined to talk to these people? They were competitors, not friends. "We need to bring the rest of the crates inside." He nodded to Miss Devereaux. "If you'll excuse us."

She waved a negligent hand. "Of course, Mr. Strauss. We wouldn't want to keep you from your work, after all."

The words were cool, but Henry had the distinct impression she was laughing at him. Silently seething, he turned and led the way back outside to the wagon.

"Here's your room, Mr. Night," Bamforth said a short time later.

Vincent nodded, striving to keep his expression from betraying how fast his heart beat or how badly he wanted to run from the house and never return. "Thank you."

"Let me know if you need anything, sir."

Vincent nodded again, as if he were used to receiving this sort of deference. "I will."

The bedroom, which had originally been one of Reyhome Castle's guest rooms, was larger than the main room of his apartment back in New York. Whatever the condition of the rest of the house, Bamforth and his hired cleaners had put a great deal of effort into making the guest rooms inhabitable: scrubbed walls and floors, clean windows, fresh mattresses, bedding, and curtains. A huge wardrobe lurked in one corner. Lavender and rose water scented the air, but a trace of dust and mildew lingered despite Bamforth's best efforts.

Vincent dropped his bags on the bed and strode to the wardrobe, flinging it open. It was empty, of course: nothing inside but shadows and air.

With a muffled groan, he sat on the edge of the bed and drew his silver flask from his coat pocket. Why had he come here? Why had he let Lizzie talk him into this? The second he'd seen the house, he'd had an overwhelming presentiment of evil, as if the place was waiting for them. For him.

But it was just an illusion. He didn't possess even a trace of precognition. The feeling was simply born of his own disordered nerves. His mouth tasted only of the cinnamon cachous he always carried with him; if any spirits walked these halls, they hadn't yet drawn near.

And yet he couldn't shake off the lingering sense of dread. Of something terrible waiting to happen.

There came a loud thud against the wall across from him, and he jumped. A moment later, Strauss's voice filtered through from the other side. "Careful! We don't want to break anything."

Vincent sighed. Not a spirit making itself known. Just one of the mysterious crates Strauss had forced his poor cousin to help haul up two stories of steps.

When he'd read Gladfield's letter, Vincent had formed a mental image of the scientist who meant to challenge them. Old, gray, and sour-faced. The reality had proved quite different. Strauss's thick hair, tousled from his journey on the train, was the color of honey. Beneath his neat, if somewhat worn, clothing, his body appeared intriguing.

As for the cousin, she wasn't what Vincent had expected, either. He'd grown up around too many black women who worked as servants or laundresses to find the relationship itself odd. But such ties were always illegitimate, unacknowledged, at least by the white half of the family. For Strauss to go about introducing the girl as his cousin—not to mention his laboratory assistant—was surprising. Surely he must be aware such acknowledgement would lower him in the eyes of men like Gladfield.

Apparently there was more to Mr. Strauss than Vincent would have guessed. Of course, the man had immediately proceeded to insult him… but at least he'd apologized for it. Had even seemed ashamed of his assumptions, which was a damned sight more than Vincent was used to. Not to mention that the flush tingeing Strauss's pale skin had made Vincent wonder what he'd look like naked in the throes of passion.

Especially since the flush had only deepened when they shook hands, and he'd caught the way Strauss's gaze lingered on him just a fraction longer than it strictly should have. Vincent had grown up in a place where accurately spotting a man who fancied a bit of buggery meant the difference between a hot meal and a beating, and he'd bet every dime of Gladfield's prize money Strauss was one such man.

Which might come in useful. No matter how admirable Vincent might find his treatment of his cousin, Henry Strauss was still a competitor, someone who meant to replace the whole of mediumship with whatever gadgets he had packed away in his precious crates. A bit of subtle flirtation to keep him off his balance might be just the thing.

Not to mention it would provide a welcome distraction to Vincent as well. He looked again at the open wardrobe. The last time he'd slept with any doors closed had been the night before Dunne died. Before he started to fear what might have followed him back from that accursed house.

The ghost had been gone when he'd regained consciousness. Typically spirits stayed in one general locale, somewhere they'd known in life, or the spot where they'd died. But some of them—the strongest and most evil—occasionally attached themselves to certain people and followed them over vast distances.

He hadn't sensed the spirit in all the months since. Nevertheless, he slept with all the doors and windows salted, and he never took off his amulet.

Just in case.

Vincent took another swig from the flask before reluctantly putting it away. Yes. A little distraction by the way of the good Mr. Strauss might be precisely the thing he needed.

Henry hurried down the stairs to the floor of the grand hall, pleased not to be the last to reconvene. Neither of the mediums had arrived yet—he'd glimpsed Night talking to his partner, probably discussing how to best ply their tricks, now they'd seen the house.

Were they partners of a more intimate sort as well? Not that he cared, of course. It was simply a matter of curiosity, and he would dismiss the thought from his mind. He had far more important things to concern himself with, after all.

Gladfield, Bamforth, and Jo already waited in the grand hall, chatting in front of the fireplace. Another young lady, perhaps twenty years of age, stood with them. Miss Prandle, no doubt.

"Ah, there you are," Gladfield said as Henry approached. "And here come our mediums as well. Allow me to make introductions. This is my niece, Miss Wilma Prandle, whom some of you already know." He smiled at her affectionately. "As soon as she heard of my plans, she insisted on accompanying me here to observe."

"The séance in New York was fascinating," Miss Prandle said to the mediums. "I look forward to seeing even more of your work over the next few days."

"We were glad to be of service," Miss Devereaux said. So this was why Gladfield had chosen these two—they already had a connection with his family.

Would Gladfield favor them for it? Henry folded his hands at the small of his back, fingers tightening on each other. It didn't mean anything. He'd have to work even harder to prove himself, but if he revealed the mediums as frauds, perhaps Gladfield's opinion would shift. Had they bilked poor Miss Prandle in some fashion? Or just dazzled her with the usual tricks—asking leading questions, performing a bit of sleight of hand, that sort of thing?

Curse the detective for not sending along his findings in a timely fashion.

Night arched an eyebrow at Henry. Damn it, he'd been staring. Henry made certain his expression was a glare. Night glanced at the others as if to make sure their attention was elsewhere…then shot Henry a deliberate wink.

What the devil? The effrontery of the scoundrel! Was he attempting to put Henry off his balance, or…

Or did he know about Henry's proclivities, somehow? Mediums doubtless communicated with one another. If Night was clever, he might have asked Gladfield for Henry's name, just as Henry had asked for the mediums' identities. What if Night knew Isaac, had asked him about

Henry?

The familiar mixture of anger and shame coursed through Henry, and he hardened his glare, fist clenching at his side. Maddeningly, Night's full lips only curved up into a lazy smile.

"Well, now we're all acquainted," Gladfield said, "allow me to welcome you to Reyhome Castle."

"Will you give us the history of the house now, Mr. Gladfield?" Miss Devereaux inquired. Henry noted it was she who seemed to take the lead between the two mediums.

"Not yet." Gladfield grinned like a boy pulling a prank. "In the interests of thoroughness, I thought it would be best if everyone began with a blank slate, as it were. No expectations of what might be found."

Night frowned and shifted. Clearly this didn't sit well with him. "But the house is said to be haunted, correct?"

"Oh yes. To the point where it hasn't been inhabited for thirty years, and spent the entire time draining the family's coffers." Gladfield clasped his hands together. "I intend to renovate Reyhome Castle into a resort hotel where those of means can retreat during the summer. For my dream to become a reality, the place must be cleared of ghosts, using whatever methods prove necessary."

"It will be," Henry said firmly.

"Confidence—I like that in a man." Gladfield beamed. "Well, if you are all ready, let's begin."

CHAPTER 4

VINCENT'S HEART pounded in his ears, and he forced himself to take several calming breaths. Lizzie needed him. The shop needed him.

But Gladfield's refusal to tell them what might lurk in the house left his gut unsettled. The man wanted them to go into this blind, without any idea of how powerful—or how angry—a spirit they might encounter.

And it must be powerful or angry. No one would abandon a mansion like this otherwise.

Vincent forced himself to concentrate on Gladfield's words as their host led them across the enormous open hall. "As you can see, the house was built around the hall," he said. "But the hall isn't quite in the center, and the layout itself is uneven, with the bay window slightly closer to one end than the other."

Subtly off—that described the whole damned house.

"We'll begin on the eastern side of the hall," Gladfield went on. "You saw the door to the right when you came in—it leads to the tower. Here in the east wing, we have the library, drawing room, and morning room, respectively."

They shuffled into the library. Light came through the small bay facing the front of the house, but it seemed to struggle through the thick panes. Two walls were lined with bookshelves, while a desk and chair lurked in the bay. The air was cold, the fireplace unlaid, and everything stank of dust and mice.

"Feel free to borrow any of the books the silverfish and mice haven't gotten to," Gladfield said, indicating the shelves.

Vincent crossed the room slowly, swirling his tongue around the inside of his mouth. Waiting for some foreign taste to burst upon his tongue, warning of a watching spirit.

Despite the efforts of the cleaners to freshen the place, the air of the house was thick and oppressive, heavy against his skin. Vincent stopped at the desk. Stuffing hung from the seat of the chair, mice having used it as a nest. He pulled open the center drawer; it came out with a shriek, the wood warped from years of hot summers and freezing winters. A few scraps of paper lay inside, chewed to illegibility by mice and insects.

"Forty degrees," Henry Strauss said. He and his young assistant stood together, she recording in a notebook while he read the temperature from the thermometer he carried.

Vincent grinned to himself. He'd managed to knock Strauss off his stride earlier, all right. His suspicions had been entirely correct. He watched the cousins from the corner of his eye as they worked. Although Strauss issued orders and the young lady obeyed, he didn't behave as if he thought her his inferior. Did the rest of the family embrace her as well, or was Strauss the exception?

Not that it mattered. It wasn't as if they'd ever be friends, after all. Still, Strauss's predilections weren't the only intriguing thing about him.

After the library, they went to the drawing room, which had an even larger bay looking out over a patio and the remains of the once extensive gardens. Strauss again measured the temperature, while the rest of them milled about.

"Do you sense anything?" Lizzie murmured, sidling up to him.

Vincent shook his head. "No. You?"

"I'm not certain." She turned her gaze to the ceiling and the shadows clinging to the corners. "It feels as though something here is watching us."

"Yes." But was it just nerves?

He would have known, once. Half a year ago, before he'd learned to fear the things lurking in the dark.

They trooped to the morning room, again finding nothing of interest. From there it was back out into the grand hall and to the rooms on its western side. "Here's where we'll take all of our meals," Gladfield said, flinging open the doors to the dining room. The huge chamber was decorated much like the grand hall, meant to recall a medieval castle. Bamforth and the hired women had clearly been at work here, with the long wooden table scrubbed and polished, the chairs in good order, and the cobwebs swept from yet another huge iron chandelier. "Breakfast will be served at nine, a light lunch at one o'clock, and dinner at six."

"Including tonight?" Miss Strauss asked hopefully.

"Jo, don't be rude," Strauss said with a frown. Did the man ever smile?

Miss Strauss flushed. "I'm sorry, Mr. Gladfield—I don't always think before speaking."

How had Strauss come to be in charge of his cousin? Poor girl—she appeared to have a boisterous nature, and finding herself in the care of a dour creature like him couldn't be easy. At least he seemed to treat her well otherwise.

Vincent shifted closer to Lizzie. "The girl," he murmured. "Do you think there will be a problem?" Spirits drew upon the energy of young people far too easily, which was why poltergeist hauntings almost always centered around a boy or girl past puberty, but not yet an adult.

"I hope not. If you think Mr. Strauss would listen—"

Vincent snorted. "I doubt it. But if it becomes an issue, I'll mention it to him."

They left the dining room behind. "The butler's pantry," Gladfield said, opening a discreet door.

As they passed into the chamber, Vincent frowned. Leaving the furniture behind in the house, he understood. But the serving dishes and silverware?

Miss Prandle apparently had the same questions. Picking up a tarnished fork, she said, "Why in the world is this still here? With a bit of polishing, it would look grand on your table, uncle."

"Indeed," Gladfield said ruefully. "But the last inhabitants left everything in the house as it was, and my father was a superstitious sort. He feared removing anything of value would only make the situation worse."

"How cryptic," Vincent murmured. He'd meant to direct the comment at Lizzie alone, but Strauss looked up from his perusal of the china cabinet. For an instant, their eyes met in agreement. Behind the lenses of his spectacles, Strauss's irises showed a deep blue, like the waters of a still pond. Pretty.

Strauss blinked and averted his gaze quickly.

A door opposite opened directly onto the servants' part of the household. Just on the left side of a short passage, a stairway let out. As he reached the foot of the stair, the air around Vincent went from cold to downright icy. The acidic bite of lemons and vinegar stung his tongue.

He grabbed automatically at the amulet beneath his shirt, the silver disk suddenly cold against his skin. "There's something here."

One moment, the tour was proceeding normally. The next, Night's eyes went wide and he shrank back from the foot of the stairs. "There's something here," he exclaimed, clutching at his chest. Dear God, could the man be any more theatrical if he tried?

In contrast, Miss Devereaux remained calm. Her eyes narrowed, and she blew out a puff of air. It turned to steam in front of her face.

"A cold spot!" Henry rushed forward with his thermometer. "At last!"

The two mediums hastened out of his way. He thrust the thermometer into the cold spot, feeling the chill bite into the back of his exposed hand. The mercury fell steadily, and he had to suppress a grin at the sight. "Thirty—no, it's still dropping—twenty-eight degrees!" he said, and Jo hurried to scribble down the results in their notebook. "A difference of twelve degrees from the rest of the house we've measured thus far." Of course, they'd have to rule out any natural causes, but they finally had a phenomenon to investigate.

"Lemons," Night muttered, making a sour face. He took a tin of cachous from his pocket and popped one into his mouth. A moment later, Henry caught a faint whiff of cinnamon.

But no lemons. What on earth was the man on about? Miss Devereaux only nodded thoughtfully. Perhaps it was some sort of code between them.

Gladfield looked interested. "Lemons, did you say? Did you get any other impressions?"

"What do you mean?" Jo asked. "What's this about lemons?"

Night's mouth lifted into a half smile. "The talent I have is known as clairgustance. Some people—clairvoyants—can see things others can't. Clairaudients might hear a spirit whispering to them. I receive impressions through my sense of taste."

Jo's eyes went wide. "You *taste* ghosts?" She sounded delightedly horrified.

"In a way." Night smiled ruefully. "Spirits are creatures of energy. The way the energy is perceived varies by the individual medium. In my case, it's taste."

"All the more reason the Electro-Séance will be an improvement over the current way of doing things," Henry said smugly. "Properly calibrated, gauges and instruments always respond in the same manner. There will be no guesswork, no uncertainty introduced by the varying perceptions of mediums."

"No humanity," Miss Devereaux shot back.

"No imperfections. No tricks."

"Enough," Gladfield said with a laugh. "Testing which method is best is what this week is all about. Unless either of you want to study the area further at the moment, let's move on."

"Agreed," Henry replied, a bit stiffly. The rest of the group shuffled after Gladfield. As Night passed by, his hip brushed against Henry's.

"You don't like for things to be out of your control, do you?" Night murmured, the words almost lost beneath Gladfield's booming voice as he led the way down the hall.

Henry scowled and tried to ignore the rush of heat to his groin. Why did the man have to be so handsome? "Who does?"

"Why, no one, Mr. Strauss." The grin Night gave him seemed to promise all sorts of intimacies. "But sometimes losing control can be… invigorating."

"I'm sure I don't know what you mean."

"Really?" Night turned half away, then glanced back. "Such a shame. And here I thought once you finished measuring your ghosts, you might like to measure something of mine."

With a last, wicked grin, he sauntered away down the corridor, leaving Henry to stand flustered until he regained enough control to catch up with the others.

Perhaps fortunately, the rest of the servants' quarters proved unremarkable. They encountered no other presences, with the exception of Bamforth in the kitchen preparing their dinner. From the servants' quarters, they rounded off the first floor with a stop in the billiard room, which lay directly to the west of the front door.

From there, they made their way up to the second floor. A wide balcony overhung the grand hall on all four sides and provided access to the rooms. "These were the family's quarters," Gladfield explained.

"Is there access to the tower?" Night asked. Henry avoided looking directly at him.

"Only on the first floor," Gladfield replied, leading the way to the eastern cluster of rooms. "This first room belonged to Mrs. Reyer, the lady of the house."

Unlike the guest rooms, these had been left unaired. As they stepped inside, Henry's eyes were drawn to the gauzy hangings around the bed, now tattered from mold and the passage of time. They hung limp around a bed reeking of mice. No doubt wildlife of every sort had made use of the down mattresses and bedding. A portrait lay on the floor, having fallen from its place on the wall. Something had chewed away part of the canvas, leaving only the image of a woman's hair and shoulders around the gaping hole where her face had been.

As they'd done in the other rooms, Henry carefully measured the temperature while Jo recorded his findings. He glanced up once to find Night watching him with a bemused smile. Henry flushed and looked away quickly.

Really, the fellow was intolerable.

Once Henry finished his measurements, they moved to the next room, which proved to be Mr. Reyer's study. Henry wracked his memory for the surname—obviously the man had been wealthy to afford such an enormous house—but came up with nothing. There was no knowing how long ago Reyer had died. If it had been some time ago, and his only accomplishment in life had been to amass a small fortune, his name might already be lost to history.

Henry's name wouldn't be so lost. Future generations wouldn't recall the quacks and frauds who had sullied the study of the spirit world with their acts, but everyone would speak of Strauss's Electro-Séance, which finally brought the study of psychical phenomena out of the Dark Ages. He'd make sure of it.

The study was dark and rather gloomy, even more so than the library downstairs. Much like the library and the bedroom, there proved to be nothing whatsoever of interest inside.

"And lastly on this side of the house, we have Mr. Reyer's chamber and dressing room," Gladfield announced, opening a heavy door of some dark wood.

Miss Prandle stepped through—and immediately wrapped her arms around herself. "Another cold spot!"

Before the mediums could approach, Henry lunged forward to measure with his thermometer. It was like thrusting his hand into a snow bank; even the density of the air felt different. He'd have to bring in the barometer to make measurements as well, after this initial tour. "Twenty-four degrees," he said triumphantly. Jo scribbled it hastily in the notebook.

Miss Prandle rubbed at her arms as Henry advanced into the room. "I don't like this place," she murmured.

"Indeed. Now you see why I took one of the guest rooms instead of staying here," Mr. Gladfield said with a chuckle.

It was, Henry had to admit, incredibly gloomy. The carvings on the massive bed resembled the ornaments of a gothic cathedral. The curtains lay on the floor as if they'd been wrenched down with some violence. A layer of dust coated everything, but unlike the other bedroom, there was no smell of mice and nothing else seemed disturbed. A man glared out at them from a portrait on the wall, seeming almost to sneer at them, as if he observed their efforts and judged them lacking.

Henry did a slow patrol of the room, discovering three more cold spots: twenty-nine degrees, twenty-five degrees, and twenty-four degrees. As with the one downstairs, he'd have to thoroughly investigate the room and rule out any other causes. Still, it was impossible not to feel a surge of excitement. At last, after years of studying and tinkering, he would have the chance to test his theory, that the science of electromagnetism would allow mediums to be replaced with machines, with what seemed a genuine haunting.

Night walked around the room as well, a faint look of disgust warping his full lips. He ate another one of the cachous but said nothing aloud. Miss Devereaux watched him closely but remained silent as well, clearly content to let him keep his own counsel for the moment.

After leaving the bedchamber, they walked along the northern balcony to the western cluster of rooms. Another cold spot, this one quite large, made itself known just before they reached the end of the balcony.

"What's that stain?" Jo asked, nodding at the floor. Wooden boards showed beneath a rat-chewed runner, the ones at the cold spot marked with an irregular patch as if something dark had seeped into the grain itself.

Night's eyes narrowed. "Blood," he said flatly.

Henry sniffed, but smelled only dust and age. Going down on his knees, he touched the stain, but detected nothing to indicate its origins. "Don't be preposterous," he scoffed. "You can't possibly know. You're only saying it because it sounds dramatic."

The glare Miss Devereaux leveled at him would surely have felled him had she the power to do so. Night, however, leaned casually against the balcony rail, not far from where Henry crouched. The position gave Henry a rather…interesting…view. "Take a close examination, Mr. Strauss. I'd like to hear your expert opinion."

"It could be from anything," Henry said, hastily directing his gaze back to the floor. "An attempt to apply new varnish to cover a repair, which didn't age the same as the rest. An incontinent rat. A glass of wine."

"Of course," Night murmured, but something in his tone made Henry certain the man laughed at him.

Gladfield said nothing, only looking keenly interested. Did he know the source of the stain? What if it was blood? Henry's stomach went sour —had he just made a fool of himself for no better reason than to argue with Night?

"It hardly matters," he declared, rising to his feet. "The cold spot suggests there may be phenomena worth investigating here, whatever the nature of the stain."

"On that we agree," Night said. A rueful smile flickered across his face, there and gone again so fast Henry must have imagined it. "What else do you have in store for us, Mr. Gladfield?"

Gladfield led the way to the next door; this room must be directly over the dining hall downstairs. Flinging open the doors, he said, "See for yourself."

CHAPTER 5

VINCENT TOOK a deep breath and felt as if his lungs were fully able to expand for the first time since he'd set foot in the house. The big room had little furniture remaining in it, but the desk and chairs seemed made for a child. Bright paint still clung to the walls, along with the faint outline of marks in a childish hand, no doubt scrawled in pencil and never quite scrubbed away.

"The atmosphere is lighter here," he said. Going to the marks, he crouched down and traced them with his fingers. "Tom."

A sweet taste of lavender competed with the fading cinnamon of the cachou, tinged with the unmistakable tang of blood. He'd sensed this spirit on the balcony, at the location of the bloodstain.

"Some sort of schoolroom," Strauss observed. "No cold spots over here."

The flavor vanished. Interesting.

"The atmosphere does seem a bit different," Strauss lectured on. "I'll take pressure readings later in addition to the others I'd planned. Good thing I thought to pack a barometer."

Of course he had. The man had probably brought a catalog's worth of scientific instruments.

Gladfield waited patiently by the door as they wandered about, but there was nothing more to be discovered. Still, Vincent felt regret when he shut the doors behind them as they left, and the oppressive air of the rest of the house closed in again. Perhaps if the gloomy atmosphere grew too much, he could retreat into the schoolroom for a rest.

Then he remembered the taste of lavender and decided against it.

The westernmost portion of the building was given over to servants' quarters and storage. Past the servants' stair—which thankfully remained spirit free as he stepped past—laid the tutor's room and the nurseries. Once again, they reached the front of the house, above the vestibule.

"The third floor you've already seen," Gladfield said as they gathered at the stairs leading down to the grand hall. "Above your rooms is nothing more than attic space. There is also a basement, with a wine cellar linked to a root cellar. I think the first two floors offer more than enough to investigate at the moment. Let us retire to freshen up for dinner, and reconvene downstairs in the dining room in half an hour. The contest can begin in earnest tomorrow morning."

Miss Strauss brightened visibly at the mention of food. Gladfield left them and went to check on Bamforth in the kitchen, and the rest of them trooped up the stairs to the third floor. Since his room was directly beside Strauss's, Vincent dawdled at the door until the other man approached.

"Let me know if you need any help with your…collar," he said.

A pink flush instantly appeared on Strauss's neck and face. "I don't need any help," he hissed in a low voice as he yanked open his door. "What I need is for you to stop."

"Stop what?" Night asked with feigned innocence.

Strauss growled at him and slammed the door. Grinning to himself, Night crossed to the rooms on the opposite side of the balcony and knocked on Lizzie's door. When she called for him to enter, he slipped inside.

She'd taken off her shoes and removed a fresh dress from the wardrobe. "What didn't you want to say in front of the others?" she asked, laying the dress aside and sitting.

"There are three spirits in the house." He leaned back against the door, arms folded over his chest. "One at the bottom of the stairs. A different one on the balcony and in the schoolroom. And a third in Reyer's bedroom."

A smile lit up Lizzie's face. "Ha! Let's see Mr. Strauss measure that with his stupid thermometer." She cocked her head. "You aren't smiling."

"No."

"What's wrong?"

"Two of the spirits seemed…ordinary, as spirits go." God, it was hard to explain this to anyone, even another medium. "The one near the stairs tasted like lemons and vinegar, and the one on the balcony like lavender with a little bit of blood."

Lizzie made a face. "I'm reminded yet again why I'm glad I don't have your talent. And the third?"

"It was fainter than the other two. For which I'm profoundly grateful." Vincent shivered. "It was like I'd licked a rusty iron nail. And there was a sense of…of malice. I think it might be angry."

"Interesting." Lizzie laced her fingers together and leaned forward. "But you said it was fainter than the others?"

"For now." But the longer living people were emitting energy in the house, the stronger all of the spirits would grow.

"Keep me informed." She rose decisively to her feet. "And you were right not to hint to Mr. Strauss about the multiple spirits. If his devices fail to detect the differences…well, his Electro-Séance won't get very far if the users are trying to contact dear old Aunt Hetty and find themselves with Uncle Bob spewing profanities at them instead."

Vincent smiled reluctantly at the mental image. "A good point. Mr. Strauss certainly is enthusiastic, isn't he?"

Lizzie snorted. "Not the word I would have used. You don't admire him, do you?"

"No, of course not," Vincent said hastily. "I just meant to comment."

Her eyes narrowed. "Please don't tell me you have designs on the man."

"I'm insulted you should even suggest such a thing!" He tried to look deeply affronted, but failed miserably. "Not as such, anyway."

Lizzie shook her head. "I won't bother telling you what a horrible idea it would be, since you won't listen anyway. Instead I'll bid you farewell so we can both change for dinner. Try to find something suitable to distract our dear Mr. Strauss, won't you?"

Vincent laughed and let himself back out into the hall.

Dinner was simple fare, consisting of three courses: potato soup, roast chicken with turnips and carrots, and chocolate cake. Henry tucked in with relish; given the erratic hours he spent in the shop, most of the meals he shared with Jo consisted of sandwiches or a quick bite from a lunch wagon.

"Delicious—my compliments to you Mr. Bamforth," he said.

Bamforth served more wine to Mr. Gladfield. "Thank you, Mr. Strauss. Just doing my job, though."

"Don't be so modest," exclaimed Miss Prandle. Bamforth blushed, and Henry winced. If Bamforth had feelings for the girl…well, falling in love with his employer's niece could only end in dismissal. "This cake is truly divine."

"May I have another piece?" Jo asked, blinking her big eyes at Bamforth.

"Of course, miss." He served another slice, and she beamed at him. Well, the fellow was rather attractive, although he couldn't hold a candle to Night.

Curse it. Henry shouldn't think such things.

As if his thought had loosed an ill genie in the room, Miss Prandle said, "I wanted to compliment you, Mr. Night. You speak English very well. Where did you learn it?"

Was it Henry's imagination, or had Night's expression become somewhat fixed? He'd changed into a sober coat for dinner, but his scarlet vest more than made up for the charcoal gray velvet. Unfortunately for Henry, the color suited Vincent, contrasting wonderfully with his dark skin and eyes.

"Thank you, Miss Prandle," he said. "To answer your question, my father was a white trader who fell in love with a Mohican princess. At first her tribe didn't wish her to marry an outsider. But her grandfather was a great medicine man, and spoke with the spirits, who told him they should wed. They were very happy together for a time, but alas died when I was still quite young. Fortunately, a pair of missionaries happened to be visiting the tribe at the time and took pity on me. They adopted me as their own son and brought me to live with them in New York."

"Your grandfather was a medium as well?" Jo asked.

Henry shot her a reproving glance, which she either didn't see or—more likely—ignored.

"In his own way," Night said.

"How fascinating!" Miss Prandle exclaimed.

Jo chewed thoughtfully on her cake. "Most mediums are women, aren't they?"

"Jo, I'm sure Mr. Night doesn't wish to answer your questions," Henry snapped.

"I don't mind," Night said. Of course he'd be contrary. "It's true the fairer sex commune most easily with the spirits. Supposedly because they are more…"—his dark eyes met Henry's gaze—"*receptive* to their intercourse."

Henry gripped his fork hard and struggled to ignore the swelling in his breeches. Bad enough the man had somehow divined Henry's interests, but to flirt with him at the very table courted disaster. True, mediums were given more leniency in their conduct. Night must know he and Miss Devereaux had no chance in this contest, and hoped to either distract Henry or to charm him into relinquishing the prize.

Well, he'd soon learn Henry Strauss couldn't be charmed. Not by any medium.

Not again.

That night, Henry opened his eyes and discovered he couldn't move.

His groggy mind flailed—where was he? Through a gap in the bed curtains, he just glimpsed the room beyond. The shapes of the furniture, the position of the window letting in dim moonlight, didn't match the configuration of his small bedroom above the shop.

He was somewhere else. Reyhome Castle. The haunted house.

And he couldn't move.

He tried to take a deep breath, but some force pressed down on his chest. The same pressure kept his limbs pinned to the bed. Not so much as a finger would obey his frantic command to move.

He'd been tired when he'd fallen asleep—this must be a dream. A horrible nightmare. He'd wake up any moment now.

There was someone else in the room.

He'd drawn the bed curtains against the winter night, but he *felt* a presence on the other side. The air against his face grew colder, and the curtains billowed gently. It looked as if someone was running a hand along them while pacing closer and closer to the head of the bed.

He struggled to breathe, to call for help. But no sound escaped his straining lungs.

A figure appeared in the gap between curtains. The shape of a woman, clad in a dress thirty years out of fashion. She leaned in, closer and closer. Like the mouse-chewed portrait in the bedroom, she had no face.

"Leave this place," she whispered. "Before it's too late."

And she was gone.

The force holding him to the bed vanished instantly. He shot upright, a wild cry escaping him. Hurling back the curtains, he staggered out of bed. The room lay silent and still around him, with no sign of any intruder.

A sharp knock sounded on the door, sending his heart lurching against his ribs. "Strauss?" Night called, his voice gravelly with sleep. "Are you all right in there?"

"I…I think so." Henry sank down on the edge of the bed. His spectacles lay on the night table, and he fumbled them on, bringing the room into focus.

The door opened, and Night stuck his head in, his sleep-tousled hair illuminated by the light of the candle in his hand. "I thought I heard you cry out."

God, the room was cold. Henry wrapped his arms about himself, shivering. "I did. I thought…I thought there was a woman here in the room with me. She said to leave."

Night frowned, and the sleep left his eyes. He strode into the room, holding the candle aloft, sending the shadows retreating. Without asking permission, he went to the door connecting to a maid's room—the chamber had originally been meant for female guests—and Henry cursed himself for not thinking of it sooner. "Locked," he murmured.

Meaning nothing, if an accomplice had shot the bolt from the other side. Miss Devereaux, perhaps. But some force had held Henry to the bed, and whatever tricks mediums might employ, they couldn't exert control over his body. Certainly not without mesmerizing him first, and there was no way to accomplish such a thing without his knowledge.

The only logical conclusions were that he'd had a very detailed nightmare…or an otherworldly visitation.

Shivers took him, and he pulled his legs onto the bed, seeking warmth. Footsteps padded rapidly across the room, and a moment later the mattress bowed slightly under Night's weight.

"Are you all right?" the medium asked, leaning forward as if to get a clear look at Henry's face. Dark fingers touched the back of Henry's hand, hot against his skin. "You're freezing—I can go to the kitchen and make some tea, if you'd like."

The note of concern in his voice caught Henry off guard. In the soft light of the candle, Night looked somehow different than when Henry had first seen him in the daylight of the grand hall. His features softer, perhaps, or maybe it was the way his raven-black hair tumbled loosely over his forehead. He wore an oriental-style robe of plum silk, decorated with embroidered dragons and birds, a glimpse of white nightshirt beneath it. The scent of some citrusy cologne rose from his skin: oranges and musk.

Henry was suddenly acutely aware of the heaviness of Night's weight on the mattress beside him. What would it feel like stretched out on top of him in this bed? Were Night's nipples much darker than the rest of his skin? His prick?

Heat flushed Henry's body; he no longer felt at all cold. Quite the opposite, in fact. "N-no. You're kind to offer, but I'm feeling much better already."

Night's fingers lingered for a moment on the back of his hand. Then they withdrew, Henry's skin going cold where their warmth had been. "I'll leave you to your rest."

Henry laughed ruefully. "Not much chance of that. I'll spend the hours until dawn wondering if every sound is the work of some otherworldly visitor."

The bed creaked as Night rose to his feet. "I don't think you'll have another visitation. Our presence is slowly charging the atmosphere of the house, but we haven't been here long enough for the energy to truly build up. An apparition like the one you saw takes power. Likely it exhausted what it had gathered from us already and won't have the strength to trouble you again. At least not tonight."

The words were spoken kindly, lacking the hidden laughter Night had directed toward him earlier. The man could have taken the chance to fluster Henry further by claiming the room haunted and Henry unlikely to sleep another wink. Either he was a very poor fraud, or…

"Thank you," Henry said.

Night paused at the door. "You're welcome. May I ask if you've ever been visited by a spirit before?"

Henry swallowed against the tightness in his throat. "Yes. I don't wish to speak of it."

"Of course." Night started out, then turned back. A slow, hot grin curved his full lips. "I'll be right next door if you have further…need…of me."

Before Henry thought of a response, Night slipped out, taking his candle with him and leaving Henry sitting alone in the dark.

Vincent sat up for an hour after he'd left Strauss, sipping from his flask. He'd relaid the line of salt he'd disturbed in rushing out the door. No spirit would be visiting him in his sleep, not tonight or ever.

The more he saw of the house, the less he liked it. They hadn't even been here for twenty-four hours, and already a spirit had appeared to Strauss, of all people. Telling him to leave.

Although it had lost the energy to manifest, Vincent caught the last of its presence when he'd entered the room. The taste of lavender had matched the spirit he'd sensed near the schoolroom. This one moved about the house. And, according to Strauss, seemed to be a woman.

Why had she appeared to Strauss? Had his room contained some special significance to her, or had it been a random choice? Did he possess a touch of clairvoyance, not quite enough to make him a medium but enough to allow spirits to contact him more easily than everyone else?

Strauss. Either sleep improved his disposition or he wasn't quite as much of an ass as Night had first supposed. Sitting on the bed with him had been a mistake, though; Vincent had wanted nothing more than to shove the man back into the blankets and warm him up the old-fashioned way. Strip away the stuffy exterior and make him moan and writhe.

Vincent shifted and ran a hand over his swelling cock. Strauss thought he was a fraud, was determined to destroy the livelihood on which Lizzie and he both depended. Determined to replace them with some soulless "Electro-Séance," as if spirits were nothing more than the voices recorded on a phonograph, to be called up on demand and dismissed when the listener grew tired.

But they weren't. They were people, or had been.

Had the ghostly woman meant her words to Strauss as a threat—or a warning?

They ought to demand the history of the house from Gladfield. But Gladfield wouldn't budge, certainly not before they'd had time to investigate tomorrow.

He knew already what Lizzie would say. They could afford to wait. Whatever was happening here wasn't dangerous.

Yet.

CHAPTER 6

OVER BREAKFAST the next morning, Henry told the others about his ghostly visitor.

Miss Prandle dropped her fork in her eggs, one hand fluttering over her chest in horror. "Dear heavens! I would have been frightened to death."

"It offered me no physical harm," he assured her.

"Still, perhaps Jo would like to stay with me," she said. "I'd simply die if something appeared in the room and I was alone! And she could help me with my hair—I had an awful time with it this morning."

Noting the rather fixed look on Jo's face, Henry said, "I may need to conduct experiments at any hour of the night. I'd hate to wake you should I require Jo's assistance on short notice." He certainly wasn't going to let Miss Prandle treat Jo as some sort of servant, there to fix her hair or lay out her clothes or whatever else the woman was used to having maids do for her.

"Oh. Of course." Miss Prandle deflated, but didn't argue. Night, however, cast him a curious look.

"What is your plan of investigation for today?" Gladfield asked as Bamforth topped off his coffee.

"Jo and I will set up instruments in various parts of the house, for the monitoring of phenomena," Henry said. "I must ask no one enter the area once the equipment is in place."

"How inconvenient," Miss Devereaux remarked, sipping her coffee.

"But necessary to prevent any tampering."

"I'm sure we'll all be able to restrain ourselves from touching your equipment," Night drawled. "No matter the temptation."

Night lounged back in his chair, nothing on his plate but a piece of dry toast, as if breakfast was simply too much effort to put forth at this hour. The green coat was back, paired with a striped vest and dark trousers. Henry's thoughts flew back to the scene on the bed, the feel of Night's weight beside him, the masculine smell of his skin.

"Better to ensure a fair test whose results cannot be disputed," Gladfield said. "Where do you propose to set up your instruments, Mr. Strauss?"

"Three places." Henry's voice scraped slightly coming out, and he cleared his throat. Across the table, Night gave him a little smirk. "Mr. Reyer's bed chamber, the schoolroom, and the base of the servants' stair on the first floor. Those should give us a good start, I would think. If you would like to accompany us, Mr. Gladfield, I'd be happy to give you an explanation of what I intend to do."

"Excellent." Gladfield rubbed his hands together happily. "And what of our mediums? Miss Devereaux, shall you and your colleague do any investigating of your own?"

She exchanged a glance with Night. "We spoke before breakfast. I intend to traverse the grounds outside, in case the spirits haunt the gardens or outbuildings as well."

The scene outside the bay window wasn't promising: overcast and gray, with a layer of old snow blanketing the ground. Henry's estimation of Miss Devereaux increased. Whether a fraud or not, she was at least committed, to brave such miserable weather.

"As for Vincent," she went on, "with your permission, Mr. Gladfield, he'll search the basement, attics, and tower."

"Go anywhere you wish," Gladfield said with a wave of his hand. "As long as it isn't one of the bedrooms occupied by another guest, you are all free to venture as you will."

"Do you mind if I accompany you, Mr. Night?" Miss Prandle asked.

A plate rattled as Bamforth, who was cleaning up, let it slip from his hand. "Sorry," he said, snatching it quickly.

Night glanced at him, then back to Miss Prandle. "Your company will be most welcome. If nothing else, it will lighten the dreariness of the day immeasurably."

Henry ground his teeth together. The man was an utter devil! First he flirted with Henry, and now with Miss Prandle? Well, at least Henry knew none of Night's innuendos were to be taken seriously.

And he wasn't disappointed by the fact. Not at all. It wasn't as if anything could possibly have come of them. Henry was far too canny to the wiles of mediums to be taken advantage of again.

No, he wasn't disappointed at all.

"Well," Gladfield said a short time later, "I must confess, I'm quite fascinated as to all of your little gadgets, Mr. Strauss. I anticipate seeing them in action."

They stood within the bedroom which had once belonged to the master of the house. While Gladfield spoke, Jo moved around the room, quietly remeasuring the cold spots they'd located the day before and recording her findings.

"None of these instruments are of my invention," Henry said, although Gladfield's praise warmed his insides. "But the use I intend to put them to is, I believe, novel. Before utilizing the Electro-Séance, we must confirm the presence of spirits."

"But you saw one yourself last night!" Gladfield exclaimed.

"I believe I did," Henry agreed. "However, the possibility remains it may have been an extraordinarily vivid dream. Or even a bit of trickery—not to suggest I think such is the case here," he added hastily, remembering Night's unexpected kindness. The man might be a cad, but he was a cad who'd offered to make a trek to the kitchen in the middle of the night just to fetch Henry tea. "However, the point of the Electro-Séance is to rely solely on scientific measurements, rather than human senses. A thermometer has no imagination to run away with it, after all."

"True, true." Gladfield drew a cigar case from his pocket and set about lighting one—without asking for Jo's permission, as he should have done in the presence of any lady. "And what would you consider evidence of a spirit?"

"Cold spots whose presence cannot be explained by drafts or other phenomena," Henry replied, forcing himself to disregard Gladfield's rudeness. Chastising the man would only risk costing them the contest, after all. "Electromagnetic fluctuations without a lightning storm or electrical wire to account for them. Highly localized changes in barometric pressure. I may devise other tests in the future, but for the purposes of this contest, I will consider any two of these sufficient evidence to proceed with the séance. When it comes to the séance, an area with higher evidence of spirit activity would be better than one with lower."

"Such as your bedroom?" Gladfield said.

"It's one possibility." Jo had returned, so he asked, "What have you found?"

She grinned, her eyes bright. Although she'd been interested in constructing and testing their equipment in the shop, their current circumstances seemed to have awakened a true investigatory zeal in her. "The cold spots we recorded yesterday are still there." She held out the notebook for him to examine her findings. "All of them within a degree or two of our original measurements."

"Good work," he said, and her smile grew wider. "Now, let's set up the Franklin bells."

They dragged a table to the center of the room and began to set up the apparatus on it. "What will these do?" Gladfield asked, drawing closer. Cigar smoke wreathed his head.

"In simple terms, it will alert us to any changes in the room's electromagnetic field." The device consisted of a wooden stand with a pair of small bells hanging from it. Wires were attached to both bells. In between the bells was suspended a metal ball approximately the size of a grape. "One of the wires will be grounded to the lightning rods on the outside of the house," he said, indicating the right hand bell. "The other will be left exposed to the atmosphere. Any change in the electromagnetic status of the air—say, if a thunderstorm were to approach—will affect the electrical charge on the bells, causing the ball to swing back and forth between them."

Gladfield scratched the side of his head. "I must say, this is all quite beyond me. What does it have to do with ghosts?"

"Spirits give off—or are—electromagnetic fields. It's one of the reasons they're disrupted by other forces such as sunlight." Henry carefully adjusted the wire before stepping back, satisfied. "Thunderstorms in January are exceedingly unlikely; therefore, if we hear any of the bells ringing, we can safely take it for evidence of spirit activity in the vicinity. However, there is one other precaution I wish to take. The starch and thread, Jo?"

Jo pulled a box of powdered starch from their bag and handed it to him. "This will make certain no one is able to sneak into the room and interfere with the bells," he explained. Going to the window, he shook out a line of starch. When he had finished, Jo ran a thread across the window, about a foot above the sill, securing it to either side with a bit of wax. Now no one could enter without breaking loose the wax.

"Do you imagine Miss Devereaux means to climb up the outside of the house and come through the window just to interfere with your experiment?" Gladfield asked with a laugh.

"Of course not." Henry gripped the box of starch more tightly. A bit puffed out, leaving a streak of white on his tie. "But this must be done as thoroughly as possible. I don't want to give any doubters an opening to declare our experiments invalid."

"An excellent point," Gladfield agreed, although Henry suspected he still thought they were being paranoid. "Continue on."

Henry and Jo sealed every window and the fireplace before leaving the room. Once outside, they sealed the doorway as well. "There," Henry said. "Now all we have to do is keep an ear out for the bells. At least the open center of the house means the sound should carry well."

"Indeed. If I hear them, I shall alert you at once," Gladfield said. "Thank you for your indulgence, Mr. Strauss. I'll leave you and your able assistant to your work."

He departed, and they made their way to the schoolroom. This time, Henry brought a barometer with him, and he and Jo took readings at various points in the room. He'd spend the afternoon taking measurements in other parts of the house, once the Franklin bells were in place and ready.

They set up the second set of bells, once again sealing the schoolroom against any possible intrusion. Once they finished, they descended the servants' stair to the first-floor landing, where Night had sensed a spirit the day before. Or tasted it, or whatever he did. What a bizarre ability to have—or claim to have.

How were Night's investigations proceeding? Or was he investigating the person of Miss Prandle instead?

It was an unworthy thought, at least in regards to Miss Prandle. Henry banished it quickly from his mind. He needed to concentrate on his scientific work, not on the infuriating Mr. Night.

The remainder of the starch outlined a wide strip around the landing, but there wasn't enough to coat the descending steps. "Blast," he said. "Jo, will you get another box from our supplies while I finish affixing the thread in the passageway?" The blockage would no doubt inconvenience Bamforth, who would have to detour through the grand hall to perform his kitchen duties, but it couldn't be helped.

"Of course," Jo said and sped up the steps like a gazelle. Henry shook his head and turned back to his work. If only he had half her energy.

God, that made him sound old. Barely a decade her senior, and yet it felt as if a chasm separated them.

Had he done the right thing, bringing her here? Making her his assistant in the first place? He hadn't known what to do when she showed up on his doorstep two years ago. What did he know about raising a young woman? Was he doing the right thing by encouraging her to learn about machines and math, or should he steer her toward finding a suitor? Surely she'd wish to marry someday…or would she? Just the thought of broaching the topic of male attention made him feel faint. He'd worry about it later. Possibly much later.

He needed to return his mind to work. A thread of just less than waist height would keep anyone from stepping over it without disturbing the seal, and the starch on the floor would show if anyone crawled beneath. Crouching down, he attached one end of a thread to the wall with wax—

Jo's scream echoed down the stairs.

Vincent descended from the attics with Miss Prandle. Cobwebs clung to his coat, and he brushed at them ineffectively. "Nothing but shadows and spiders," he said. "But at least we know now."

Just as they reached the third-floor landing, a young woman's scream split the air.

Vincent leapt down the last few steps before his brain even registered that the shriek belonged to Miss Strauss. She stood near the stone chimney piercing the balcony from the grand hall below. The discreet door beside it, leading to the servants' stair, hung open. As for Miss Strauss herself, she stood frozen, her arms drawn in tight, her eyes wide with fear.

"Miss Strauss! What happened?" he asked.

She flung herself into his arms with a frightened sob. Startled, he caught her. Her body trembled with fear, and her teeth chattered. "Have you been harmed?" he asked urgently.

"N-no." She pulled just far enough away to blink up at him. "The mirror on the wall—by the chimney."

The glass now showed nothing but their forms and that of Miss Prandle hurrying up behind them. "What of it?"

"I'd come upstairs to get something, and as I passed by the mirror, I looked up and—and there was a woman standing behind me!" Miss Strauss bit her lip. "She was unearthly pale, and her head just lolled to one side, like her neck was broken!"

The spirit he'd sensed at the bottom of the stair? Perhaps a maid had fallen and suffered a snapped spine?

"Jo!" exclaimed Strauss, bursting out of the door leading to the stairs. "Are you all right? I—"

He stopped when he saw his cousin in Vincent's arms. For an instant he went even paler than usual—then spots of angry color appeared on his cheeks. "Unhand her at once!"

Vincent's mood turned sour. He released the girl and stepped back. "I wasn't the cause for her scream."

"I'll let Jo be the judge of that," Strauss snapped, putting a protective hand on her shoulder.

Of course Strauss had only seen him as a savage redskin manhandling a young woman. Why had he ever imagined Strauss would view him differently?

"I'm all right, Henry," Miss Strauss said shakily. "I only saw something in the mirror." She repeated her story to her cousin.

"You poor thing," Miss Prandle said. "You should go to your room and rest."

"No." Miss Strauss straightened her back determinedly. "Thank you, Miss Prandle, but I have work to do."

She certainly didn't lack for backbone. Still. "Miss Strauss," Vincent said, "if I may, I have some exercises to help calm your mind. Spirits are notorious for feeding off the energy of young persons your age, and—"

"Absolutely not!" Strauss exclaimed. His eyes flashed angrily behind the lenses of his spectacles, and he took his cousin's arm as if he meant to drag her bodily away from Vincent. "Jo doesn't need some mediumistic hocus-pocus."

Vincent drew himself up. "I'm trying to help."

"Keep your 'help' to yourself. I know how your sort operates, and —"

"Mr. Strauss!" Miss Prandle exclaimed. "Control yourself. This is my uncle's guest you're insulting."

As if she hadn't insulted him last night over dinner, with her careless comment about his ability to speak English. Or earlier today in the attics, when she'd guilelessly asked if he knew Buffalo Bill Cody.

"No matter, Miss Prandle." Vincent bowed to her, careful to keep the heat seething in his chest from showing on his face. "I'm going to finish my investigations of the tower. If you'd be so good as to stay with Miss Strauss, it would put my mind at ease."

Before Strauss objected, he turned on his heel and marched to the main stairs, leaving the group behind him.

Once Night had vanished, Henry turned back to Jo. "Now that he's gone—"

"You—you cur!" Jo glared up at him, her lower lip thrust out pugnaciously. "Mr. Night was trying to help me, and you came charging up like some overgrown bull."

What could he say? That he'd seen before how men took liberties with Jo that they would never consider with a white girl? And although it seemed he'd been mistaken in his initial assumption, Night's offer to help calm her mind put him back on his guard. Wasn't that how Isaac had begun?

"These mediums are nothing but fakes," he retorted. "Any concern on his part was just an act."

"You don't know that! Miss Prandle, you saw everything."

"Yes, and I agree your cousin isn't being at all fair to Mr. Night," she soothed. "Still, there's no reason to harangue poor Mr. Strauss."

Of course Miss Prandle had come in on Night's side—she was no doubt as swayed by his charms as Jo. "I know how these mediums behave," Henry said. "Mr. Night is probably some sort of cad. You shouldn't be alone with him again, Miss Prandle."

She let out a long sigh. "Mr. Strauss, with all due respect, I have far more experience with cads than you. Our family is rather well off financially. Do you imagine my station fails to attract suitors of rather dubious character?"

He didn't want to admit it, but… "I suppose it would."

"Let me reassure you, Mr. Night might play the rogue, but it is no more than an act." She patted Jo on the shoulder. "Besides, it was your cousin who flung herself on him, not he who clasped her first."

"I was frightened," Jo said, shamefaced.

The last of Henry's anger drained away. Perhaps he hadn't been fair to Mr. Night after all. "I've behaved like a beast," he said. "Forgive me, Jo."

"I'm not the one you need to apologize to," Jo said. "I believe Mr. Night indicated you could find him in the tower?"

"Oh, I'm sure he wouldn't want an interruption," Henry said hastily. At her look, he sighed. "Very well. I'll go to him at once, if it will make you happy."

He descended to the first floor, where the only entrance to the tower lay to the east of the front vestibule. The tower door stood open for the first time since they'd come to Reyhome Castle. Henry stuck his head cautiously inside, hoping to spot Night right away.

Of course he didn't. The servants hadn't gotten around to cleaning out the tower, and cobwebs and dust filled the simple stone interior. An iron stair clung to the walls, spiraling up into darkness above. For some reason, the tower had been built without windows, and the only light leaked down from the open platform high above. If only he'd thought to bring a candle.

"Mr. Night?" he called tentatively. The still air swallowed his words, giving him not even an echo in return.

Well, there was nothing for it but to start climbing. Jo would hound him if he didn't offer his apology. And…well. He had been unduly hard on the man, perhaps. Would he have been as resentful of Night if he wasn't so accursed handsome and flirtatious? So much like Isaac?

It didn't matter. Henry thrust the memories away and began to climb the steps. Even the ring of iron beneath his shoes seemed oddly muted, as if the tower resented any loud sounds.

Cold air flooded from above, stirring his hair and biting deep into his bones. He should have worn his overcoat, but he'd forgotten the top of the tower was exposed to the elements, save for where the pointed roof offered some small protection.

Something brushed against his sleeve. Just the wind, curling down from above.

Wasn't it?

He froze in place, acutely aware of his heartbeat. Uncanny silence surrounded him, broken only his ragged breathing. He might have been the only one left in the house.

Maybe he was. Perhaps everyone else had fled something terrible.

A floor below him, the tower door slammed shut.

CHAPTER 7

HENRY OPENED his mouth to cry out, but no sound issued forth. He gripped the iron rail, peering down into the dimness below him. Someone was having a prank at his expense, nothing more. Or they'd closed the door accidentally, not realizing anyone was inside.

The sound of footsteps ascending the stair came from below.

Every hair on his body stood up, bristling against the fabric of his shirtsleeves, his trousers. The turn of the stair kept him from seeing whoever it was, but the tread was heavy. A man's.

Just Gladfield. Or Bamforth, come to make some inquiry about dinner preferences. Or even Night himself, returning to continue his exploration of the tower after some brief errand.

The footsteps drew closer. They were right at the bend. In a moment, he'd be able to see who it was.

Closer. They were in front of him now, just a few steps below.

No one was there. But the footsteps kept coming.

Henry flung himself up the stairs, taking them two and three at a time. The thunder of his shoes on the iron now rang throughout the tower, muffling the sound of any pursuing steps. His breath ached in his lungs, and a wave of cold washed over him. At any moment now, he'd feel a hand grasp his collar and wrench him backward.

He came around a turn and collided with a dark shape.

The cry locked behind Henry's teeth burst forth, and he shoved wildly at the figure, trying to free himself from its grasp.

"Strauss! It's me. Calm down," Night exclaimed.

Henry clutched at the solidity of Night's arms. "There's something on the stairs—the door slammed—I heard footsteps, but no one was there."

Night frowned slightly, tilting his head to listen. Henry did the same, although he could barely make anything out over the pounding of his heart and the raggedness of his breath. The winter wind moaned across the parapet above them, but otherwise there was nothing. Silence.

"Whatever it was is gone now," Night murmured. But he didn't move away.

The scent of citrus and musk rose from warm skin, and Henry breathed it in deep. Had he been cold only moments ago? Now his skin burned, drawing fire from the heat of the man next to him. His prick stirred, and his treacherous heart sped once again, this time with excitement rather than fear.

"I-I came to apologize," he said, but his voice shook. "For earlier."

A speculative look came into those dark eyes. "Did you?"

"Yes." He swallowed against a dryness in his throat. "It's my duty to be protective of Jo, and…well. Men seem to often think the color of her skin means she's available to them for…things."

Night arched a brow, but he still didn't move away. "And all the lurid dime-novel tales of Indians carrying off hapless women surely didn't help."

Embarrassed heat flooded Henry's face. "No! I know you might think so, given how I spoke to you on our first meeting. Please, accept my apology."

Night seemed taken aback. "I don't think I've ever had an apology from a white man."

Now Henry felt even more wretched. "Living with Jo has made me consider things in a way I had no cause to before."

"I see. Then I accept your apology." Night moved nearer, forcing Henry back until his shoulders met the stone of the wall. The man was far too close, his lithe legs pressing lightly against Henry's, his hands still on Henry's arms. Henry realized dimly that he still clutched Night in return, but he couldn't quite seem to make himself let go.

"And did you only come to say you were sorry?" Night murmured, his voice gone deep and husky.

"Yes." He had to be firm about this. Had to. "I…I should go. I w-wouldn't want to deprive Miss Prandle of your company any longer."

Night bent his head. "But I don't want to do this with Miss Prandle," he said. And before Henry did more than part his lips to ask what he referred to, Night kissed him.

His full lips moved sensuously against Henry's even as their bodies pressed tight. The hard line of Night's erection pushed against Henry's hip, and Henry moaned involuntarily, rubbing them together. Night took advantage of the moan, slipping his tongue into Henry's mouth, and oh God, he'd missed this. He never kissed any of the men he met in the back alleyways, and Night's lips on his were like the fall of rain on drought-stricken soil. The medium tasted of cinnamon and warmth, his tongue exploring Henry's mouth with a thoroughness which turned his knees to water.

Night drew back, his breathing uneven. He let go of Henry's arm with one hand, running his thumb lightly over Henry's lips. Henry bit at the tip, sucked it, but he couldn't look away from Night's dark eyes. This was madness—foolishness—it was Isaac all over again.

Yet he couldn't seem to make himself stop.

There came a loud squeal of hinges from below, and they both froze. In the heat of the moment, Henry had forgotten about whatever had come up the stair behind him, forgotten everything except for the man whose prick still pressed against his through their trousers.

"Henry?" Jo called. "Are you up there?"

Night released him and stepped back. Henry cleared his throat, fighting past the bands of lust tightening his chest. "Y-yes?" Night grinned at his discomposure, and Henry shot him a scowl. "I'm here!"

"Come down quick, and bring Mr. Night with you! The bells are ringing!"

Vincent stood back with Miss Prandle, Gladfield, and Miss Strauss while Henry—he couldn't help but think of Strauss as such—inspected the thread and the line of starch across the doorway leading to what had been Mr. Reyer's bedroom. The Franklin bells had ceased ringing by the time they'd arrived, but it didn't seem to dampen Henry's excitement in the slightest.

"Everything here is intact," he verified, and Miss Strauss scribbled something in their notebook. "No one entered the room to tamper with the equipment, at least through this doorway. I'm removing the thread now in order to enter."

The gleam of genuine excitement in his eyes made Vincent suppress a somewhat rueful grin. Whatever Henry might think of mediums, there was no denying he enjoyed using his science to achieve similar ends.

No denying either the way he'd returned Vincent's kiss in the tower, like a man dying of thirst finding an oasis in the desert.

Vincent shifted his stance and took a deep breath to calm his pulse. He'd never intended to kiss Henry, hadn't meant to do more than flirt. But once he'd had Henry in his arms, he hadn't been able to resist. Neither, it seemed, had Henry. If Miss Strauss hadn't interrupted, things would have gone a great deal further.

The mental image of Henry kneeling in front of him had his prick hardening again. He had to think of something else—anything else.

Fortunately, the rustle of skirts sounded behind him as Lizzie approached. Glad for the distraction, he stepped away from the gathering to greet her.

The cold air outside had reddened her nose and ears, and the hem of her skirt was damp. Her gaze went past him to the bedroom. "Has Mr. Strauss made some sort of discovery?" she asked. "Or is he just showing off his instrument?"

Night snickered. "The former, actually. Maybe. His spirit-detecting bells went off, and he's making certain no one else had access to the room."

"And does it actually prove anything we didn't already know?" she asked, folding her arms over her chest.

Oddly, he found he wanted to defend Henry to her. "I think it does. Whatever his intentions, Mr. Strauss's methods are ingenious. The bells alerted us to the presence of a spirit, without needing a medium to be on hand. In a case such as this, where there are only two of us and multiple spirits…"

"Hmm." Lizzie didn't seem so convinced.

"The spirit here was the weakest before," Vincent added. "I hesitate to suggest it, but could the fact its presence stirred the bells mean it's growing stronger?"

"Hardly a comforting thought," she muttered.

"I know." He glanced over his shoulder to make certain everyone else was still occupied. "Did you find anything?"

"No. I tramped around in the snow for nothing." Her lips turned up into a wicked grin. "Perhaps I should tell Mr. Strauss I sensed something in the pond. Let him freeze his fingers off trying to measure a cold spot on the ice."

"He'd do it," Vincent agreed ruefully.

"I'll keep the thought in mind in case we need entertainment later."

"Don't be cruel, Lizzie."

She gave him an odd look. "He's our competition, Vincent. No matter what else you might get up to with him, he's not your friend, or mine."

The thought was dispiriting. Henry's kindness to his cousin, his willingness to apologize to Vincent for a slight, suggested Vincent's original assessment of Henry had been wrong. He wanted to get Henry alone again, not to kiss—although he'd certainly relish the opportunity—but to talk. To find out more about that clever mind and unexpectedly warm heart.

But Lizzie was right. "There's something else you should know," he said and told her of the apparition Jo had glimpsed in the mirror. "Henry and I exchanged words, and I went to investigate the tower."

"Henry?" she asked sharply.

Damn it. "Strauss," he said hastily. "He came to find me, and the tower door slammed behind him. Then he reported hearing disembodied footsteps coming up the stairs."

"Did you hear these steps?"

"No," he admitted. "And I didn't sense anything. But something frightened Strauss. I suppose it might have been his imagination."

"Hmm." She continued to look at him askance. "I've known you for a long time, Vincent Night. There's something you aren't telling me."

"The tower…I think it bears closer inspection." He lowered his voice conspiratorially. "Regardless of whatever Mr. Strauss heard on the stair, the small room at the top of the tower is a locus of spirit activity of some sort." The taste of rusty iron nails had been so strong in his mouth he'd almost gagged.

Until the kiss washed it away with the sweetness of another's lips. Then he hadn't tasted anything but Henry.

A short time later, everyone drifted into the dining room for lunch. It was less formal than their earlier meals, and at the moment only Henry, Jo, and Night were present; the others' footsteps and voices sounded on the stairs and in the hall.

Henry scarcely believed the Franklin bells had worked. Of course theory said they should, and he'd been confident in it…but there had always been a little seed of doubt.

Not now. He'd create his own model of the bells and patent it as a "ghost detector." Strauss's Sure-Fire Spirit Finder—that sounded good, didn't it? *Sleep peacefully, without fear of unseen spirits*, the ad might say. Of course, he'd have to find some way of insulating it from lightning storms, or else legions of customers would end up convinced that they were haunted every time the weather turned foul.

But those were just details, to be figured out later. For now, the point was that the device had worked.

Bamforth laid out a selection of cold meats, cheeses, and bread for them on the long side table. Henry assembled a sandwich from them and dropped into one of the chairs at the table.

Vincent Night sat down directly beside him.

Bands tightened around Henry's chest, and his hunger dissolved. Or rather, his hunger for the food. Even not looking directly at Night, he was keenly aware of the medium's body inches from his, just as he would have been the heat from a fire. He reached hurriedly for his coffee with his right hand even as Night reached with his left. Their elbows bumped, and Henry felt in his groin the shock of the casual touch.

"Pardon me," Night said, giving no indication that Henry's presence had any effect on him at all.

"Of course," Henry replied, striving to sound cool. Which was impossible, considering all he could think of was the heat of Night's lips on his, the press of his erection through their trousers.

No. He had to fight this. The man was a fraud and a liar at worst, an archaic purveyor of superstition at best. How many widows had Night tricked out of their inheritances, leaving them destitute? How many young men had he taken advantage of, claiming to care for them?

Except he'd gone out of his way to reassure Henry last night in the bedroom. Offered to make him tea. And this morning, he'd tried to help Jo, at least until Henry had intervened. Those seemed less like the actions of a fraud, and more like the actions of someone concerned about those around him.

"Are you quite all right, Mr. Strauss?" Miss Prandle asked as she entered the room.

Henry blinked back to the here and now and realized he'd been clutching his coffee and glaring at his plate without either taking a sip or eating a bite. "Quite fine, thank you," he said and brought the coffee cup to his lips.

"I'm sure Mr. Strauss is merely excited by the morning's events," Night said blandly.

Henry choked on the coffee in his mouth, succeeding in bringing it up his nose. Jo helpfully pounded him on the back.

"Indeed," he said, mopping his face with his napkin. "*Science* is always thrilling. Far more so than most other activities one might undertake."

"Of course," Night replied, pausing to take a bite of bread. "There is nothing quite so rousing for a man as to have his bells played with."

Jo giggled, and Miss Prandle covered an unladylike snort behind her hand. Thank heavens Gladfield had only just come in and hadn't overheard. Even given the loosened boundaries allowed mediums, he might have objected to Night's talk.

Henry's neck and cheeks flushed hot. He bit savagely into his sandwich, imagining it was…well, he wouldn't want to really bite Night. Although…

Damn it.

Bamforth reemerged from the kitchen with an offering of fresh coffee, distracting the company. Miss Devereaux entered the room, making their gathering complete. Night turned his attention to Miss Prandle, asking something about a misplaced will. Too flustered to follow the conversation, Henry concentrated on his meal, glad to be left in peace for a few minutes.

Once finished, he tossed down his napkin and drained the rest of his coffee. "Come along, Jo. As we've gotten results in the bedroom, I wish to set up the barometer inside. We'll monitor it throughout the afternoon."

They climbed the stairs to the second floor. Henry's mind was already half on the experiments he intended to run, when Jo grabbed his arm and let out a gasp. "Henry, look!"

Startled, he raised his head. They'd come up the easternmost of the double staircases, which let out directly facing the wall of Mrs. Reyer's bedroom. High up on the wall—higher than any human could easily reach, at least without a ladder—someone had scrawled "Kill the whores."

CHAPTER 8

Vincent stood in front of the wall, staring up at the uneven letters. He breathed deep, but smelled only chalk and dust, tasted only the milk-cut coffee from lunch. "I don't know," he said slowly. "I don't sense anything."

"Don't be daft." Henry cut him a sharp look. "This…filth… certainly wasn't here when we went down to lunch, or else we would have seen it. The starch and threads on the servants' stair weren't disturbed, and with the doors to the dining room open, no one could have gone up the main stair without us spotting them. It's impossible for any human agency to have done this."

"Mr. Strauss is right," Bamforth said. "It had to be a spirit." He swallowed and glanced at Miss Prandle. "Do you…do you think the ladies are safe staying here?"

Vincent refrained from saying he didn't think any of them were safe. Was it possible he'd lost his skill? In refusing to channel the spirits, had he somehow let it atrophy like an unused muscle? First he hadn't heard the steps on the tower stair, and now he didn't sense any lingering presence.

Everything else had been so clear—the three spirits, their distinct flavors. So why couldn't he sense anything now?

"Spirit writing doesn't necessarily indicate the ability actually carry out any threats," Lizzie said. Her mouth turned down into a frown, however, her brows drawing together.

"Surely it doesn't bode well, either," Bamforth argued.

"I say we put the matter to our experts," Miss Prandle said. "Mr. Night, Miss Devereaux, Mr. Strauss—what do you think?"

"I would prefer to gather more preliminary data," Henry said with a glance at Gladfield. "But if necessary, for the safety of the ladies, I'm willing to perform the Electro-Séance and banish the spirit for good."

He made it sound so damnably easy. "You've never faced an actual haunting in your life, have you?" Vincent asked.

Color stood out high on Henry's pale cheeks. "I don't see that it matters. My theories—"

"Mean nothing." God, the man didn't even know they were dealing with more than one spirit. Whatever good qualities he possessed, his arrogance was unbounded. "An angry ghost isn't a-a machine you can turn off or on."

"Perhaps, when it comes to the *old* way of doing things." Henry's lip curled. "But this is the nineteenth century, not the Middle Ages. Progress has given us more than adequate tools for dealing with such matters, if we but use them."

"*I* think," Lizzie interrupted, "if this spirit is eager to communicate, we should give it the opportunity."

Gladfield had stood back and listened to the argument without interference. Now, however, he cocked his head to the side. "What do you mean?"

"Spirit writing," Vincent said flatly. "Lizzie, you can't. It's too dangerous."

"Nothing here has attempted harm to us," she said calmly. "The apparition in Mr. Strauss's room was fearful in aspect, but it merely spoke to him. Jo's sighting, and the sound of footsteps on the stairs with Mr. Strauss, might have been startling, but were hardly perilous. As for this..." She gestured negligently at the ugly words. "I've had far worse vitriol directed at me in broad daylight on the very streets of New York."

On the surface of things, she was right. But Vincent couldn't shake the feeling of menace. Of something watching which meant them real harm. Was it real, though, or just the product of his own paranoia? "It's your decision," he said at last.

"Indeed it is." She turned to Gladfield. "If you'll have Bamforth remove this, I'd like an hour to meditate in my room. After, I propose we try contacting this spirit through automatic writing."

Henry's eyes narrowed, and Vincent knew he was trying to come up with some reason to object. "My experiment—"

"You can continue with it," Lizzie said. "I'm certainly not going to stop you."

"I'll sit in and watch the automatic writing, if I may," Gladfield said.

Despite everything, Vincent struggled to suppress a grin. A point to Lizzie; surely she'd known anyone would prefer to watch a medium in trance over a man staring at a barometer. Henry knew it as well, given the way his face darkened into a glower.

"Oh, can we watch too?" Miss Strauss asked excitedly.

"Of course," Lizzie replied with the air of a queen granting favors.

Henry all but swelled with indignation, and for a moment Vincent wondered if he'd make some outburst or force his cousin to attend him instead. Miss Strauss must have sensed the same, because she turned big eyes on him. "Please, Henry?"

Henry seemed to deflate. "Very well. We'll attend this 'automatic writing' session of Miss Devereaux's. With barometer and Franklin bells," he added. "It will help to verify whether any spirits actually attend or not."

The devil? "Are you calling Lizzie a liar, sir?" Vincent asked. He took a step forward.

Henry failed to step back, but instead glared up at him. "It doesn't matter what I think of Miss Devereaux. My aim is to scientifically measure—and manipulate—spirit phenomena."

Lizzie turned to Gladfield. "Surely this isn't fair—Vincent and I don't hover over his experiments! Why should he be allowed to use my efforts to bolster his case?"

"Miss Devereaux does have a point," Miss Prandle said, looking to her uncle.

Gladfield stroked his mustache as he considered. "True, true. But the aim of the contest is to rid Reyhome Castle of this spirit activity. Mr. Strauss's measurements won't affect your séance, and shall be allowed."

Vincent's stomach turned sour. Of course Gladfield had always been in Henry's corner. The whole purpose of the contest had been to give Henry the opportunity to prove his theories, not to vindicate the work of reputable mediums. If the lure of five hundred dollars had obscured the truth from him before, it was certainly clear now.

He turned to Lizzie, wondering if maybe they should just leave, and to hell with Gladfield and Henry and everything else. Except…

Except if they did just abandon everyone, and the haunting went bad…Henry might have more than his share of confidence, but Vincent had glimpsed his capacity for kindness and loyalty, at least when it came to his cousin. Vincent couldn't abandon him, let alone Miss Strauss or Miss Prandle, to face an angry ghost.

Lizzie's scowl did nothing to conceal her anger. But she nodded once, stiffly. "As you say, Mr. Gladfield. Let's reconvene in an hour."

"Where?" Henry asked immediately.

Vincent half expected her to suggest the master bedroom. But instead she said, "The schoolroom."

"Why there?" Miss Prandle asked.

Lizzie offered nothing but a thin smile. "Medium's intuition," she said before turning her back on them all and walking away.

"You don't have to be cruel, you know," Night said from behind him.

Henry paused, his hand on the latch of his bedroom door. Vincent—Night—stood close behind him, like something materialized from the shadows. "I don't know what you mean," he told the boards of his door, not daring to turn around. Not daring to put himself in such close proximity.

The boards creaked as Night drew closer. "Whether you approve of us or not, this is our livelihood. If you win this, it will see Lizzie and me out on the streets."

Henry swallowed hard, his fingers tightening on the latch. He found he didn't wish to sound unsympathetic. "How many candlemakers found themselves out of a job when gaslight was introduced?" he asked. "Progress marches on, whether we will it or no. Clinging to the shadows of the past will help no one in the long term. I'm sure a woman as clever as Miss Devereaux will find her footing in no time."

Night let out an explosive hiss of breath, so close that the hairs on Henry's neck stirred. "As always, you miss the point. At first I thought you had no heart at all, but your conduct with your cousin convinced me otherwise. Yet you insist on challenging us—belligerently—on every point. Could you not just quietly stand back for one moment?"

Henry wavered. All too well, he recalled Jo condemning his behavior as beastly only hours before. "I'm sorry. But this contest is important to me."

"And to me as well. But not for the reasons you think."

Henry snorted. "You're here for the money, the same as the rest of us."

"Lizzie is," Night corrected. "I came to protect her. I'm here because I want to save both the living and the dead. Can you say the same?"

Night stepped away, and Henry felt the loss of warmth against his back more keenly than he would have guessed. "I didn't mean—that is—it isn't just the money," Henry protested. "The prize is the means to an end. The Electro-Séance will make people's lives better."

"I believe you." Night stepped away, then paused. "But we all know what the road to hell is paved with. I only hope you know which direction your good intentions will ultimately lead."

They gathered in the schoolroom. Vincent and Bamforth hauled a table and chairs from the third-floor parlor while Lizzie hung heavy curtains over all the windows to block out as much light as possible. A thick cloth shrouded the table, its hem brushing the floor, its black surface drinking up any stray light. Henry and Miss Strauss installed a set of their infernal bells at one end of the table and took readings from a thermometer and a barometer.

"Jo, I'd like you to measure the temperature outside the room," Henry ordered when they were done.

Miss Strauss's face fell. "But I want to see the séance!"

Vincent barely restrained himself from rolling his eyes. Did Henry think they'd somehow corrupt his young cousin if she remained?

"Her youthful energy would be a useful addition to our company," Vincent pointed out. "Even though Lizzie will be the point of contact, the spirit will draw from everyone present."

Henry shot him a scowl. At a guess, Vincent's disparaging remark about good intentions had stung. "Allow me to conduct my experiments as I see fit, and you may conduct your séances as you see fit."

Looking disappointed, Miss Strauss took a thermometer and a notebook outside and shut the door. Lizzie sat at the head of the table, a pencil and paper in front of her. Everyone else crowded around, knees bumping, Vincent to her left and Gladfield to her right. A bit of subtle maneuvering on Vincent's part ensured that Henry sat to his left.

Gladfield wore an air of expectation. Something significant in the house's history must have happened in this room. Had they been the frauds Henry feared, Gladfield would have been an easy victim.

"Whenever you're ready," Gladfield said grandly, as if he had command of the spirits.

Vincent wiped his hands surreptitiously on his trousers. He hadn't attended a séance since the night Dunne died. True, Lizzie had chosen this room in order to interact with the lavender spirit, not the more threatening one Vincent had sensed in the bedroom, which hopefully meant there was less risk.

But what if something went wrong? What if he turned around and found something else wearing Lizzie's skin? What if the amulet didn't work, and something else ended up using his body like a puppet? Something cold and evil, staining him from the inside with slime and rot…

"Will this be like the trance in New York?" Miss Prandle asked. Startled out of his thoughts, Vincent jumped. Henry shot him a concerned look.

Lizzie nodded. "Very much like. Mr. Gladfield, would you put out the light?"

Darkness shrouded the room, with only the faintest glimmer of muted sun filtering through the twin draperies of cloud cover and heavy curtains. "Now, if I may have silence from everyone," Lizzie said. "I'm ready to begin."

Henry let out a soft snort as if he thought it easy to go into a trance state. Lizzie ignored him. "If everyone would please join hands. Vincent, Mr. Gladfield, both of you will take my right hand to leave the left free to write."

Vincent did as instructed, taking Lizzie's hand in his right and Henry's in his left. Hopefully his palm wasn't sweating too badly. As no one else could see in the dark room, he ran his thumb slowly across the back of Henry's hand and was rewarded with a hitch of breath.

If they were to be deprived of the youthful energy Miss Strauss would have brought to the circle, sexual energy would do just as well.

"Spirits of this place." Lizzie's voice seemed to float above them in the darkness. "My hand is prepared to write your words. Draw from the energy of this circle and direct my pencil as you will. I stand ready to receive you."

Vincent slowly traced the length of Henry's thumb with his own, taking his time. Exploring a callus, caressing the cuticle of the nail, mapping the creases of flesh above the knuckle. Henry's fingers tightened on his, breathing quickening even as Lizzie's slowed. Her chair creaked as she leaned back, body relaxing into trance. There came the soft scratch of pencil on paper—only looping now, idle circles which would resolve into words if the spirit took the chance to communicate thusly.

Lavender in his mouth, with just a hint of blood. The spirit was responding.

Might as well give it more energy. If Henry could use their skills to further his own goals, surely it was only fair to use Henry in return.

He shifted his grip on Henry's hand slightly, running his thumb over the vulnerable skin of the palm. Henry's breath caught audibly. A moment later, his chair creaked, as if sitting had grown uncomfortable. His pulse fluttered in his wrist beneath the swipe of Vincent's thumb.

Henry's grip shifted, and Vincent grinned at the feel of a hesitant caress across the back of his own knuckles now. He ached to draw Henry's hand to his mouth, to plant kisses over it before kissing him more thoroughly. That would be noticeable even in the darkened room, though. Instead, he tugged Henry's hand off the table and slid their joined fingers into Henry's lap.

The taste of lavender grew stronger.

Henry jumped slightly as Vincent found the outline of his prick. Vincent slowly drew their clasped fingers up and down the length, feeling it go harder beneath the barrier of cloth separating them. Henry's fingers tensed but he didn't pull away.

Blood spiked the lavender. The scratch of the pencil shifted, going from the idle loops to something more deliberate, and the Franklin bells began to ring. Henry tensed, so Vincent deliberately ran the nail of his thumb over the rigid outline of the head of the other man's cock. A startled gasp escaped Henry, largely covered by the bells, and his hips shifted. Vincent grinned into the dark, imagining how Henry must be fighting the need to move, trying to keep his left hand from shaking and giving anything away to Bamforth.

The bells rang more and more frantically, and Lizzie's hand tugged against his with the violence of her movements. On his other side, Henry tried to pull away, to break the circle. His fingers shook in Vincent's—he must be close.

Vincent gripped his fingers hard to keep him from pulling away and ran a final, firm caress down Henry's prick, from head to base—

Lizzie cried out sharply, the pencil snapping, bits flying away. The racket of the bells crescendoed, the suspended ball striking them so fast as to be deafening. Vincent's mouth was lavender and blood. Henry's head arched back in a silent cry.

Then nothing. The bells fell silent, as if a hand had reached out and stilled them. The only sound was of ragged breathing from both Lizzie and Henry—albeit for different reasons.

"L-light, please," Lizzie said, sounding tired. "The spirit has left.

Let's see what it had to say."

As Gladfield pulled open the curtains to let the gloomy daylight inside once more, Henry hurriedly dropped Bamforth's hand. Had he given himself away? He'd tried not to, but that damnable Night…

He shot a glance at the man beside him. Night's lips were turned up in a smirk. Although it was hard to tell given the color of his skin, Henry thought his face was flushed. Still, he seemed composed enough, although the voluminous tablecloth hid any evidence of arousal.

Henry's burning cheeks grew even hotter. He should have pulled away or forced their hands back up onto the table. He was supposed to be observing the séance scientifically, and instead he'd let Night use the cover of darkness to bring him to orgasm. And allowed it to happen in the middle of a group, where they might have been caught at any moment. Had he entirely taken leave of his senses?

But it had felt so good he hadn't been able to bring himself to make Night stop. Now he'd have to leave the room last and make certain the hang of his coat covered any wet spot. And put up with Night's knowing smirk.

Of course, Night probably wasn't feeling terribly comfortable at the moment. A small revenge, but he'd take it.

Damn it, he was supposed to be recording data, not staring at Night. Turning hastily to the equipment, he checked the barometer. "A slight change in pressure. Temperature decrease by four degrees," he said, hoping his voice sounded natural and not like a man who'd just come in his drawers like an untried youth.

"Your bells performed quite adequately," Night put in.

Henry flushed again, but answered the comment as if there had been no double meaning to it. "Assuming no one broke the circle during the séance in order to play a trick on us."

"I certainly couldn't have if I'd tried," Bamforth said. "You've got quite the grip there, Mr. Strauss."

Perhaps he'd just die from shame and become a spirit himself.

"What does the writing say?" Gladfield asked, rescuing him from further humiliation.

Miss Devereaux stared down at the pad, her mouth pensive. "See for yourself," she said and passed the paper to Gladfield. He frowned and handed it across to Night. Henry peered across the table.

The upper portion of the paper was covered in nothing more than loops and swirls, scrawled without lifting the pencil. Gradually, however, the scribbles became more and more defined, until they were first linked words, then finally separate ones.

Getoutgetoutgetout get out Get out.
Leave now.
Leave.
I can't hold him back much longer.
Leave.
Before he comes for you.

CHAPTER 9

"WE NEED to leave," Vincent said before Lizzie could vanish into her room.

They'd retreated from the schoolroom to dress for dinner. Rather than go to his own quarters, Vincent had hurried after the other medium, desperate to talk to her as soon as he could get her alone.

"Because of the spirit writing?" she asked.

"That's part of it. The house is Gothic Revival, so it can't be any more than fifty years old. Nonetheless, it's haunted by multiple spirits, one of whom is warning us to get out before 'he' comes for us." Vincent shook his head. "We need to get out of here. And quickly."

Pity flashed in Lizzie's green eyes. "Vincent," she said, her tone far too gentle, "have you considered that your reaction to the house might be…compromised…by your experience of last summer?"

"You're starting to sound like Strauss," he shot back. "Next you'll be saying machines are more reliable than people."

"But you haven't *been* reliable, have you?" Lizzie scowled, although at least the pity was gone from her expression. "You refused to channel the ghost of a little girl for her parents. I thought bringing you here might help you remember the medium you used to be, but it's only made you more paranoid."

Vincent ground his teeth together. "The spirit told us to get out. The same spirit as came to Strauss last night."

"Not an unusual thing for a ghost to tell the living," she countered. "How many hauntings occur because the old inhabitants of a house are confused by new owners living there? Intruding on what they see as their home?"

"And the part about leaving before 'he' comes?" Vincent demanded.

Lizzie's confident mask slipped. "That does concern me," she admitted. "But we knew this might be a difficult exorcism. There's no compelling reason for us to leave yet."

She hadn't been in the house with Dunne and him. Hadn't felt the malevolence first hand, beating down on her.

Hadn't opened her eyes, cold and drained almost to the point of death, only to find she'd killed the one person who'd ever really given a damn about her.

He touched the amulet through the layers of his clothes, pressing the circle of metal against his skin. Maybe she was right. Maybe he was paranoid. The long nights of hiding behind lines of salt, wondering if—when—the dark ghost that had killed Dunne would come back for him, had taken their toll. All of his instincts were off.

If their positions were reversed, would he give serious credence to the fears of someone too frightened to channel even the most docile of spirits, or read cards, or interact with the spirit world in any way? Or would he dismiss them and press on, reaching for the gleaming dream of the five-hundred-dollar prize held out before him?

"Perhaps you're right," he said at last.

She touched him lightly on the shoulder. "Go and dress for dinner, Vincent. We'll discuss things further."

Not certain whether he should feel foolish or alarmed, he slunk across the balcony to the door of his chamber. But before he could open it, Henry Strauss emerged from the next room. Catching sight of Vincent, his eyes narrowed sharply. "How dare you!"

Vincent glanced about automatically, but Henry was no fool, and no one else stirred on the third floor at the moment. Well, if nothing else, sparring with Henry might provide him with a diversion from his fears. He leaned his shoulder casually against the frame of Henry's door, looking down at Henry with only inches separating them.

Henry retreated, but only a little. His blue eyes flashed fire from behind the protective shield of his spectacles. Vincent had the sudden urge to pull them off, lean down, and kiss the frown off of Henry's mouth.

"How dare I?" he asked instead. "You'll have to be far more

specific, as I've done so many things to offend you."

Rather to his surprise, Henry grasped his arm and pulled him inside the room, shutting the door behind them. "You know what I'm talking about," he said in a voice no less angry for its low pitch. "At the séance. When you…"

Vincent grinned at Henry's reticence to speak the words aloud. "When I what? Put my hand on your cock?"

Henry's nostrils flared. "Y-yes. Are you insane? What did you think to gain from—from manhandling me?"

"I'm insulted." Vincent folded his arms over his chest. "My technique was far better than 'manhandling,' don't you think?"

"Devil take you, Night. What are you about?"

Vincent sighed and ran his hand tiredly back through his thick hair. It needed trimming again. "Spirits utilize the energy of the circle to manifest. Sexual energy works very well, and you seemed receptive. And I confess I found the possibility of touching you difficult to resist. Did I truly force something you didn't want?"

Henry's anger seemed to drain away. "No," he muttered, eyes on Vincent's shoes.

"As I thought." Vincent caught his chin lightly, tipping his head back. Henry's lips were slightly parted, his breath warm and smelling of mint dentifrice. "Do you want me to kiss you?"

"Why are you doing this?" Henry's Adam's apple bobbed as he swallowed convulsively. "What do you want?"

"I find you handsome. And I like you."

Henry looked skeptical. "Why do I have trouble believing that?"

"You're clever, and I admire that." Vincent slowly traced the line of Henry's jaw, feeling the lightest scratch of stubble. "You've a fascinating mind. You don't think the way everyone else does, and I find you intriguing. More, it's obvious you genuinely care for your cousin." Vincent smiled wryly. "I think you truly do mean well, even if I can't agree with your methods." Then he let his hand fall. "But I'll keep my distance if you wish."

"No," Henry protested, his body swaying forward at the loss of contact.

The gong sounded from below, signaling dinner. Vincent expected Henry to use it as an excuse to usher them both out of the bedroom as quickly as possible.

Instead, Henry caught hold of Vincent's tie and pulled him closer, down, until their lips met. He tasted of the dentifrice, of warmth and maleness. Closing his eyes, Vincent returned the kiss, parting his lips and letting Henry's tongue dart in, a quick swirl against the roof of his mouth. His pulse leapt in his throat, echoed below his waist as his cock grew heavy.

Henry pulled back, seeming a bit dazed. "We should go downstairs," he said, voice husky with desire. "Before anyone comes to find us."

Vincent didn't want to go down to dinner. He wanted to shove Henry back on the bed, unbutton his trousers, and feast on his prick. But the other man was right. "Very well," he said and dipped his head for another quick kiss. "We'll continue this later."

Once at dinner, Henry made certain to seat himself between Miss Prandle and Jo, in case Vincent—Night, damn it—got any more creative ideas. Or in case he found himself tempted by ideas of his own.

What was wrong with him? He hadn't kissed a man since Isaac, certainly hadn't pursued anything more than an anonymous tug in a back alley. He'd shared those alley encounters with all sorts of men, from handsome clerks with soft hands to scarred longshoremen with fingers callused and chapped from their work. A few awkward moments punctuated by the sharp pleasure of release, before carefully departing in the opposite directions. He'd certainly never wanted to drag any of them back to his workshop and the bed inside.

Vincent entered the room, and Henry found it impossible not to watch. The medium was built like a dancer, all long limbs and lean muscle, his movements infused with unconscious grace. Flexible as a cat and just as hard to pin down.

Vincent's gaze met his, and the corner of his full mouth turned up into the familiar, insufferable grin. Henry looked away quickly. The nerve of the fellow…but Henry had been the one to seize Vincent's tie and drag him in for a kiss not half an hour ago, rather than the other way around.

God. Henry had known it was insane. Known he should hold firm, make it clear there were to be no more intimacies of any kind between them. But confronted with the warmth of those dark eyes, the roguish curve of that smile, he'd crumbled. Vincent had even offered him the chance to walk away, and yet he hadn't been able to force himself to take it. To deny what he wanted one more time.

Miss Devereaux sat across from Miss Prandle, with Gladfield between them. Vincent, predictably by now, chose to settle in the chair directly opposite Henry. He lounged back, watching Henry from under lowered lids while Bamforth served the soup. Henry pretended not to notice, and doubted he was at all successful at doing so.

"Quite an exciting day!" Gladfield declared as he tucked into the soup.

"I wouldn't put it quite in those terms," Vincent murmured. The quiet tone surprised Henry, and he glanced across the table to find the medium frowning down at his dish. He hadn't sounded at all his normal, cocky self. Rather, he'd seemed worried. Afraid, even.

No one else seemed to have noticed. Certainly their host hadn't. "Does anyone have any theories they would like to share?" Gladfield asked, casting his gaze first at Miss Devereaux, then at Henry.

Blast, he'd been so absorbed by Vincent, he hadn't even considered his report. Henry took a sip of his coffee to buy time. "It seems clear the house is genuinely haunted, and it is possible the spirit wishes to make contact," he said.

"Possible?" Miss Prandle asked. "I'd say after the séance this afternoon, it is indisputable."

Henry's grip tightened on his cup. Ordinarily, he wouldn't feel odd about saying this aloud, but the woman was Vincent's partner…

And the fact he'd even had the thought spoke to his questionable judgment more damningly than anything else. "I did monitor a change in temperature within the room, which Jo didn't record just outside," Henry said. "However, we have only Miss Devereaux's word the sentences she wrote came from a spirit."

Miss Prandle's eyes widened slightly, as if she were shocked at his boldness. Across from him, Vincent's dark gaze flicked up. "And mine."

Damn it. This was the sort of game Isaac had played. *"Trust me. Take my word. Don't question."*

"I understand," Henry said levelly. "Nonetheless, I cannot consider it to be indisputable evidence in my investigation. It's nothing against you or Miss Devereaux. I can't consider my own visitation as evidence, either, as there were no measurements to corroborate it."

"What do you suggest for our next move?" Gladfield asked with a smile that said he rather enjoyed their sparring.

"Another séance," Henry said. "Using the Electro-Séance, of course. We'll attempt to speak to the ghost and get actual data."

"Which one?" Vincent asked, his voice pitched to sound innocent.

"What do you mean, 'which one?'" Henry's gut tightened—Vincent was up to something, he was certain of it. Did he mean to imply the spirit Jo had glimpsed in the mirror was a different ghost than the one that had visited his bedroom?

Vincent raised a brow. Taking a flask from his pocket, he deliberately poured a measure of liquor into his coffee. "How many spirits would you say are in this house, Mr. Strauss?"

The formality sent a foolish little pang through him. "What are you suggesting, Mr. Night?" he replied, refusing to be put on the defensive.

Vincent sipped his coffee. "There are at least three spirits present," he said. He spoke to the room as a whole, but his dark gaze flicked over the rim of his cup, pinning Henry in place. "It seems like something one would need to know if one meant to thoroughly exorcise the house."

All the blood seemed to drain to Henry's feet. Was Vincent speaking truthfully? Because if he was right…the instruments had no practical way to differentiate. The oversight could be great enough to cost him to the contest.

"Three spirits," Vincent repeated. "In a house not fifty years old. Not impossible, but it does make me wonder if some larger tragedy happened here and is responsible for the haunting."

Gladfield clapped his hands. "Well done, well done! I think you've scored a point against our Mr. Strauss."

Henry shot a glare at Vincent, but to his surprise, the medium didn't look at all triumphant. "I'll question the spirit I raise using the Electro-Séance," Henry said, trying desperately to make up some of the ground he'd just lost. "I'm sure it will be able to tell us of any other spirits in the house, including the one it seems to be attempting to warn us against."

"About that," Miss Devereaux said. "Mr. Gladfield, although I appreciate why you withheld the history of the house, I think the time has come to share it with the rest of us. After the automatic writing this afternoon, it seems likely the spirit in Mr. Strauss's bedroom was attempting to warn rather than threaten him. Between these warnings and the fact there are multiple spirits on the premises, Mr. Night and I are concerned."

"Concerned about what?" Miss Prandle asked as Bamforth refilled her coffee.

"Some spirits are dangerous." Vincent stared at his coffee cup, but not as if he really saw it, instead seeming to gaze into some other place and time. "They can become violent. Throwing objects. Hitting or pinching. Sometimes they even kill."

Pain underlaid his voice, barely perceptible, like a current through a wire. Had one of his previous séances gone wrong?

Unless he was only trying to scare the rest of them. It was possible.

Isaac had been a good actor, too.

Somehow, though, Henry didn't believe Vincent was acting. Maybe it was the shadows in Vincent's eyes, or the way his fingers trembled as he lifted the coffee to his lips. Or the memory of how he'd tried to comfort Henry last night, instead of trying to frighten him further.

"The warnings of the spirit to get out before 'he' comes for us seems to suggest a dark force in the house." Miss Devereaux glanced briefly at Vincent, then back to Gladfield. "The longer we're here, the more our energy will seep into the house, making it easier for any spirits to manifest."

"Hmm." Gladfield considered for a long moment. "But surely, in order to rid the house of the spirit, you'll have to confront it."

"Perhaps," Miss Devereaux said, her tone carefully neutral.

"And what do you say, Mr. Strauss?" Gladfield challenged.

Henry would have preferred more time to think things over. But he'd already been made to look like a fool once during this meal. "Technology doesn't care about the provenance of a ghost," he said. "Or whether it desires to be helpful or harmful. I believe I can rid the house of the various spirits whether I know anything about its history or not."

Vincent shook his head. "You're rushing headlong into danger."

"I disagree."

"Perhaps we should compromise," Gladfield said, lifting his hands in a gesture for peace. "You will all have tonight to conduct whatever further experiments or investigations you wish. Tomorrow morning, after breakfast, I'll reveal the house's history, and each group can decide what to do from there. How does that sound?"

Henry immediately nodded. "Most fair, Mr. Gladfield." Across the table, Vincent rolled his eyes, but Gladfield didn't seem to notice.

"Very well," Miss Devereaux said, sounding rather unhappy about it.

"I wish to set up the Franklin bells again, including in my room," Henry said quickly. "In case the spirit reappears there."

"It won't, without you inside," Vincent said.

"You don't know for certain."

"It's trying to warn us. Why warn an empty room?"

Henry glared. "If it's trying to warn us, why appear to me and not you?"

Vincent's smile was thin, just a fragile mask which might have cracked at any moment to reveal darkness beneath. "Because I take certain precautions when I sleep, Mr. Strauss."

"Afraid for your virtue?" The words were out before Henry could stop them.

"Of course." Vincent's smile shifted, became less pained and more like his usual lazy grin. "I'm but an innocent lamb lost in the woods."

"More like a wolf in sheep's clothing," Henry muttered.

"Enough sparring, gentlemen," Gladfield cut in. "We don't want bad blood, after all." He dabbed at his lips with his napkin, then pushed back his chair. "I intend to retire to my room for the evening, so allow me to bid you all goodnight. You have until dawn."

CHAPTER 10

"THANK YOU for mentioning my concerns over dinner," Vincent said as he settled into a chair across from Lizzie, near the roaring fire in the grand hall. The wind had strengthened after sundown, and branches of overgrown shrubs rubbed against the glass of the huge bay window. When the gusts blew in a particular direction, a soft keening came from the tower. Henry had trooped up with his poor cousin to investigate and had come back half an hour later, shivering and miserable, to report it was nothing but the wind blowing around the open parapet.

Lizzie shifted, the silk folds of her dress whispering together. "You were a good medium once," she replied quietly. "I don't want to you to feel as if I'm dismissing your warnings altogether, or rushing headlong into danger without a second thought."

"No, we have Mr. Strauss for that," he replied with a wry smile.

Lizzie shook her head. "I think you're becoming far too fond of him."

"He's not a bad sort. Deep down."

"*Very* deep," she agreed. She indicated the hairbrush which lay on the table between them. "Shall we begin?"

As darkness fell, he and Lizzie had gone to the servants' quarters and made a second survey, not for spirit activity but for objects left behind. It seemed likely the ghost he'd sensed on the servants' stair, and who Miss Strauss had seen, had been a maid.

Their search had uncovered a great many empty beds and barren dressers…and one space with women's clothing left in both a trunk and drawers. Odd, to say the least. After a few moments of handling various objects, Lizzie had chosen the hairbrush.

At least psychometry wasn't like spirit writing. There was no direct channeling of the spirit, the object itself forming the conduit of communication. The results were more limited, but still might be useful.

Lizzie closed her eyes and put her hands on the brush. Her breathing gradually became deeper and slower as she slipped into trance. Vincent watched her carefully, the pencil in his hand poised above a sheet of paper, ready to take note of anything she might say. Around them, the house creaked in the rising wind. The firelight threw flickering shadows, the movement making the skin between his shoulder blades crawl. He had to resist the urge to glance behind him.

There was nothing there. Nothing coming up behind him in the shadowy hall.

A shiver ran through Lizzie, dragging his attention back to her. A faint acidity, like vinegar and lemons, coated his tongue.

Lizzie's brows drew together. "Cold. Dark. She's trapped."

Vincent's pencil scratched softly on the paper as he recorded her words. Outside, the wind strengthened. The winter-bare branches tapped harder against the window, like skeletal fingers seeking entrance.

"It's dark here," Lizzie went on. Her frown deepened, lips drawing tight against her teeth. "There was a light, but he wouldn't let her go to it. She can't leave."

All the hair stood up on Vincent's neck. "She can't leave…?"

"The house."

There came a loud snap as one of the dozens of windowpanes on the bay cracked in half.

Vincent jumped violently, and Lizzie's eyes flew open. They both stared at the broken window, but nothing further happened. The wind died down, and the violent strikes of the bushes against the glass calmed.

Vincent barely bit back the impulse to swear. "Lizzie…"

"I know."

"The lavender ghost was worried 'he' would come for us. Now this other one is trapped in the house, unable to move on, because 'he' won't let her." Vincent tossed the pencil down. "This is getting worse by the minute. This goes beyond any paranoia of mine. We have to leave."

Lizzie sighed. "There's nothing to be done tonight. For now, I'm going to bed—and laying a good line of salt down across the door first.

Tomorrow morning we'll hear the history of the house and make any necessary decisions."

He wanted to argue, but she was right. There was nothing else to be done at the moment.

And who knew? Maybe Henry was having better luck with his measurements and devices. "I think I'll see what mischief Mr. Strauss is getting up to."

Lizzie arched a brow. "Well. That should be entertaining."

Henry leaned out the window, trying to attach the copper wire in his hand to the lightning rod outside. If he was to prove the action of Strauss's Patented Ghost Grounder, it had to be, well, grounded.

He'd used the same lightning rod for the Franklin bells earlier in the day, but at the time the weather had been relatively mild. Now it was practically blowing up a hurricane, with every surface slick with ice and snow. The windowsill he'd perched on earlier had become too treacherous to trust, unless he wished to tempt both gravity and fate.

"Do you need assistance?" Vincent inquired from the door to the schoolroom.

Henry was half tempted to refuse. But in truth, he did need help, and with Jo busy taking readings, he couldn't exactly turn Vincent away. "If you don't mind. I need to lean out a bit farther than I'm comfortable. I'd take it as a kindness if you'd keep me from plummeting to my death."

Vincent grinned. "Any chance to manhandle you again."

Henry glared in response. "Perhaps I should rethink things. I trust you have no desire to murder me in order to win our contest?"

"I might." Vincent ambled closer. "But shoving you out the window would be rather pedestrian. If I choose to do you in, Mr. Strauss, the fashion won't be nearly so common."

Henry snorted. "I think sometimes you say things just to hear the sound of your own voice. And it's Henry." He wasn't certain why he offered the familiarity, except it seemed absurd to stand on formality when the man in question had made him spill in his trousers.

"I do enjoy hearing myself talk," Vincent agreed shamelessly. "Please call me Vincent." He smiled with what seemed like real pleasure, though, his teeth very white against his copper skin.

"Then, as I am safe from simply being tossed out the window, I accept your offer of assistance, Vincent." Henry uncoiled the wire. "Come over here and hold my legs."

"Bossy. I like that in a man." Vincent strolled over and did as ordered. His grip on Henry was warm and firm, and Henry did his best to ignore it. At least the icy air whipping in through the open window cooled any ardor he might have otherwise felt.

As Henry leaned out into the cold air and began to attach the wire to the lightning rod, Vincent said, "May I ask you a question?"

Now? The man had a dreadful sense of timing. "If you must."

"You said you'd seen a spirit before. What caused you to pursue the secrets of the hereafter in this fashion?"

Henry gritted his teeth. His fingers were clumsy from the cold, and he swore mentally when the wire slipped loose. "You mean scientifically?"

"Yes."

Henry didn't owe the medium anything. He could simply say it was none of Vincent's business and tell him to be off.

But Vincent, for all his impertinence and lack of shame, had shown genuine kindness last night when he'd come in response to Henry's fearful cry. He'd comforted Jo after her encounter this morning.

He'd called Henry clever, praised the way he thought. The words had warmed Henry even more than the kiss they'd shared a few moments later. Who would have imagined the first person to appreciate his ingenuity would be a medium?

"My family was never wealthy, but we had more money than most." Henry finally got the wire into place. "Nothing like Mr. Gladfield, of course. My father was the president of a bank and did quite well for himself…at least until he died."

"I'm sorry."

Henry pulled himself back inside. For once, Vincent let go and stepped away instead of pursuing anything more. Henry hurriedly closed the window as much as he could given the wire running outside. His fingers were like ice, and he jammed them beneath his armpits in an attempt to warm them.

"As am I, but he…he came back. To reassure me, I think. I was fifteen, and only just fully realized I was…different…from other lads." He looked up to see if Vincent took his meaning. A small nod assured him that the medium did. "I was confused and afraid, and I couldn't help but wonder if it wasn't just as well my father had died. If he'd ever found out, surely it would have broken his heart. One night, I woke up and discovered him standing at the foot of my bed."

Vincent cocked his head to one side. "Were you frightened?"

Henry laughed ruefully. "I should have been, shouldn't I? But all I felt was a sense of warmth and love. As if he'd come to tell me everything would be all right. Then he was gone, but I heard something hit the floor. I jumped out of bed, and what did I find but an emerald stickpin?" Henry began to pace, trying to work some warmth back into his limbs after the chill of the outside. "He'd been buried with the pin—I knew he had, I'd seen it myself as they shut the coffin. There was no explanation for how it arrived on my floor, except as an apport from a spirit. From him."

"It makes sense." Vincent perched on the edge of a school desk, watching Henry pace. "Young people like you were—like Miss Strauss is now—generate a great deal of energy. Given your emotional distress, it was probably even higher than usual. Concentrated as it was around a single spirit, it gave your father enough energy to cross the veil and apport the pin. To say goodbye."

Henry came to a halt, his eyes fixed on the wall in front of him. Faint marks revealed the old vandalism left behind by some child, not quite removed by subsequent scrubbing. "Yes."

Vincent folded his arms over his chest. "But it doesn't explain why you're determined to replace me with a machine."

Henry wanted to protest that he didn't. Not Vincent. But that would be the effect of winning the contest, whether he wished it or not. "When Father died, Mother was utterly devastated," Henry said. "I told her about my vision and showed her the stickpin. It got her hopes up, I suppose. She longed to see him again, too. So she hired a medium. Isaac Woodsend, or at least that was the name he went by."

"Oh dear." Vincent winced. "A fraud?"

"In every possible way. Only we didn't know it." Henry laughed, but there was no humor in the sound. "He took us in completely. Within a week, Mother was convinced not only that she could talk to Father again, but that she might do so any time she wanted. Almost as if he wasn't dead, but just on a long journey. Isaac moved in with us—the house was quite large, and there was plenty of room. Before long, he said Father wanted us to do things—little things to begin with, like give Isaac his diamond cufflinks. Over time the gifts became more extravagant: money, clothes." He lowered his voice. "Me."

"Shit," Vincent said, with a sort of soft viciousness. His eyes blazed with dark fire.

"He didn't say as much in front of Mother, of course," Henry said hurriedly. "But privately…and since I knew Father still loved me, it seemed reasonable. Not least because I wanted it, too. Isaac was handsome and charming. I was fifteen and stupid."

"The man was a scheming bastard who took advantage." Vincent's cold anger seemed an impossibly sharp contrast to the languid amusement he generally displayed. "I hope this story contains a bad ending for Mr. Woodsend."

The sentiment warmed Henry even as he shook his head ruefully. "Quite the opposite. Isaac drained our bank accounts and took everything—even the emerald stickpin." Somehow, that hurt the most, even now. "But I determined I wouldn't let anyone else fall prey to such an unscrupulous ruse ever again. The Electro-Séance is important, not just to me, but to everyone who has been taken in by a fraud. If I can keep one other person from going through what my family did, it will all have been worth it."

A small, sad smile played on Vincent's mouth. "I won't deny your devices may have some use. But if you could replace every doctor with an automaton, would you? For no better reason than that there are quacks as well as trained professionals?"

Oddly enough, Henry still remembered the smell of Dr. Jones's tobacco when he'd attended Father during his last hours. The kindly old man's soothing voice telling Mother it was over and Father hadn't suffered at the end. The weight of his hand on Henry's shoulder. *"You're the man of the house now, lad. But don't worry. Your father and I were old friends, and he was always proud of you. He still is."*

"It isn't the same," Henry said.

"Isn't it?" The smile grew even sadder, more wistful. "Maybe you're right, Henry. Maybe machines can replace us all. Maybe if they did, Dunne would still be alive."

"Who?"

"It doesn't matter." Vincent turned back to the closed doors of the schoolroom. "If you've made your preparations, let's see what this device of yours can do."

Vincent leaned against the balcony railing, watching while Henry finished setting up what he referred to as his ghost grounder. Listening to the man's story hadn't been easy. The thought of someone taking advantage of people—of Henry—in such a way, while real mediums like Dunne died trying to make the world a better place, made his chest hot with anger.

No wonder Henry had turned to machines. They would never break his heart.

"Are you ready, Jo?" Henry asked. His cheeks were still flushed from the cold, but his eyes sparkled with anticipation. As did Jo's—despite the differences in the color of their skins, in many ways the cousins were more alike than not.

Henry had connected his wire, now trailing from beneath the schoolroom doors, to a thick copper rod. The rod he handled with a heavy rubber glove. They'd gathered at the cold spot on the balcony, set up a thermometer, and noted the temperature. The faint taste of lavender spiced Vincent's tongue—this cold spot belonged to the ghost who had tried to warn them. It was a connection to this world where she could draw energy from the ambient air. Given the dark stains on the floor, he thought it likely she'd died here.

Of course he didn't say as much to Henry. They were still competitors after all, and he doubted Henry would care, given his tart remarks about "provenance" earlier.

Vincent held up his hand. "One moment, if you please. What exactly do you mean to do here?"

Henry, of course, jumped on the opportunity for a lecture. "Ghosts—or their manifestations on this side of the veil—are electromagnetic in nature. They interact with our fields of energy, and with those naturally present all around us. Cold spots form when spirits drain the ambient energy out of the air."

"And your ghost grounder?"

Henry beamed. "We use the ghost's connection with a certain place in our world against it. The copper rod will ground any sort of energy in the area—it doesn't distinguish between that generated by a static charge or a spirit. By introducing it into the cold spot, it will make contact, if you will, with the energy of the spirit and begin to drain it. When the ghost loses sufficient energy to keep up contact with this side, the cold spot should return to normal temperature."

There was a certain amount of genius to Henry's ideas. "And the spirit?" Vincent asked. "How will she feel? Will it hurt her?"

"No more than when a séance's circle is broken and the energy no longer available to the summoned spirit," Henry said.

"I see." Vincent arched a brow at him as Miss Strauss turned away to check one of their instruments. Lowering his voice so only Henry could hear, he said, "Then by all means, give us a demonstration of your thrusting rod."

Henry's cheeks reddened again, with something other than the cold now. "Ready, Jo?" he asked, turning his back deliberately on Vincent.

"Cold spot is at twenty-seven degrees," she reported, her pencil hovering over the notebook, ready to spring into action.

"Then let us begin."

Henry carefully aimed the tip of the copper rod into the center of the cold spot. There came the tiny flash of a spark and a soft *crack*, like touching a door latch after shuffling over carpet.

"Thirty-one degrees!" Jo said.

The taste of lavender began to fade.

Jo recited changes in temperature at regular intervals. Henry's eyes all but glowed in triumph, but his hand remained steady, keeping the copper rod in place until at last Jo declared their two thermometers read the same, both in the former cold spot and a few feet away.

Vincent swirled his tongue around his mouth. No lavender, just the lingering flavor of cinnamon cachous.

She was gone. Or rather, her connection to this place was gone.

"Well done," Vincent said softly.

Henry looked uncertain, as if he thought Vincent might be mocking him. "Thank you."

Vincent gave him a small bow before leaving Henry and his cousin to clear away their things. But as he laid down lines of salt across his bedroom door and window, and checked inside the wardrobe one last time, he couldn't help but think back to that terrible night last summer. If Dunne had something like the ghost grounder, might things have gone differently? Might he still be alive?

By competing against Henry, were Lizzie and he potentially dooming future mediums to the same death?

CHAPTER 11

"ALL RIGHT, Mr. Gladfield," Miss Devereaux said as Bamforth cleared away the breakfast plates the next morning, "it's time to keep your promise. Tell us the history of Reyhome Castle."

Henry leaned forward in his chair. Even though, as he'd said yesterday, the house's history made no difference to his experiments, he couldn't help but find himself curious.

Gladfield settled back in his chair, seeming to enjoy prolonging their suspense. "Very well. You've all been remarkably patient," he said. "The history of Reyhome Castle began in 1846. Francis Reyer had made his fortune in timber, and once he felt the hand of age upon him, he decided to marry. As fate would have it, he settled upon a much younger woman for his bride, a Miss Martha Hargrave. For the first year of their marriage, the couple lived in New York while Reyhome Castle was built. The house was intended as a summer home only, except things began to go wrong."

"What happened?" Jo asked eagerly.

"Nothing terrible at first." Gladfield sipped his coffee. "Reyer had always been somewhat paranoid, but never to an extreme—just enough to keep him sharp in business. But with such a young, pretty wife, he began to display jealousy toward any other man who met her socially. He seldom allowed her to leave their New York home, and never without his company. She couldn't even see her cousins without his presence as chaperone. And as soon as Reyhome Castle was finished, they moved here on a permanent basis."

"I suppose this far out in the country, he believed there would be fewer temptations for his wife," Henry suggested.

Gladfield nodded. "No doubt. In due time, the family was joined by two more souls: a boy and girl who were the delight of Mrs. Reyer. Alas, their arrival marked the beginning of Francis Reyer's descent into madness."

Miss Devereaux's flowing skirts rustled as she shifted in her chair. "Madness?"

"Indeed." Gladfield watched them over the edge of his cup. "Reyer became completely unhinged. He barred even the few visitors they had and fired every man on staff, including his own valet. Supposedly, he became convinced the children weren't really his and flung the most horrid accusations at his wife. His paranoia became so extreme, he withdrew a small fortune from the bank to have the money on hand. That way, he wouldn't have to leave the house even for a few hours."

Miss Prandle shivered. "His poor wife. And children."

"Trapped in a house far from anyone else, with a lunatic in complete control of their fates," Gladfield agreed. "Inevitably, things ended badly. One day Reyer lost what little grip he retained on sanity, took up a knife, and swore he'd kill the children, as he was certain they weren't his. His wife died on the second-floor balcony, in front of the schoolroom, trying to save them."

So Vincent was right—the stain on the floor had been blood. Henry suppressed a shiver.

"Once he was done with her," Gladfield went on, "Reyer went into the schoolroom. The tutor was badly wounded in the defense of her charges, but to no avail. He murdered his little son and daughter."

"How terrible," Henry said, but it came out a horrified whisper. This was far worse than anything he'd imagined. Perhaps it would have been better not to know after all.

"The handful of remaining servants fled in terror," Gladfield went on. "Within a few hours, a group of local men returned, determined to overpower Reyer and take him to face justice for his crimes. They were too late—Reyer hanged himself, either from remorse or as a final phase of his lunacy, who can say? Reports vary as to where his body was found. Some say in this very room, dangling from the chandelier above our heads."

Henry glanced up reflexively. The dark iron seemed suddenly, unspeakably sinister. Jo let out little gasp, but she seemed more fascinated than frightened. "Where else?" Henry asked.

"The top of the tower is the other place Reyer might have done himself in. The fortune he'd supposedly kept on hand was never found. If it existed at all, the men who discovered the body probably took it." Gladfield shrugged. "By the time of the deaths, the house had been occupied for less than ten years. After, it passed into the possession of Reyer's sister, newly married to my father. As my parents already had a country home, they rented the property to friends for the summer. The friends remained for less than a month, reporting cold spots, figures glimpsed in mirrors, and other things which left them deeply uneasy. They finally departed when the head maid fell down the servants' stair to her death. They were convinced a ghost had pushed her. The house has lain undisturbed since."

Silence lay over the room for a long moment. Then Miss Devereaux asked, "When?"

"Pardon me?" Gladfield asked.

Her eyes were like chips of green ice, and there was no mistaking the low urgency in her voice when she spoke. "When did the murders and suicide occur? The date, sir."

Gladfield smiled. "The twelfth of January. The anniversary is tomorrow night."

"We need to leave. Right now." Vincent's heart drummed in his chest, and waves of alternating hot and cold washed over him. Lizzie was saying something, but he couldn't hear over the sound of screams and mad laughter. Breaking glass. He tasted rot and slime on his tongue. If he turned his head just a little, he'd see Dunne staring back at him with sightless eyes.

"Vincent?" A hand landed on his arm. He jumped and found he'd risen to his feet without even realizing it. Henry stood beside him, blue eyes staring worriedly up. "Are you well?"

Of course he wasn't well. His knees trembled, threatening to give way. Every instinct he possessed screamed at him to grab Henry and Lizzie, and run.

But Henry didn't understand—his puzzlement said as much. Bitter laughter welled in Vincent's throat, but he choked it down. Instead, he turned to Gladfield. "You have no idea the sort of danger you've put us all in, do you?"

Gladfield frowned severely. "I suggest you watch your tone, Mr. Night. Your savage blood does not excuse such behavior."

Henry drew in a harsh sip of breath as if he meant to protest.

"Vincent, sit down," Lizzie ordered before Henry could speak. "Forgive my colleague, Mr. Gladfield. He didn't mean to speak sharply."

Vincent wanted to object. To tell Gladfield to go to hell and take the house with him. But doing so would only end with him being thrown out.

And wouldn't it be for the best? He'd have an excuse to walk away. One absolving him of all guilt when it came to the fate of those left behind.

"Yes." He sank back into his seat. "Forgive me."

"What Mr. Night meant to say," Lizzie went on, "was, while most spirits are entirely harmless, save for giving the occasional fright to the unwary, such isn't always the case. There are instances when spirits can become violent and do injury to people, mediums and ordinary souls alike. Given the death of the maid—"

"Which may have been an accident," Henry pointed out quickly.

Lizzie arched a cool brow at him. "Given our circumstances, such an assumption is dangerous to make, Mr. Strauss. If the ghost of Reyer walks these halls, if it has killed once already, we are in peril."

"*If*," Henry said. Leaning back in his chair, he folded his arms over his chest, radiating skepticism. Vincent clenched his fists and tried to resist the urge to grab the man and shake sense into him.

"Do you think Reyer was the 'he' referred to in the spirit writing?" Miss Strauss asked.

Lizzie nodded. "I think it likely. It seems to me his wife may have been trying to warn us, both through her writing and her appearance to Mr. Strauss."

Gladfield set his coffee aside. "What do you suggest?"

Lizzie glanced briefly at Henry, then back to Gladfield. "Reyer is not a spirit any of us want to encounter. My advice to you is to end the experiment immediately, begin packing, and have us all on the train south by nightfall."

Vincent sagged in relief. Lizzie agreed, so his alarm hadn't just been a product of the fear that had stalked him for months.

"Are you saying you refuse to conduct a séance to try to exorcize Reyer's ghost?" Gladfield asked.

For a long moment, Lizzie didn't reply, the struggle clear on her face. No doubt she thought of the five hundred dollars, of all the things the money could buy. Of saving the shop, the last thing they had of Dunne.

Her shoulders slumped fractionally. "Yes, Mr. Gladfield. It's simply too dangerous."

A surprised grin slowly spread across Henry's features. "You're forfeiting the contest. I've won!"

"Are you insane?" Vincent turned to look at him full on, and the sight of elation on Henry's face was like a blow to his chest. "Didn't you hear what Lizzie said? What I said? Even with your ghost grounder, we can't risk this!"

Henry's smile faltered. "I…"

"Mr. Night." Gladfield wasn't pleased with him, not at all. Right then, Vincent didn't particularly give a damn. "Perhaps you don't understand what's at stake here. This is a very valuable property, and I mean to have it exorcised. One of the best times for contacting a ghost, unless I am mistaken, is the anniversary of its death, which is why I chose this week for the contest. If Mr. Strauss is willing to make the attempt, he shall, without any further interference from *you*." Gladfield's annoyed gaze moved to Henry's face. "And Mr. Strauss, don't get ahead of yourself. You'll have your five hundred dollars only when—and if—you dispose of the ghost."

Henry glanced at Vincent, uncertainty in his eyes. For a moment, Vincent let himself hope Henry realized what a terrible idea this was.

Then Henry's shoulders went back. "I intend to, Mr. Gladfield. We'll conduct the Electro-Séance as soon as I can put my equipment in place. This house will be free of ghosts by sundown."

"Pardon me, Mr. Strauss," Bamforth said from the doorway. "A man just came from the train station—he delivered this packet for you."

Henry stood in his bedroom, straightening his collar in the mirror. He and Jo had spent the last two hours moving their equipment into Reyer's bedroom, which seemed the most likely place to summon the spirit, given the activity noted by the cold spots and the Franklin bells. Having finished all the preparations, he had retreated to his own room, determined to look his best for his moment of triumph.

Miss Devereaux had helped prove the case for the weakness of the human element, and had done so without any prompting from him. The way to victory was now clear. He had only to operate the Electro-Séance effectively, and the five hundred dollars would be his. He'd convert the repair shop into a full laboratory where he could invent ever better ways of bringing the spirit world under control, banishing superstition and fear to the dusty past where they belonged. Jo's future would be secure.

Best of all, the Psychical Society would be forced to admit he'd been right all along. Perhaps they'd even beg him to become society president, a post he'd regretfully have to decline, as his work would keep him far too busy.

Yet his triumph came at the cost of Vincent's loss. Its shadow prevented him from savoring it as he should have.

Vincent. The genuine alarm on his face had given Henry pause. He'd said something last night about a death. But of course the medium hadn't seen the Electro-Séance in operation, didn't realize how powerful it could be. Once he did, he'd surely come around to Henry's side. He'd see science could make things safe, realize he'd been fighting for a way of life that brought harm instead of helped.

"Thank you, Bamforth," Henry said, taking the mail. Bamforth nodded and left, shutting the door behind him again.

The large envelope weighed heavy in Henry's hand, and a quick perusal revealed it was the packet he'd been expecting from the blasted detective. Not much point in looking at it now, as it was too late to be of any use. Still, there might be something of interest…

A sharp knock sounded. "Henry?" Vincent demanded. "Are you in there?"

Curse it. Henry hurriedly tossed the packet onto the bottom of the wardrobe and shut its door. "Yes—come in."

Vincent strode purposefully into the room. The medium's copper skin was flushed, and his black brows drawn down. "Are you insane? Didn't you hear anything we said? Or have you convinced yourself we're a pair of frauds, no better than Isaac?"

Henry stiffened at the anger in Vincent's voice, as well as the mention of Isaac. "I might have believed you a fraud at first, but I don't think so any longer," Henry replied, fighting to keep his voice calm. "And yes, I heard you."

"You just don't believe us."

"I didn't say that."

Vincent shut the door and crossed the room. Henry stepped back, his shoulders colliding with the wardrobe. Vincent took advantage, hands closing on Henry's arms, pinning him against the wooden doors. "Listen to me," Vincent said. Their thighs brushed together. "You wish to prove your gadgets can dispel a haunting? Do so. But not this one."

Henry stiffened. His heart beat faster at Vincent's closeness, and he cursed the treacherous organ. "I'll not turn my back on five hundred dollars without good reason."

"Good reason?" Vincent's hands gripped his arms, almost tight enough to bruise. "What about your cousin's safety? Miss Prandle's? Bamforth's?"

"I understand you're concerned. I'll take every possible precaution, I swear."

"People have *died* trying to exorcise violent ghosts." Vincent's lips pressed together as if to hold in the next words. "My own mentor among them, and he knew more about the spirit world than I will in a lifetime."

As Henry had suspected—the death Vincent had mentioned did play into his reluctance to accept Henry's assurances. "Tell me," Henry said. "Please."

Vincent's eyes lowered as if he couldn't bring himself to meet Henry's gaze. "Do you know what a medium is? Really?"

"Someone who can sense spirits, of course."

But Vincent shook his head. "We're holes in the veil between the lands of the living and the dead. Some are pinpricks, open to receiving vague impressions or the occasional premonition. But others of us… we're walking, talking gateways, just waiting for something to come along from the other side and use us. Without proper training, we're vulnerable to possession, psychic sickness, insanity, and a host of other horrors."

The darkness in Vincent's eyes tugged at something deep inside Henry's chest. "I didn't realize."

"Many of us end up dead or in madhouses before anyone ever realizes we have a talent in need of training." Vincent bit his lip in a flash of white teeth. "Lizzie and I were lucky. We both had the same mentor. James Dunne. He was a good medium, but more. A good man. The best I ever met."

The anger had drained from Vincent's voice, leaving behind only weary grief. "What happened?" Henry asked softly.

Vincent's grip relaxed, and he bowed his head. "Dunne and I went to remove what we thought was a simple poltergeist. It had tormented a family, particularly their young son, for months. No one else had been able to help. The ghost was violent. Angry." A shudder went through Vincent's slender frame. "But I was confident. I talked Dunne into staying despite all the dangers."

There was only one way this story was going to end. "Things didn't go as planned, I take it."

"You might say that." Vincent released Henry and stepped back. Folding his arms across his chest, he turned away and stared out the window. Fat flakes of snow drifted past lazily. "When I opened myself to the spirit, it took control of me completely. Not like when Lizzie did her spirit writing, but a full possession. It used my body, my energy, to attack Dunne, and I couldn't stop it. I was a prisoner inside my own skull. I couldn't even scream."

Oh God. Henry tentatively touched Vincent's shoulder. "I'm sorry." It sounded inadequate, but what else could he say?

Vincent flinched away as if he couldn't bear any gesture of comfort. "It killed him. Wearing my skin. Dunne did everything for me, and that was how I repaid his kindness. Believe me when I say I understand the danger this ghost poses to all of us."

Henry's breath caught in dismay. Poor Vincent. How must he feel? What horrors must still visit him in the small hours of the night? "You were very brave to come here at all."

For a moment, Vincent looked surprised, as if it had never occurred to him. Then he shook his head. "I'm not brave. Stupid, perhaps. Desperate, certainly. What good is a medium afraid to channel spirits? I haven't so much as read the cards for anyone since. I try to be useful to Lizzie, but the truth is, I'm just dragging her down with me. I killed Dunne, and now because of me, we're going to lose his shop, the only thing we have left of him. Lizzie thought if we won the five hundred dollars..." He sighed. "But the money isn't worth dying for."

"Of course not." Henry moved closer, and this time Vincent didn't pull away from his touch. "Don't you see, though? The Electro-Séance isn't a person. It can't be possessed. What happened to your mentor—to you—was terrible. Tragic. But I can prevent such a tragedy from ever happening again."

"Maybe you can." Vincent's agreement took him by surprise. "But find another haunting to test your theories. A ghost that doesn't realize it's dead, or one enacting the scene of its demise again and again—one that isn't violent, isn't dangerous. Not this one."

Henry sighed. "Your experience has colored your reaction. No matter how dangerous or violent this ghost was in life, it still must obey certain principles now. The Electro-Séance—"

"Curse you, listen to me." Vincent's expression hardened. "You still think spirits are—are cogs in a machine. Chemicals you can combine and get a known reaction from. But they aren't. They used to be human—perhaps still are—and they have plans and minds of their own. You think you can call them up and banish them at will, like some sort of party trick. The way Isaac pretended to call up your father on demand. But you're wrong, dangerously so, and I fear to contemplate who else will pay the price for your hubris."

"It isn't hubris to try and help people," Henry shot back. "As long as you refuse to allow even the possibility of scientific help, more people will suffer. At least I'm doing something to change things for the better. What are you doing except hiding from your fear?"

Vincent's eyes widened—then narrowed sharply even as his cheeks darkened with anger. "I see. Very well. Good day to you, Mr. Strauss."

The door slammed behind him, leaving Henry alone in the room.

CHAPTER 12

VINCENT STOOD at the doorway of what had been Francis Reyer's bedroom on the second floor. Of course Henry had decided to set up his séance equipment here, where evidence of spectral activity had been high. Henry might have tried to draw the ghost somewhere else, like a hunter luring a beast from a cave. But such a plan would have been too sensible—why not just march right into monster's lair instead?

Henry and his cousin had dragged the furniture back to the walls, save for the desk, which they'd put near the center of the room. They'd placed their Wimshurst machine on the desk, along with a host of measuring instruments: galvanometer, thermometer, barometer, even a water-filled contraption Henry referred to as a dispeller.

Vincent glared silently at Henry as he checked the equipment a final time. Vincent had revealed the most painful moment of his life, opened his heart, and what had Henry done in return? Accused him of hiding, of not doing enough. Of not even trying to make things better. As if Vincent hadn't been doing his best to keep them all safe, even when no one wanted to listen to his warnings.

Well, the devil could take Henry Strauss for all Vincent cared.

"We should have packed and been out the door, on the way to the train station," he muttered to Lizzie, who stood beside him in the doorway. Everyone else had crowded into the room to watch Henry and Miss Strauss prepare for the séance.

"Perhaps," Lizzie murmured back. "But I wish to view the operation of Mr. Strauss's Electro-Séance. It may yet catch fire or fail to perform." She hesitated. "And Dunne wouldn't have just left Miss Prandle and Miss Strauss to suffer the foolishness of others."

"Dunne recruited me," Vincent said, pulling his flask from his pocket. "So what did he know?"

Lizzie gave him a quelling glare, which he ignored in favor of sipping from the flask. The amulet hung heavy around his neck, reminding him of the consequences of failure.

Maybe that was why he was still here. As long as he wore the amulet, he couldn't be possessed. If he was a gateway, as he'd told Henry, the amulet was the seal keeping it shut. He didn't have to be afraid, for himself at least.

And if his hand shook so badly it took two tries to screw the cap back on the flask…well, he wouldn't think about it. He'd concentrate on the séance and pull Miss Strauss and Miss Prandle clear of the room should things go awry.

And perhaps things wouldn't. Maybe Henry was right, and he and his untried equipment could handily remove the angry ghost of a man who had killed before and after death. At the moment, Vincent devoutly hoped things would go just as Henry believed, with the ghost removed and Henry strolling away with the prize money. Certainly it would be a far better outcome than the one Vincent feared.

"We're almost ready to begin," Henry declared. "We've set the desk beneath the strongest cold spot. We'll ground the rest of the cold spots, then begin the summoning. Jo?"

She picked up the thermometer. Henry pulled on his heavy rubber glove and picked up the copper rod, whose wire was already attached to the lightning rod outside the window. The two cousins went around the room, finding the surplus spots and draining their energy.

Vincent pulled his amulet from beneath his clothes, wrapping his hand tightly around it until the edges almost cut into his palm. Sick fear whispered along his nerves, and he tasted old metal and rust.

Something in Reyhome Castle had taken notice of Henry's actions.

"There we are," Henry said, sounding satisfied. "All extraneous cold spots taken care of, so any spirit we summon won't be able to draw off the energy of the room through them. Now, there is one more step before we attempt contact."

As Henry spoke, Jo began to set up a strange device, almost like a telegraph line: wooden posts surmounted by glass insulators, with wires connecting them. Soon they formed a circle around the table. "I call this the phantom fence," Henry said proudly. "Once the spirit manifests, we'll attach the wires to a battery. The current will prevent the spirit from crossing out of the circle."

"Why not just use salt?" Gladfield asked.

"Salt is too easily disturbed," Henry replied. "An accidental scrape of the foot or a gust of strong wind, and suddenly the spirit is free. The phantom fence removes all uncertainty."

"I'm not sure I understand how it works," Miss Prandle said with a small frown.

"Being composed of electromagnetic fields themselves, ghosts can be disrupted by other, stronger fields." Henry patted one of the fence posts like a proud father. "At the moment, the wires are inert, but as soon as a current moves through them, a field will be generated. The ghost won't be able to approach without dispersing itself."

The idea, Vincent had to admit, was clever. Maybe even brilliant. Lizzie tilted her head toward Vincent. "He certainly seems to have thought of everything."

"Yes," Vincent murmured. The taste in his mouth grew stronger, and the back of his neck prickled.

Gladfield noticed their quiet conversation. "Come now, won't our mediums draw nearer? At least join the rest of us outside Mr. Strauss's fence. No reason for Mr. Night to stand there imitating a cigar store Indian."

For the first time since Vincent had taken up position in the doorway, Henry looked at him. The gaslights threw reflections across his spectacles, but his mouth turned down into an unhappy frown.

God. Vincent was an idiot to let it affect him. To care what Henry thought. But he found himself shuffling closer, Lizzie behind him.

"If you'll shut the door, please, to keep out the light?" Henry asked. The man sounded uncertain, as if he thought Vincent might yell at him to close the damned door himself.

With a sigh, Vincent shut the door. Henry smiled, perhaps taking the action as an indicator Vincent was no longer angry with him. "Thank you. Bamforth, if you'd be so good as to draw the curtains and put out the lights except for the candle."

A swish of curtains, and the gloomy sunlight vanished, along with the sight of snow slowly piling up against the panes. Within moments, the room had been plunged into near darkness, with only the dim candle to provide any illumination. The tang of iron grew sharply stronger, and

Vincent leaned back against the door, feeling the solid wooden planks against his shoulder blades. A chill passed over his skin, the small hairs of his ears vibrating in response, as if something unseen had let out a nasty chuckle.

"Jo, crank the Wimshurst machine," Henry ordered.

She did as he asked. The tick-tick of the machine's rotating disks sounded in almost total silence, as if everyone in the room held their breath. The first loud crack of electricity leaping from one metal ball to the other made Vincent's heart jump; given the small motions from Miss Prandle and Lizzie, he wasn't the only one startled.

"We wish to make contact with the spirit of Francis Reyer," Henry proclaimed in a clear voice. "If the one known as in life Francis Reyer is here with us, use the energy provided by the machine and show yourself!"

Henry's pulse fluttered in his throat. Now was the moment—either Reyer would respond and the séance would proceed, or he'd suffer humiliation in front of Gladfield and everyone else. Drawing a deep breath, he started to repeat the invocation.

A wave of freezing air poured over him, shocking in its cold. The thermometer's reading plunged, and the galvanometer showed the charge vanishing from the air. "Keep cranking, Jo!" he cried. "It's working!"

His words came out in a breath of steam. Frost coalesced on the surface of the table, raced along the Wimshurst machine, and gathered on the copper wires surrounding the table. A thin skin of ice formed over the dispeller's water bowl.

Jo let out a cry and jerked her hand back from the crank. "It's too cold!"

No—they couldn't fail now. Henry lunged at the crank, grasping it with his gloved hand. "Jo—attach the wires to the phantom fence. Quickly, before the spirit leaves!"

She rushed to carry out his instructions, but he kept his eyes fixed on the air of the original cold spot. Was it his imagination, or was there a sort of shadow there, like the ripple of a heat wave, only darker?

There came a soft hum as the fence came to life. At the same moment, the ripple seemed to thicken. A translucent substance, not quite smoke and not quite solid, took shape. A sickly, yellow-green glow clung to its edges, allowing him to make out its form in the dark room.

"We have ectoplasm!" Henry exclaimed. Someone—he thought it might have been Miss Prandle—clapped in delight.

A pair of eyes appeared amidst the ectoplasmic swirl. Not human eyes, but spots burning with some unholy light. They fixed upon Henry.

He stopped cranking, the Wimshurst machine letting out a few last cracks as it slowed. "Francis Reyer?" he asked. "Your presence is no longer welcome here."

A soft laugh, like the skittering of skeletal fingers across his ear, came from the form.

All the little hairs on the back of his neck tried to stand up. Pushing back his fear, he said, "Be gone, or you leave us no choice but to force you out."

The eyes blazed, and malevolence struck him like a physical force. The spirit began to advance on him.

Instinct screamed that he needed to back away, to run, to put as much distance as possible between them. This thing wanted to hurt him, to break his will, to lay greasy fingers upon his very soul.

He had to hook the dispeller to the battery. But his every muscle locked in place. He couldn't move, could barely breathe.

It was only inches away. Was this the last thing the maid had seen before she'd fallen to her death? These soulless eyes, full of hate and rage?

"Henry!" Vincent cried from somewhere beyond the phantom fence.

The spirit's attention snapped away from Henry. He sagged, knees turning to water. His hands slammed into the desk, palms catching him from collapsing altogether. From beneath the desk came a pitiful squeak. Jo had taken refuge under there—thank heavens she wasn't hurt.

And Vincent? Why had the spirit turned from Henry? Did it realize Vincent was a medium—a gateway open to spirits, as he'd said earlier?

Oh God. Vincent.

Henry forced himself straight just in time to see Reyer rush the fence. For a horrified second, he thought the spirit would surely slip past the wire. How could he ever have imagined simple copper and current would hold back such hate?

Just inches from the fence, the roil of ectoplasm stopped, jerking away from the wire and its current. Another pulse of rage and hate beat against Henry, and Jo moaned.

"You have it trapped!" Gladfield shouted. He sounded like a spectator at some entertainment, unaware or uncaring of the horror saturating the very air inside the fence. "Finish it off, Mr. Strauss!"

Finish it. Yes. A hurried glance at the galvanometer showed the charge in the air had dipped far below normal levels. The water for the piezoelectric dispeller had frozen, but there was no more energy within the circle for the ghost to draw from. Save for him and Jo, at least.

The ghost grounder. Where was it?

A growl vibrated through the air. The spirit turned from its futile attempts to breach the fence, its baleful eyes fixing on Henry once again.

"Don't look at it, Henry!" Vincent cried. "Damn it, let go of me! We have to stop this!"

"Hold him, Bamforth!" Gladfield roared. "He's trying to sabotage Mr. Strauss!"

Obeying Vincent's command, Henry dragged his gaze from the spirit's. Some life returned to his limbs, and he stumbled away from Reyer, although the fence prevented him from going far. Was Jo still safe? Where was the damned ghost grounder?

Something struck him in the back, sending him sprawling to the frost-covered floor.

The skin of his palms burned, either from cold or friction. His chin clipped the floor, teeth clacking together and a spike of pain jarring through his skull. Beneath the desk, Jo huddled, the whites of her eyes gleaming in the darkness along with her pale blouse.

And in front of him, just inches away, lay the copper grounding rod.

Henry snatched it up in his gloved hand. Even as the sense of malevolence beat at his back, he rolled over and thrust the grounder deep into the heart of the presence looming above him.

Frost raced across the rod's surface, and sparks leapt around it, blindingly bright after the darkness. The sickly light faded from the ectoplasm, energy leaching away along the copper rod. The growl came again, deep and thrumming in Henry's bones, but it seemed less intense.

The grounder was working.

The glowing roil of ectoplasm gathered itself—then shot across to the side of the circle opposite Henry.

Was Reyer trying the fence again? Henry staggered to his feet, intending to pursue the spirit if he had to in order to sever its connection to this world once and for all. The fence had repulsed it earlier—it would again.

Except the ghost wasn't trying the fence. Instead, it fell upon the batteries powering the device.

Horrified realization crashed into Henry. "No!" he shouted, but it was already too late.

~ * ~

Henry stared aghast as the spirit drained the energy from the batteries, replacing everything he'd taken from it and more. The hateful, glowing eye spots flared, and there came a nasty chuckle.

But he'd nearly stopped it before. If he could only get the ghost grounder close again—

"The fence!" Jo shouted in dismay.

Oh no. Without the batteries, there would be no current. And with no current…

The spirit was no longer confined to the circle.

"Run!" cried Miss Devereaux, and she hurled open the door.

The ghost seemed to expand, tendrils of sickly ectoplasm streaming through the room. The mirror on the wall shattered. Paintings fell in a cacophony of snapping frames and ripping canvas.

A violent wind filled the room, like a blast straight from the arctic, so cold it stole Henry's breath. The Wimshurst machine hurtled from the table, smashing against the wall. One of the fence posts uprooted and struck Henry in the back, sending him to his knees. Shards of glass stung his cheek, and he cried out involuntarily. Where was Jo? Was she safe? He had to get to her out of here, but how? He couldn't see, couldn't even stand.

Daylight flooded the room, even the dim illumination of a snowy afternoon blinding after the darkness.

There came a vibration like an angry roar, shaking the walls and floor, but the storm of glass and broken furniture died away. Blinking dazedly, Henry slowly lowered the arm he'd flung up against the sudden brightness.

A warm hand closed on Henry's chilled one, accompanied by the scent of citrus and musk. Vincent.

"Can you stand?" the medium demanded. No doubt it was he who'd thought to open the curtains.

"Yes," Henry said through chattering teeth.

Vincent hauled him up, then, one arm around his waist, dragged him out of the room. Henry stumbled beside him in a daze. How had things gone wrong this quickly? What had happened to the others?

"Jo," he said as they emerged from the room. "Where is she?"

"Everyone else had the sense to run," Vincent replied. "You were the only one to stand there and get knocked about."

"I didn't stand there! I—"

The door to the bedroom slammed shut behind them, cutting off Henry's words. Vincent flinched. "Well. It looks as if Mr. Reyer isn't accepting any more visitors today."

Before Henry could reply, Jo hurled her arms around him, almost knocking him from his feet. Relieved beyond words, he hugged her back. "Jo! Are you injured?"

"No." Her hair had half come out of its bun, forming a wild nimbus around her face. "Just frightened. But what of you?"

Henry's cheek stung where flying glass had caught him, and his back ached from the impact of the post. Even so, he managed a reassuring smile. "I'm fine."

"If Mr. Night hadn't helped you…"

Now they were safe, fear began to be replaced by a sinking feeling. Vincent had saved him—Vincent, who had warned him not to do this in the first place.

Vincent, who, it seemed, had a point.

The medium stood a few feet away now, near the rest of the group. Beside him, Miss Devereaux's hair was disarranged, but otherwise she seemed calm—if angry. Miss Prandle's eyes were huge, and her hand fluttered above her breast.

"Oh!" she said. "Your séance had quite a bit more excitement than one usually sees."

"Indeed." Bamforth hovered near Miss Prandle, but his gaze went to Henry, tight and angry. "You've given the ladies a terrible fright, Mr. Strauss."

Heat crept up Henry's neck. "I won't pretend things went according to plan."

"Then I am reassured," Vincent said. The flying glass had nicked him as well, and spots of blood stood out here and there against his bronze skin. "If that had been the Electro-Séance's intended mode of operation, I would have to recommend against it most strongly."

Henry wanted to make some acerbic reply, but as Jo had pointed out, he owed Vincent a great deal. "Thank you, Mr. Night, for your timely intervention. Without you, I fear my injuries might have been worse."

Vincent waved his hand languidly. "Think nothing of it."

"What went wrong?" Gladfield asked with the air of a man inquiring about some minor issue. Apparently, he didn't feel the need to apologize for accusing Vincent of trying to sabotage Henry earlier.

Curse the man. Henry took a deep breath, forcing his shoulders to relax. "The battery. The spirit—Reyer—drained the battery connected to the fence, both energizing itself and removing the only thing keeping it in check at the same time. It never occurred to me…"

He trailed off miserably. This was supposed to be his moment of triumph, and instead he'd made a fool of himself in front of everyone.

"And now you've awakened, fed, and set loose a dangerous entity." Miss Devereaux's eyes flashed emerald fire. "Were I Mr. Gladfield, I'd demand you pay *me* five hundred dollars for making things infinitely worse!"

Stung, Henry stiffened his posture. "I'll make things right. Jo and I will repair the equipment and try again."

"And you think you can force the spirit to do your bidding? You couldn't when it was weak—how do you propose to try now?" she shot back.

Would she not even give him a chance to put things right? "I made a mistake, yes, but I intend to fix it. Which is a sight better than standing about complaining!"

"We need to leave." Vincent pushed himself off the wall, his dark gaze traveling over the company. "This is the ghost of a madman who murdered his own wife and children. It's dangerous, and it's angry. Depending on precisely when Reyer hanged himself, we have approximately twenty-four hours before the hour of its death makes it even stronger. We should pack our things and depart for the next train south. Reyhome Castle belongs to the dead now."

Of course Vincent had no confidence in Henry's ability. Why should he, given how badly the séance had gone? Still, Henry struggled to keep the hurt from showing in his voice. "I will fix my mistake. But I won't ask you to stay."

"Don't be absurd—I'm not leaving you here," Vincent snapped as if insulted at the very suggestion.

"I…oh." He wasn't certain how to respond, except Vincent's words brought a foolish warmth to his chest.

"We should at least remove the ladies," Bamforth said, with a glance at Miss Prandle.

Miss Devereaux's mouth twitched in annoyance. "I'm more qualified to deal with this situation than anyone save Mr. Night."

"And I have to help Henry," Jo put in loyally. Henry started to protest, but fell silent. In truth, if they were to put the situation to rights, he needed someone who could help repair their ruined equipment.

Miss Prandle turned to Gladfield. "Well, uncle? Shall we stay?"

"Of course!" Gladfield said, as if any alternative were preposterous. "I'm not leaving a valuable property just because of a few broken mirrors and thrown bits of furniture. The experience was startling at the time, but no one was hurt, beyond a few scrapes and cuts. The real damage was done to the furniture and poor Mr. Strauss's equipment. I see no reason to call off the experiment, especially as conditions now offer a true test of ability."

"There you have it," Miss Prandle said. "We are all resolved to stay."

CHAPTER 13

"YOU NEED my help," Vincent told Henry.

They stood in the schoolroom, where Henry, Jo, and Bamforth had brought the broken equipment from Reyer's bedroom. Jo and Bamforth had departed, leaving Henry standing alone, his back to the door, his arms folded and his gaze fixed on the jumble of wires and rods. How badly the devices had been damaged, Vincent couldn't tell, but the breakage certainly looked severe to his untrained eye.

At Vincent's words, Henry turned to face him. Like Vincent, he'd washed the blood from his face, and only a small bit of plaster, decorating a cut on his pale cheek, betrayed the danger they'd faced an hour ago. "Do I?" he asked waspishly.

Curse the man. Couldn't he see Vincent only wanted to help?

Vincent shut the door behind him and stalked across the room. Henry's eyes widened slightly, and he backed up until his shoulders met the wall.

"Yes. You do." Vincent crowded him, not quite touching, but close enough to feel the heat of Henry's body through the inch of air separating them. "If you won't do the sensible thing and get the hell out of this house, you need all the help you can get."

Henry lifted his chin, lip jutting slightly. "I've made a mess of things. It's up to me to fix them. I'm not going to beg for your assistance now after I spurned it earlier."

Of course he wanted to stay. Henry cared—about other families who might be ruined by frauds, about his cousin, even about Vincent. Just like Dunne had cared.

Dunne would have stayed to help the dead as well as the living. And he certainly wouldn't have abandoned anyone to face Reyer's ghost alone. Even if it got him killed. Even though it *had* killed him.

"You seem to have mistaken my statement for a request." Vincent leaned in further, thighs brushing together now. Henry's breath caught softly. "It wasn't."

He kissed Henry, and that, too, wasn't a request. For a moment, Henry held out against his insistent probing—then his lips parted, and he sucked on Vincent's intruding tongue. Vincent pinned him tight against the wall, sliding his thigh between Henry's, his hands braced against Henry's shoulders. Henry shifted against him, his growing erection hard against Vincent's thigh. One hand clutched at Vincent's hair while the other encircled his waist, pulling him even closer.

Vincent ached. He wanted to get this man in bed, feel their skin together, learn all the things that would make Henry whimper and beg for more.

Vincent drew back just far enough to break the kiss, bodies still locked together from the chest down. Henry's breath came raggedly, his eyes wide with lust behind smudged spectacles. "Why did you save me earlier?" he asked, breath soft against Vincent's cheek. "You might have run with the others. Left me in the room to deal with Reyer's ghost by myself."

"Because I wouldn't have been able to fuck you later." It was a lie, but it sounded good and brought a scarlet flush to Henry's face.

"You seem awfully sure I'll let you."

Vincent rocked his thigh against Henry's erection and received a gasp of pleasure in return. "I think my confidence is not without reason."

Henry slid a hand between them, pushing against Vincent's chest. "It's not why you didn't leave me. Gladfield thinks I wouldn't have been seriously injured, but…I'm not so sure."

"Gladfield is blinded by his vision of what this house could be," Vincent said flatly. "Of the money it would make as a resort hotel. If he was the only person to worry about, I'd have left already."

Henry glanced down to where his hand rested on Vincent's chest, directly above his heart. "You were right earlier—I was too confident," he admitted. "Although I don't think I'm quite the fool you take me for. Yet now you refuse to leave me, and demand in fact to help. Why?"

"Because I'm an idiot?" Vincent suggested.

Henry shook his head. "Not a good enough answer."

Vincent sighed. His glibness had served him well in the past, but Henry wasn't the sort of man to take it for an answer. He had to get at the heart of things and find out what made them work. "You're brilliant. Your fence and grounder might have worked, under other circumstances. But your very cleverness makes you foolhardy, because you aren't used to being wrong."

He laid his palm against Henry's jaw, thumb lightly tracing the other man's bottom lip. "You mean well, though. You accepted your error and are trying to correct it." Vincent smiled ruefully. "You care about people. You're a good man, even though I want to strangle you at times."

"*You* wish to strangle *me*?" Henry exclaimed. "When you are the one who—"

There came the click of the door latch. Vincent dropped his hand and stepped back in a flash, composing his expression as he turned to the door. A moment later, Miss Strauss stuck her head tentatively around the edge. "Is everything all right in here?"

"Yes, of course," Henry said, sounding flustered. "Mr. Night and I were just discussing our next course of action."

Miss Strauss brightened. "Oh—are you going to help us, Mr. Night? I rather thought you wanted to kick Henry down the stairs."

"I haven't yet ruled it out," Vincent replied mildly.

Henry shot him a glare. "Come inside, Jo—we need to repair the phantom fence and other devices as quickly as possible."

"The fence didn't work in this case," Vincent pointed out. "I said it might have in other circumstances, because I thought it was rather obvious it didn't in these."

"It *did* work," Henry corrected, seeming unperturbed by the note of exasperation in Vincent's voice. "At least until the ghost drained the batteries. If we can find a way to keep the batteries away from the ghost, it will function as intended."

"I'll start working," Jo offered. "Mr. Bamforth laid out a buffet in the dining hall, since we missed lunch. He didn't think you'd want to take the time for a sit-down supper."

"Very thoughtful of him." Henry straightened his spectacles, which had gotten slightly askew when Vincent had kissed him. "Would you like to come with me? We can lay our plans over a quick bite."

Vincent nodded. They left the schoolroom behind and went out onto the balcony. The cold spot above the bloodstain hadn't returned after Henry drained it. Further evidence there might be something to all the technology Henry seemed determined to force onto the spirit world.

On the opposite balcony, Lizzie stood in front of the door to Reyer's room, putting down lines of salt and scribbling protective signs in chalk while Miss Prandle watched. Henry nodded in Lizzie's direction. "Do you think it will do any good?"

"Probably not." Vincent shrugged when Henry gave him a surprised look. "I didn't sense Reyer when you went back into the bedroom to get your equipment. He's already slipped free and gone elsewhere."

Henry's expression fell. "Oh. I was so relieved not to be attacked, it didn't occur to me to wonder where he'd gone."

"It won't hurt, though," Vincent added. "If nothing else, it will be yet another room we can keep Reyer out of, as long as the salt line holds. If we can box him in, perhaps…"

He let the words die. Perhaps what? What did he truly imagine happening? Was it really possible to force a spirit to the other side of the veil and seal it there without using a medium as a gateway?

In the bedroom earlier, it had been everything Vincent could do not to bolt out the door when the ghost manifested. The darkness, the malevolence, emanating from it had turned his stomach and sapped the strength from his arms and legs until he'd thought he might faint.

His soul recoiled at the idea of being touched by something so inhuman. Whatever Reyer had been in life, death had stripped away what little humanity and sanity he may have retained. Reyer was nothing more than an entity of hate and rage…and far too reminiscent of the poltergeist that had killed Dunne.

And when the fence had failed and Reyer's spirit burst free, the only thing Vincent had been able to think was that it was all happening again.

It was why he'd gone in after Henry. To keep history from repeating.

No other reason. Certainly not because of how much Henry obviously cared for his cousin, or because he wanted to make the world a better place, or any of the other things about him that tugged at Vincent's heart.

Henry cheered up at his words. "We can trap the ghost? Good thinking," he said as they stepped into the brightly lit dining room. The savory smell of bread and cheese wafted out, making Vincent's stomach growl with anticipation and reminding him that he hadn't eaten anything since breakfast.

Henry heard the sound and cast him a grin. "Am I to dine with a wild beast?"

"Perhaps. As you know, I'm a man of voracious appetites."

Henry flushed and shook his head. "You're a scoundrel." But he didn't sound at all as if he meant it.

A selection of meats, breads, and cheeses lay spread the length of the table. Thick towels covered the warm items, and Henry peered beneath one as Vincent went to pour coffee from the urn on the sideboard.

"Oh, look!" Henry leaned forward and took a deep breath. "Apple pie—shall I cut you a slice as well?"

As Vincent turned to answer, a loud creak and groan sounded from above. He glanced up automatically and saw the chandelier shift. He had only an instant to shout a warning before it tore loose from its moorings and plummeted directly to where Henry had been standing.

"Henry!" Vincent shouted just as the lights went out.

There came a strange crack followed by a groan as something above Henry's head let go. Acting on instinct, he scrambled back in the sudden dimness. A rush of air washed over him as something passed just inches from his face.

The sound of the iron chandelier smashing into the table was tremendous—wood cracking, iron twisting, plates shattering. It drowned out Henry's cry of terror as he fell backward over one of the chairs, his body striking the floor.

Strong arms caught him. "Shit!" Vincent gathered Henry to his chest. "Fucking hell! Are you all right?"

Henry's whole body trembled, reaction setting in as he realized just how close he'd come to dying a second time in one afternoon. "I-I—" He swallowed hard. "I think so."

The sound of running footsteps came from the direction of the hall. Henry pulled free from Vincent's embrace. Still, he left one hand on Vincent's arm to brace himself as he stood.

"What happened?" Gladfield boomed from the doorway. A moment later, Bamforth, wearing an apron over his suit, appeared behind him.

"It was the ghost!" Bamforth cried, eyes going wide with fear. "The ghost tried to kill Mr. Strauss!"

More footsteps, and Miss Prandle joined them, followed by Jo and Lizzie. "Is anyone injured?" Miss Prandle asked, surveying the wreckage in dismay by the dim light filtering through the windows.

"No—I'm fine. Shaken, but fine," Henry said. His voice trembled slightly, then steadied. "Although I fear there's little left of the feast Bamforth prepared."

"The ghost is trying to finish what it started in the bedroom." Bamforth moved to shut off the gas valve that had fed the chandelier.

Jo's eyes widened. "Oh no!"

"I warned you," Miss Devereaux began.

"No." Vincent stepped away from Henry and toward the iron chandelier, his eyes narrowed as if it contained some message for him. "It wasn't the ghost."

"Not the ghost?" Gladfield asked, perplexed.

"I'm a medium, sir. I can sense the presence of spirits. There wasn't one in this room when the chandelier fell." Vincent's dark eyes met Henry's briefly, as if trying to pass along some message. "The house has stood empty for thirty years. It's truly amazing it's as solid as it is. Rats and mice must have worked over the beam above, or else some leak let in just enough dampness to rust the bolt. As startling as the accident might have been, it was still only an accident."

"Ah." Gladfield beamed. "Good work, Mr. Night. I see now why Miss Devereaux brought you."

Henry wanted to protest that Vincent was certainly as good a medium as his partner. But Vincent merely bowed elegantly to Gladfield. "Thank you." He straightened. "Now, if Bamforth would be so good as to return to the kitchen and put together a small dinner for Mr. Strauss and me, we'll clean up this mess."

Bamforth wavered. "But sir, you have other matters to attend. Let me find you something to eat, then I'll see to it."

"We'll make a start while you're getting our plates."

"Yes, sir," Bamforth said, a bit dubiously. Henry shared his confusion.

"Are you certain you're all right?" Jo asked as Bamforth and the others left.

"I'm sure." Henry patted her shoulder. "Finish what repairs you can, and I'll rejoin you soon."

Once she was gone, Vincent hurried to the twisted iron of the chandelier. He inspected the central column before going to the walls and feeling about the baseboards.

"What on earth are you doing?" Henry asked, perplexed. "I thought you wanted to clean up this mess for some mad reason."

"Shh." Vincent continued to search for a few moments before letting out a small sound of triumph. When he turned back to Henry, he held up a length of broken steel wire.

"What the—" At Vincent's glare, Henry lowered his voice to a whisper. "What the devil is that?"

Vincent rolled his eyes, but instead of answering, he merely let the wire drop. Hurrying to the ruin of table and chandelier, he began to pick up shards of broken ceramic. Now thoroughly confused, Henry joined him.

Vincent reached for a shard of crockery, the movement bringing his mouth close to Henry's ear. "As I said earlier," he murmured, "there was no spirit in here with us. But no accident of mice and bad timing caused the chandelier to nearly crush you."

Henry picked a pile of cheese slices from the carpet. "What are you implying?"

"There's no damage to the bolt, and it's still attached to the loop of the chandelier. I think someone rigged it to fall. They waited until you were almost underneath, then released the wires holding it up."

"You...you can't be serious." Henry set aside the cheese with trembling fingers. "I might have been killed. Why would someone do such a thing?"

"To drive us from the house?" Vincent shook his head. "I don't know, and perhaps I'm mistaken. But this isn't the first incident which has struck me as wrong."

"What are you talking about?"

Vincent's eyes narrowed, and he bent to scoop up the remains of the apple pie. "The writing on the wall. There was no sense of a spirit lingering nearby, but I thought perhaps it had moved on. Yet the graffiti doesn't really fit with any of the other spectral occurrences."

"Reyer was obsessed with the idea his wife had been unfaithful," Henry pointed out.

"I know. But the writing Lizzie channeled suggested Reyer hadn't yet fully become aware of our presence in the house. And Martha Reyer or the dead maid or the children certainly wouldn't have scrawled such a phrase on the wall." Vincent gave the tiniest of shrugs, under cover of picking up more broken crockery. "It doesn't *feel* right."

There'd been no unusual measurement at the wall, either. No fluctuations of temperature or charge, such as might have been expected. "A simple pole with a piece of chalk affixed to the end could have allowed someone to write near the ceiling," Henry mused. "But it doesn't explain why we're whispering to each other."

"Because if I'm right about the chandelier, whoever orchestrated its fall must have had some means of observing the room, to know when someone stood beneath it." Vincent glanced up at him. "As there was no one else here but us, there must be a secret room or passage. They could be watching even now."

Secret passages? Some unknown assassin? It sounded like nonsense. Vincent must be mad or just paranoid or even trying to play some sort of game.

But Henry believed him.

"I see," he said. "What do you suggest?"

A tiny smile flashed over Vincent's mouth as if he understood that Henry had decided to trust him. "I think a stroll outside in the snow, to confer and clear our heads, will be most instructive."

CHAPTER 14

"NOW THAT we're out here freezing our bits off, do you mind telling me *why* we're out here freezing our bits off?" Henry asked waspishly.

Vincent suppressed a grin—not very successfully—at the sight of Henry bundled in a thick coat and several layers of scarves, with his hat pulled as far down over his ears as possible. "You look ready for a bit of Arctic exploration. Spearing seals, driving dogs, searching for the Northwest Passage."

Henry snorted. They trudged through the decrepit garden, behind the grand hall. Their breaths plumed, and the lazy drift of snow turned the shoulders of their coats and the crowns of their hats white. The weeds and overgrown bushes in the garden already bowed beneath the accumulation as if giving winter its proper due.

"You might be from Mohican stock, able to withstand such hardship," Henry said. "My ancestors hailed from Düsseldorf. I'm the descendant of fat, comfortable brewers and bakers, thank you very much."

A note of guilt, like a pluck on an untuned violin string, hummed through Vincent. But now wasn't the time for a confession. "If they were fat and comfortable, why did they come to America?"

"Unfortunately, 'fat and comfortable' all too easily becomes 'drunk and lazy.'" Henry offered him a self-deprecating smile. "But you're avoiding my question."

"Not avoiding so much as trying to discern how to answer." Vincent tipped his head back, letting the soft flakes of snow kiss his face. "I wanted to speak outside because I know we won't be overheard. Which, yes, sounds almost as paranoid as our dear friend Reyer. For the sake of argument, let's say I'm right about the writing on the wall and the chandelier."

"I don't doubt you are, but…why?" Henry tucked his gloved hands into his armpits for additional warmth. "Why would someone do such a thing?"

"To frighten us away for some reason?" Vincent suggested.

"Again, why?"

The snow creaked softly beneath Vincent's tread. "I don't know. There seems no motive—Gladfield wants the house exorcised and is willing to stay here far past the bounds of safety to see it done. Miss Prandle can only benefit from the exorcism as well, as turning Reyhome Castle into a resort hotel will increase the family coffers. Bamforth has nothing to gain or lose, other than Miss Prandle's safety, I suppose. Still, I imagine he would try other means to woo her before turning to murder."

Henry glanced at Vincent out of the corner of his eye. "I can think of two other possibilities. How well do you know Miss Devereaux?"

"What, you think she would actually try to kill you to win the contest?" Vincent wanted to laugh, but the seriousness of Henry's expression arrested him. "No. Trust me on this. I've known Lizzie for a long time."

"Perhaps." The cold air turned Henry's cheeks and the tip of his nose bright pink. "But five hundred dollars is a large amount of money. People have killed for a great deal less."

Vincent sighed. "Even if she was a murderess, it couldn't have been her. I can sense spirits, remember? She wouldn't be so foolish as to drop a chandelier on you right in front of me."

Henry brushed against one of the overgrown bushes. Its laden boughs dumped snow across his shoulders, and he let out a startled curse when some of it went down the back of his collar. Suppressing a laugh, Vincent helped brush the snow from Henry's coat. "What's your other possibility?" Vincent asked.

Henry shot him a small smile of thanks as he knocked the last of the snow from his sleeve. But his expression sobered when he said, "We aren't alone in the house."

"Ah." The thought had merit. Vincent began to walk again, and Henry fell in by him, their elbows brushing lightly. "If the secret passages are extensive enough, someone might hide in them undetected. But why? What do they want? What do they have to gain from driving us away?"

Henry shrugged. "I'm only suggesting it as a possibility. I don't have any real answers. We don't even know the passages exist."

"There's one way to find out, I suppose," Vincent mused. "Investigate the secret passages ourselves."

"Of course, how simple." Henry snorted, his breath turning into a plume of steam. "And how exactly are you going to find them, oh all-seeing medium?"

Vincent came to a halt. "Fifty-three."

Henry stared at him blankly. "What?"

Vincent grinned. "Which one of us is meant to be the scientist? If there are indeed hidden passages, the easiest way to find them will be to count steps along the outside wall, then count them inside the rooms. If the total disagrees by a large factor, we'll have an idea where they're located."

For a long moment, Henry only blinked at him. Then a slow, rather sultry smile touched his lips. "Well done. I knew there was a reason I liked you."

On the way back inside, they discussed whether or not to tell anyone else about their speculations. Since in Vincent's case "anyone else" would mean Miss Devereaux, Henry vetoed the idea. He didn't say as much aloud to Vincent, of course—if nothing else, the man was loyal. And it was also true Gladfield or Miss Prandle might have some motive of which they were unaware. Keeping silent about their discovery seemed the safest course, since whoever had rigged the chandelier was clearly willing to commit murder to further their own ends.

Fortunately, no one questioned Vincent and Henry's strange movements within the house as they went from room to room. Vincent paced off the ground floor rooms, and Henry noted his measurements in the same notebook he'd used to record his findings earlier. If anyone happened to look, they would assume the two men to be working on some way of ridding the house of the ghost.

Vincent had a fine mind to match his body. He seemed open to the advantages science could bring, at least. And he was barely a medium anymore—he'd said as much when recounting his mentor's death. Perhaps…

But friendship with a medium, even a former medium, would only cast doubt upon Henry's Electro-Séance in the minds of scientific men. The ones he most had to impress. And Vincent was clearly loyal to Miss Devereaux.

Miss Devereaux. Henry pursed his lips in a frown as he scribbled down another set of paces from Vincent. Vincent might be convinced of her innocence, but friendship could blind one. Vincent had admitted their shop was in need, and the first instance of fakery had prompted the automatic writing séance. Perhaps she'd meant to build up the ghost in order to make their triumph over it seem greater.

Of course, she'd refused to conduct a second séance of her own, but it only meant she'd come to understand the ghost was far more dangerous than she'd first thought. And if the situation grew even worse —if Henry, say, died underneath an iron chandelier—Gladfield would surely regret not having listened to her advice in the first place. Even if she didn't receive the prize money, her reputation would remain intact, or perhaps even be bolstered. Meaning more clients.

"That's it," Vincent said. They'd traversed the entirety of the ground floor. "Let's retreat to the bay window in the drawing room—even if the rest of the room is under observation, it should give us some privacy to work."

They drew up chairs as close to the window as possible. Icy drafts slipped around panes which no longer fit tightly in the weather-warped frames. On the patio outside, snow had almost filled in the footprints they'd left while traversing the outside of the building.

Henry bent over his notebook, his back to the rest of the room, and began to sketch. Vincent wandered about the room, pretending to be interested in various objects. There was something comforting to Henry about his presence, the soft whisper of the velvet coat, the scuff of his boots against the stone floor.

"So," Vincent said casually, "how did you come to be Miss Strauss's guardian?"

No doubt Vincent thought it would be a bit suspicious if they didn't speak to one another at all. Assuming anyone was watching them at the moment. A man could become paranoid as Reyer, worrying about such things.

"Our fathers were brothers." Henry checked his notes and continued to sketch. "Uncle William met Jo's mother, Georgia, while in Pennsylvania on business. She taught mathematics at the School for Negro Girls. After they married, the rest of the family cut off Uncle

William entirely. I think I met him once when I was very small, but in truth I have no real memory of him. My grandparents disowned him, and my parents never spoke of him again, except in the occasional hushed whisper."

"He must have cared for his wife a great deal." Vincent's voice held an odd note of wistfulness.

"I'm certain he did." Henry added up some figures and drew another line on his sketch. "Two years ago, William and Georgia died in a train accident. Jo had no family on her mother's side, so our Aunt Emma agreed to take her in."

"Kind of her, to acknowledge such a relationship with a black girl."

"Kind!" Henry glared up at Vincent, who stood examining a poorly executed landscape on the wall nearby. "One might think so, I suppose."

Vincent arched a brow. "But one would be wrong, I take it?"

"The woman doesn't know the meaning of kindness." Henry all but gouged the next line of the sketch into the paper. "Emma behaved as if there had never been an Emancipation Proclamation, and Jo was her slave instead of her niece. Forcing Jo to work long, hard hours without enough food, making her sleep in the barn with the animals. Letting the hired farmhands behave like fiends, with no thought of protecting her from them."

Vincent closed his eyes briefly. "How terrible. I'm sorry."

Henry's fingers ached, and he became aware he clutched his pencil as tightly as he sometimes wished to clutch Emma's neck. "I didn't know any of it, not at first," he said. "I corresponded with Emma and knew she'd taken in Jo, but nothing more. Still, I was curious about my cousin, so I sent a letter to Jo, introducing myself. A week later, she showed up on my doorstep in Baltimore."

Vincent chuckled. "That must have been a surprise."

"Quite." Henry managed a rueful grin. "I'd thought to spend my life as a quiet, lonely bachelor, and instead found myself with a fourteen-year-old girl to raise."

"And yet you took her in, despite her race." Vincent leaned his hip against one of the chairs, his expression curious.

"She had a bruise under one eye, a healing cut on her lip, and was too thin by half," Henry said. The memory caused bile to sting the back of this throat. "I wouldn't have turned away a dog in such condition, let alone a girl, no matter her race."

"She must have been truly courageous, to take such a chance," Vincent remarked quietly. "She couldn't have known you wouldn't slam the door in her face or treat her even less kindly."

"I know. Or I do now." Henry sighed. "Having Jo with me has been an education in more ways than one. Most of the family refuses to even speak to me. If I behaved as though she were a maid I'd hired, I suppose they wouldn't care, but to acknowledge her as our blood…they think I'm shaming us all. I keep trying to get them just to meet her, but they refuse."

"She's very lucky to have you."

Henry shook his head. "Quite the opposite. For all the challenges, Jo has certainly made my life more interesting. I'm fortunate to have her." He returned his gaze to the sketch. "Jo is why I want to win Gladfield's prize, you know. To secure a future for her."

"I know." The fond note in Vincent's voice made Henry look up again. "When we first met, I thought you a self-aggrandizing prick. I was wrong."

Henry shrugged awkwardly. "And I thought you a scheming liar. So we were both wrong. Now come here and tell me what you think."

Vincent dropped into the chair beside him and leaned over. Their knees brushed, and Henry wished he dared move closer. What if someone had been watching them in the schoolroom when they kissed? Or in the tower?

It was too late to worry about their indiscretions now. "Look," Henry murmured, keeping his voice low, just in case. "There are three places where the measurements don't come close to adding up. The good news is, none of them border the guest bedrooms, so at least no one has been spying on us while we sleep."

Vincent shuddered. "Thank heavens for small favors. Where are the passages, then?"

"One to the west side of the vestibule, bordering the billiard room. Another between the tower and the library. And the last between the butler's pantry and the dining room."

"The tower." Vincent tapped the blank space between tower and vestibule. "You heard steps behind you, but no one was there, and I didn't sense any spirits near you. What if it was someone walking loudly up a hidden stair?"

"What, trying to spook me?" Henry considered. "They could have slammed the door behind me, then ducked into the secret passage. I think you're right."

Vincent offered him a cocky grin. "Of course I am."

"What now?" Henry sat back. "Do we go to Gladfield?"

“Considering he’s the person most likely to have known about the existence of the passages beforehand, no.” Vincent chewed on his lower lip. “Perhaps…I’m not certain, but perhaps we can find some evidence of whoever is behind this if we explore the passages.”

“Or find ourselves face-to-face with them,” Henry muttered. “Do you think we’ll even be able to find the entrances? They must be well hidden.”

Vincent tapped the crude map. “Let’s try this one, between the billiard room and the vestibule. There must be another in the library or the tower, but I have no desire to shovel through moldy books in an attempt to find a hidden catch.”

“Very well.” Henry folded the paper and tucked it into his pocket. “I’ll fetch a lantern and meet you there.”

Vincent loitered outside the billiard room, listening for approaching footsteps. Bangs and scrapes came from the dining room as Bamforth removed the broken furniture. Lizzie had set herself to drawing wards on all of the bedroom doors, and commandeered all of the salt left in the kitchen. Gladfield and Miss Prandle watched her work, while Miss Strauss labored on the repairs to Henry’s devices. Hopefully, everyone would remain busy enough to stay out of any secret passages while Vincent and Henry explored.

Equally hopefully, they wouldn’t find themselves face-to-face with either an unknown person or Reyer’s enraged ghost. Thus far, the very last of the daylight had kept the spirit at bay, but they would be blundering around in the dark between the walls.

Still, it was a risk they had to take. If someone, either in the company or a hidden stranger, would go so far as to attempt murder, there was no knowing what they might do next. A dangerous ghost on the loose was bad enough, but at least Vincent could sense Reyer’s approach. He didn’t have an ability to tell who among the living might be a threat.

Henry came from the servants’ wing, a lantern in his hand. They slipped into the billiard room, and Vincent shut the door quietly behind them. “With any luck, no one will come searching for us,” he said.

Henry placed the lantern on the mice-gnawed felt of the billiard table. He stepped closer, slipped one hand around Vincent’s neck, and drew him into a kiss.

The gesture surprised Vincent, but he responded without hesitation. The memory of that awful moment, the chandelier falling and himself helpless to do anything, had him wrapping his arms around Henry and pulling him close. The scent of sweat and dust mingled with bay rum, and Vincent breathed deep.

Henry let go of him and took a step back. "I just wanted to do that," he said with a shaky grin. "I trust you had no objections?"

"None at all." Vincent cocked his head to the side. "Although I am curious as to what inspired it."

A light flush tinged Henry's pale face. "I was only thinking about what we discussed earlier. About misjudging one another. But other than Jo and an old friend, you're the first person who has shown real appreciation for my inventions. Even though we disagree on points, you don't hesitate to say if you do think something can be of use, and you call me clever, and you're kind, and…" His flush deepened. "I wanted to show you I value that. You."

Vincent's grin grew wider, and his ribs felt too constrictive around his heart. "I'm glad. It's nice to be valued for something other than my skill as a medium. Or judged solely on how I look." He ducked down to kiss Henry again. "As pleasant as it would be continue, however, we'd best search for the hidden door before anyone notices our absence."

They set themselves to examining the wall. A moth-eaten mount of a deer head hung there alongside a boar. Vincent pulled them away from the wall one at a time, feeling behind them for a hidden catch. There was nothing.

"What about the rack for the cue sticks?" Henry suggested.

Vincent shook his head. "It's not easily removed by a single person. The first time Reyer dropped it, the unholy racket of falling sticks would have brought half the servants in the house."

"Not very good for keeping a secret passage secret," Henry agreed. "Hmm. Hold up a moment."

Vincent stepped back. Henry studied the wall carefully before rapping on a section. Shaking his head, he went to the next, and this time he smiled. "Hear that? Hollow. Now if I were a hidden catch, where would I be?"

Going to his knees, he ran his hands across the baseboards. There came a soft click, and a section of the paneled wall popped open. "There we are."

"Brilliant," Vincent said. He wanted to kiss Henry again, but he restrained himself. As Henry eased open the small doorway, he lit the lantern and brought it over.

"Someone's been in here recently all right," Henry said, taking the lantern and shining it inside. "The cobwebs have been cleared away, except for in the corners."

Vincent peered inside. The secret passage was tiny, nothing more than the narrowest of stairs climbing up. The scent of dust and mice clung to it, but as Henry had said, someone had taken pains to clean away the worst of the grime. "I suppose it would be obvious if our culprit turned up to dinner covered in cobwebs. Assuming it is one of us."

"Quite." Henry glanced at him. "Shall we?"

"Lead the way."

They ducked through the small door and onto the stair. Vincent hesitated before pulling it shut behind them. "Hold up a moment. I don't want to get stuck in here." Taking his handkerchief from his pocket, he folded it a few times, then wedged it into the crack between door and wall. "There. Now the door won't latch behind us, but it won't be obviously open should anyone glance inside before we return."

The stairs were well constructed; even after so many years, they hardly let out a creak. No doubt Reyer had realized it would be difficult to remain hidden if other people heard him tromping around in the walls. Vincent's shoulders brushed one side wall or the other frequently through the narrow passage. The only light came from the lantern held by Henry. His body blocked almost all the illumination, leaving Vincent to stumble blindly behind him.

As they reached the first landing, Henry said, "Look."

Vincent squeezed in beside him. The yellow flame of the lantern showed another concealed door, this one with a small spy hole located at about eye level. "It should look out into the nursery," Henry said in a low voice.

Vincent cautiously peered through. The cobweb-festooned room beyond showed little but shadows, the only light that of sunset struggling through falling snow and begrimed windows. "Spying on his little children. What a charming fellow."

"The passage next to the tower probably has a peephole into Martha Reyer's bedchamber." Henry shuddered. "Everything about this house makes me want to take a copper brush to my skin."

"Agreed." Vincent stepped away from the door. "Let's see what's above us."

The passage ended on the third floor. Once again, there was a concealed door and spy hole, this time overlooking the guest parlor. "Reyer probably wanted to find out what his guests got up to when they thought he wasn't around," Vincent guessed. "Shall we exit here, or do you think it would be better to retrace our steps?"

"Retrace our steps," Henry said.

They started back down, Henry passing the lantern to Vincent, who was now in the lead. Vincent held it high; the flame flickered and cast wild shadows on the walls. His shadow danced across the boards to his right…then very slowly crept down the wall and onto the second-floor landing in front of him.

Rusted iron slid over his tongue. The quality of the light changed, the flame going from warm yellow to cold blue-white.

The madman's ghost was in the passage with them.

CHAPTER 15

HENRY FROZE. His breath plumed in air suddenly gone painfully cold. The eerie blue light of the lantern flame leeched color from the world and turned Vincent's skin gray. The shadows around them grew bigger, thicker, more like solid objects than the mere absence of light.

In the darkness of the landing, something growled.

"Run!" Vincent shouted.

Henry's paralysis broke. He flung himself back up the stairs, not caring who might hear the clatter of feet behind the wall. His body blocked the pallid illumination of the lantern, turning the stairs in front of him into a black slot. He stumbled, hands and shins colliding with the risers. The air turned even colder, and the slickness of frost met his fingers as he groped blindly up the stairs.

The growl came again. A sense of being watched by something malevolent, something that wanted him the way a lion wants an antelope, washed over him. Vincent let out a hiss.

Then there were no more stairs, and Henry toppled out onto the tiny landing. The catch—there had to be a catch to let them out into the guest parlor. He groped along the edge of the door until his fingers encountered the latch. It clicked, and he flung himself against it.

It started to open—then stopped. Some piece of furniture left by the last tenants, a table or sideboard too short to block the spy hole, must have been keeping it from opening.

"Henry," Vincent cried urgently.

"It won't open! It's blocked." Henry glanced over his shoulder.

Something came up the stair behind them. The sickly blue light of the lantern failed to penetrate the shadow surrounding it—or perhaps it *was* the shadow. It had a man's shape, huge and hulking, but a rabid dog's growl issued from it.

"Together," Vincent said and put his shoulder against the door.

Henry joined in, trying to concentrate on shoving the door open. Not thinking about the footsteps approaching behind them, closer and closer. The freezing shadow hand reaching out to touch him—

With a loud scrape of wood against the floor, the door swung open. They tumbled out into murky daylight. A final growl sounded, and Henry glimpsed the shadow dangerously near the door as he slammed it shut behind them.

"Is the sunlight bright enough to hold it at bay?" he asked, backing away from the door.

"Any sunlight will do, even given this gloom. At least until tomorrow—then he might be strong enough to come out if it remains cloudy." Vincent dropped down onto the small couch that had kept the door from opening. Henry wanted to join him but wasn't sure if he could resist the temptation to collapse into the other man's arms. Instead, he lowered himself shakily into a nearby chair.

"Well, at least no one seems to have heard us," Vincent said after a few moments.

"Yes." Henry swallowed hard and wondered when his hands would stop shaking. "And if there *is* someone hiding from us in the passages… well, I don't expect they'll remain so for long now."

"True enough." Vincent took out his tin of cachous and popped one into his mouth. "Even if the culprit is one of us, I daresay we don't have to worry about them using the passages to spring any more nasty surprises on us."

Henry's legs seemed to be working well enough again to try standing, so he rose to his feet. "Well. As the passages led nowhere—metaphorically, at least—I suppose I should see what progress Jo has made in fixing our equipment."

Vincent glanced at the window. "Be quick about it," he said.

Henry frowned. "Why?"

"Because nightfall is coming." Vincent rose as well. "Right now, he can't manifest in any rooms with windows to let in the sunlight. After sundown, Reyer will be free to prowl anywhere he likes. I think we should all be safely tucked away behind lines of salt as soon as possible."

Still unsettled from the ghostly encounter in the passage, Henry went to the schoolroom to find Jo. In his absence, she had done wonders with the repairs. The phantom fence was untangled, the snapped copper wires spliced back together. The fragile galvanometer had miraculously survived any damage from flying debris, although the Wimshurst machine was in sad shape and the dispeller utterly destroyed.

"I don't think we'll need the Wimshurst machine, at any rate," Henry said. "We've already given this ghost far too much energy as it is."

"Agreed," Jo said ruefully. She shifted from one foot to the other, her skirts rustling. "Henry…I'm sorry the Electro-Séance didn't work the way you planned."

"It's quite all right. Every new invention is plagued with setbacks."

"Still…"

She had a streak of grease on her forehead. Tsking softly, he pulled a handkerchief from his pocket and began to scrub at it. "Don't worry yourself, Jo. We're still in the running for the prize."

"Stop it," she muttered, shoving him away and wiping at her forehead with the back of her hand. "You've been working with Mr. Night all afternoon, haven't you? Won't you have to split the prize?"

Of course he and Vincent had actually been searching out secret passages, not looking for ways to stop Reyer. But they'd agreed not to tell anyone else, and if he made an exception for Jo, Vincent would no doubt feel justified in making an exception for Miss Devereaux. "We haven't discussed it," he hedged. "I suppose splitting it would only be fair. Two hundred and fifty dollars is nothing to scoff at. It will still be enough to start production on the Electro-Séance."

Jo began to put the tools away. "And you think you can do it? Get rid of the ghosts?" she asked.

"I believe so. I just have to work out a few small issues." Such as how to keep a spirit from draining the phantom fence's batteries. "Perhaps Vincent will have some suggestions."

Her mouth curved into a smirk. "'Vincent,' is it?"

Curse it. "I'm allowed to be friends with a medium," Henry said a bit stiffly.

"I didn't say otherwise." She gave him a look of wide-eyed innocence, which didn't fool him for a moment. Was it possible she had somehow heard about the scandal with Isaac? Or had Henry said or done something to give himself away otherwise?

He put the final tools away in their chest and closed it. "We'd best join the rest of the company—*Vincent* said he wished to speak with everyone."

She bounded along behind him like an energetic gazelle. It made him feel even more tired; after the day they'd had, he wanted nothing more than to curl up under the covers and sleep.

The rest of the group waited near the fireplace in the grand hall. Bamforth had laid out a small table with coffee and sandwiches, and Henry took one of each before settling in a chair near the fire. Gazing about at his companions, Henry found himself acutely aware of the fact that one of them had probably tried to kill him.

"Well, what has the afternoon brought us?" Gladfield asked when everyone had settled.

Vincent exchanged a glance with Henry. The medium ate standing up, plate in hand, his back propped against the stones of the hearth. "Very little, I'm afraid," he said lightly. "Mr. Strauss and I scoured the house and grounds, but saw no sign of any spectral activity."

"Reyer may be biding his time, conserving his energy until nightfall frees him to move about the house," Miss Devereaux said.

"Can spirits reason?" Miss Prandle asked, sipping her coffee.

"Some of them." Miss Devereaux looked toward the great bay. The snow still drifted past the windowpanes, leaving the grounds blanketed in pristine white. "Some seem more mindless forces, reenacting the scenes of their life—or death. But others, such as the ones in this house, possess intelligence. Awareness. In the case of a violent haunting such as this one, I suspect whatever remains of Reyer means to try us tonight."

"Midnight," Vincent said. "The anniversary of Reyer's death is tomorrow, meaning he'll be strongest between midnight tonight and midnight tomorrow. He may lie in wait until then."

Miss Prandle shifted uneasily. "That sounds a bit frightening."

"I've placed protective wards on all of the bedroom doors," Miss Devereaux said. "I suggest everyone lock themselves in and put down lines of salt in front of all the doors and windows."

"Perhaps we should double up in the rooms, just to make certain no one has to lie alone in the dark, waiting for something to happen," Miss Prandle suggested. "I've plenty of space, between the main bedroom and the maid's room. Miss Devereaux and Jo can stay with me."

"Capital idea," Gladfield agreed, clasping his hands together. "Bamforth will room with me, and Mr. Night and Mr. Strauss can share, if they've no objection."

Henry's heart beat faster. Share a bed? With Vincent?

"I'm perfectly happy to share my chamber, if Mr. Strauss wishes to," Vincent said.

"I…y-yes." Henry cleared his throat. "An excellent suggestion."

Vincent gave him a quick, small smile.

"Thank you for the offer, Miss Prandle," Miss Devereaux said, "but I shall remain alone in my room."

"Are you certain?" Miss Prandle asked, looking surprised. "I know you're a medium, but surely it would be best for us to stay together."

"I'm quite certain. But I think the suggestion is a good one," Miss Devereaux added with a nod in Jo's direction.

Politeness required Miss Prandle to let the matter drop. But as Bamforth moved through the gathering, taking up dishes and pouring more coffee, Henry watched Miss Devereaux closely. There seemed no logical reason for her to refuse Miss Prandle's offer.

Unless she was their would-be murderer and meant to use their fear of Reyer as cover to strike again.

Henry stood outside Vincent's room, holding a small bag containing his necessary articles in a trembling hand. Perhaps it had been quite a while since he'd had anything more than a quick encounter in an alley, but he was no blushing virgin. Why was he nervous now? Because Vincent was a medium like Isaac?

But Vincent was nothing like Isaac. Isaac would have abandoned them all at the first sign of trouble. Vincent stayed even when he thought them fools, because he wouldn't leave anyone to face danger alone. He might play the rogue, as Miss Prandle had said, but past the languid smile and easy banter, there beat the heart of a brave man. A good man. Someone Henry could imagine being friends with—someone he *wanted* to be friends with.

Once the ghost was gone and Henry busy refining and producing the Electro-Séance, there would be no reason to ever see Vincent again. And if the thought made him feel lonely now, what they were about to do certainly wasn't going to help.

Assuming Vincent even wanted to take things further. Given his previous behavior, it seemed likely, but perhaps it had all just been outrageous flirtation.

He rapped lightly on Vincent's door. It opened almost instantly, revealing Vincent in the same oriental robe he'd worn the night he'd come to Henry's room. The soft illumination of a lone candle gilded his dark skin and emphasized his high cheekbones and full lips.

Vincent stepped back, gesturing for him to enter. "Come in. Make yourself comfortable."

As soon as Henry entered, Vincent shut the door and set about laying down a line of salt in front of it. Salt already gleamed on the windowsills and in front of the small fireplace.

Henry put his bag on the floor near the bed, then stood awkwardly, not certain what to do. What Vincent expected from him. He liked Vincent too much to want to disappoint him now, either by assuming too much or too little.

Apparently Vincent felt the same. He finished with the salt before joining Henry. Long-fingered hands closed lightly on Henry's upper arms, and he sensed the heat of Vincent's body through the air between them.

"I'm sure my previous behavior has given you the impression I want to do more than sleep tonight," Vincent murmured. "And I do, don't mistake me. But we don't have to do anything. If you don't wish to take things further, I'll sit in the chair and wait for midnight."

Henry's throat had gone tight. "Why wouldn't I want to take things further with someone like you?"

"Someone like me?"

Perhaps that had been a poor way to put it. "Someone brave enough to come to this house, even after what happened to you last summer. Someone kind enough to offer to make his competition tea in the middle of the night. Someone honest enough to admit said competitor may occasionally be right about something."

"Occasionally," Vincent teased. "But nothing about my physical charms? Perhaps you'd prefer to sit and talk chastely?"

Henry snorted. "You're blasted handsome, and you know it." His fingers slipped over Vincent's narrow hips until he reached the sash keeping the robe closed. "I admire you, but that doesn't mean I don't want you, too."

Vincent gave him a lazy smile, but his eyes flashed with heat. "I'm glad to hear it." Cupping Henry's face in his hands, he leaned in and offered a kiss, surprising in its tenderness. Henry closed his eyes and gave himself over to the soft caress of lips, the lightest nip of teeth. He caught the sash firmly in his hands and untied the knot, shoving the robe open.

His fingers encountered bare skin, and he let out a gasp of surprise. Vincent chuckled and let him go, stepping back to let the robe fall open entirely. The plum silk complimented Vincent's bronze complexion, enhancing his lean muscles and dark nipples. His prick stood half-erect already, and Henry's mouth watered at the sight. God, he'd wanted this, wanted it since the first moment he'd laid eyes on Vincent. Their kisses, the firm stroke of Vincent's hand bringing him off at the séance, every touch and word had served to sharpen his desire rather than blunt it.

Henry went to his knees almost without thought, wrapping his fingers around the base of Vincent's cock. His touch brought the other man to full hardness. Vincent's fingers slid through Henry's hair, snagging on the frame of his spectacles before deftly plucking them away.

Henry stroked slowly up Vincent's prick, then down again. Vincent's fingers curled in Henry's hair, not pulling or tugging, just caressing. Henry slid his other hand beneath the open robe, palm gliding over the smooth skin of Vincent's hip and around, to cup one firm buttock and urge him forward.

Moisture gathered in the slit of Vincent's cock, and Henry deliberately rubbed it over his lips, delighting in the feel of velvety skin against his mouth. Vincent's breath caught, and a soft moan of frustration escaped him. Henry refused to be rushed, licking lightly at the glans before tracing the edge of the hood with his tongue.

"Henry, please," Vincent gasped.

"Please what?" Henry teased. He watched Vincent's face, waited for the moment some tart remark was about to issue forth—then slid his mouth around Vincent's cock and took him all the way to the root.

Whatever words Vincent meant to say turned into a garbled curse. His hips jerked involuntarily, prick hitting the back of Henry's throat. Henry swallowed to keep from gagging, wringing another strangled curse from Vincent. Henry pulled back gradually, and when the tip had almost slipped from his lips, he repeated the action, though more slowly. He savored the salty flavor of Vincent's skin, the musk and citrus of his scent, the flex of his tight buttock beneath Henry's fingers.

"God," Vincent swore, pulling away. "Stop, please."

"Oh, first it's *Henry, please*, and now it's *stop, please*," Henry said. "Someone can't make up his mind."

"I've made up my mind, all right." Vincent grasped Henry's arms, urging him to his feet. "I'm determined not to let this end until I've felt every inch of your skin against mine and heard you beg for more."

He kissed Henry fiercely even as his hands gripped Henry's coat, shoving it from his shoulders. Henry pulled away to undo the buttons of his vest with shaking fingers. Vincent let the silken robe slide to the floor with a whisper of slick cloth, leaving him naked and vulnerable in the cool air.

Henry didn't think he'd ever undressed so fast in his life.

Vincent tumbled back against the sheets, the pale linens making his skin look darker by contrast. The silver amulet gleamed on his chest. God, he was beautiful, from his lithe figure to his burning black eyes. Henry slid in beside Vincent, threading his fingers through thick, raven-wing hair. The delicious heat of skin on skin further inflamed his senses, and he rocked against Vincent, rubbing his cock wantonly against the other man's hip.

Vincent pulled the covers up over them—and vanished beneath. He bit at Henry's nipple, sending a bolt of pleasure straight to his groin. Henry gasped and clutched at Vincent's broad shoulders.

Suitably encouraged, Vincent turned his attentions to the other nipple until both were tight with pleasure. The warm pressure of his lips slid further down, across Henry's belly, making him jump when Vincent found a ticklish spot.

The heat of Vincent's mouth closed around Henry's cock. Henry closed his eyes and bit his lip, fighting for control as soft, wet lips slid down to the base of his shaft while Vincent's tongue massaged and caressed the underside. A part of him wanted to let it continue until he spent—but that would deprive him of whatever else Vincent might have in mind.

He tugged on Vincent's hair, and the other man slid back up, emerging from beneath the covers to kiss him. "What do you want?" Henry asked breathlessly once their mouths had parted again.

Vincent's fingers traced his chest, finding one pink nipple and pinching hard enough to make Henry writhe against him. "Whatever you'd like," Vincent murmured in his ear. The brush of breath against Henry's earlobe made him squirm even more.

"I have petroleum jelly," Henry managed to say. "In my kit. I brought it, in case…"

Vincent propped himself up on one elbow, grinning slyly down at Henry. "Would you like to bugger me?"

Henry's mouth went dry. "Y-yes."

Vincent kissed him. "Why don't you get it out?"

CHAPTER 16

THE BAG sat where Henry had left it beside the bed. As he leaned over and reached for it, Vincent bit him sharply on one buttock, drawing a surprised yelp from him.

"Sorry," Vincent said unrepentantly. "The view was just too tempting."

"Hmph," Henry said, but it warmed him. He wasn't the sort of man who caused anyone to look twice. It was surprisingly nice to hear that someone like Vincent found him tempting. "How would you like to…?"

Vincent stretched out on his back and shoved a pillow beneath his hips. "The dimness of the séance kept me from seeing your face when you came. I don't intend to deprive myself of the view a second time."

Heat crept up Henry's neck. He scooped out a generous dollop of petroleum jelly, warming it on his hands. Vincent drew up his legs, lips parted and eyes bright with anticipation.

Henry touched a slick finger to Vincent's hole, caressing and probing around the edges, drawing a shiver of pleasure out of his lover before pressing gently. Vincent's cock jutted against his belly, flushed dark and leaking with need. Everything about him, from his form to his scent, made Henry ache with a desire that a quick fumble couldn't possibly satisfy.

But surely *this* would be enough. It would have to be.

Soon Vincent all but writhed around his buried fingers. "I'm ready,

Henry. Ready for your cock."

Henry slowly pumped his fingers in and out, feeling the clench and relax as Vincent wriggled. "Are you sure?" he teased. "I could keep this up for a while."

It earned him a glare and a curse. "Damn it. This is payback for bringing you off at the séance, isn't it?"

"Perhaps a little." He might have continued, but the urgent ache of his own cock had grown too powerful to ignore. Sitting back, he retrieved more lubricant from the jar, slicking it generously over his prick.

Vincent watched hungrily. "God, I want you in me."

Henry's cock twitched, desire spiking at the words, the husky tone. It was strange and powerfully arousing to have someone be so open about what he wanted. So different from the veiled invitations and shamefaced mutterings of his alleyway encounters.

Henry shifted into position between Vincent's legs, gripping his cock by the base and pressing the tip lightly against his lover. "Take it," he growled and pushed in.

Vincent opened for him, and oh God, it felt good, head sliding in past the ring of muscle into slick heat. Henry bit his lip hard, letting the pain distract him from the primal desire to just shove in and start thrusting. He gripped Vincent's hips with his hands, easing slowly deeper.

"Yes," Vincent babbled, back arching. At least the only adjoining room was now empty; there was no one to overhear them but ghosts. "Yes, more, please, more!"

Henry gave him more, every inch. The legs draped loosely around him tightened, and Vincent's cock bobbed against his stomach. "Fuck," Vincent swore. "It feels good—don't stop, please!"

"I won't."

Henry rode him, no longer conscious of the cold or the house or anything except for the man beneath him, the hot, tight body gripping his prick. Vincent grasped Henry's shoulder with one hand while the other wrapped around his own shaft, stroking in time to Henry's movements. They rocked together, the soft slap of skin on skin and the gasp of their breathing the only sounds in the room. Vincent stared into his eyes, black gaze glassy with lust, the connection somehow even more intimate than that of their bodies. Henry stared back, reveling in the expressions of pleasure chasing each other across Vincent's face, until the other man arched again, thighs tensing and teeth clenching in an effort not to cry aloud. He tightened sharply around Henry's prick even as white semen spilled from his cock across the dark skin of his belly.

Henry stopped trying to hold back, gripped Vincent's hips, and pumped into him hard: once, twice, before white hot pleasure seared his vision and wrung a low groan out of him as he spent himself deep inside.

Henry blinked, his mind slowly reordering itself. He braced himself above Vincent, their cocks going soft, their breathing slowly evening out. He freed himself gently and slipped out of bed to pad to the washbasin. The air was icy and the water frigid. Having attended himself, he returned to the bed with the cloth. "It's cold," he said apologetically as he handed it to Vincent.

"But you let me stay in the warmth of the bed. Quite the gentleman." Vincent's smile was gentle, though. "Thank you."

"You're welcome."

Vincent tossed the cloth in the direction of the washstand. Henry slid back beneath the covers and immediately had an arm and leg thrown about him, Vincent snuggling in close. "You're freezing—let me warm you up."

It was strange to lie in bed together. Isaac had always left as soon as he was done, to keep Henry's mother from suspecting. Vincent behaved as if cuddling together were natural, however. Doubtless he had more experience in these matters.

"Thank you," Henry murmured.

Vincent chuckled. "You're very welcome. Thank *you*."

Henry didn't want to move or speak. Wanted to let the silence continue and pretend neither of them had checked the clock to see how few minutes they had left until midnight. But he couldn't.

"I know you're fond of Miss Devereaux," he said quietly. "But the fact she refused to share a room with Jo and Miss Prandle has convinced me she's the one who has been using the secret passages."

Vincent sighed. "I understand why it might seem thus. But I assure you, Lizzie has very good reasons to remain apart tonight."

"Oh?" Henry frowned. "Such as?"

The languid, mocking smile was back. "Surely you don't think I'd ever give away a lady's secrets, sir."

Henry's frown turned into a scowl. "This is important, Vincent. If she tried to kill me—"

"She didn't." The smile slipped away, leaving Vincent's expression vulnerable. "It's a delicate matter. I can't speak of it to anyone without her permission. Please, Henry. Trust me."

Henry wavered…then nodded. "I do."

"Thank you." Vincent's long fingers brushed Henry's hair. "There is something I'd like to tell you, though."

A heavy blow slammed into the wall.

Shock seized Henry's heart in his chest. Beside him, Vincent swore. "Damn it—midnight. Sometimes I hate being right."

They both jumped again as something struck the other side of the wall with inhuman force, nearer the door this time. Vincent moved first, eeling out of bed and snatching up his nightshirt in a single, sinuous move.

Bam.

The overwhelming sense of being a hunted animal washed over Henry. There was *something* just outside his den, and it wanted nothing less than his death.

No. No, he had to think rationally. Not let the malevolent presence affect him. Not panic.

Vincent pressed cloth against his skin. Startled, Henry looked down and found Vincent had taken his nightshirt from his bag.

"Thank you." Somehow Henry's voice didn't shake, although he didn't dare do more than whisper. He hauled the shirt over his head, then fumbled on his spectacles.

Bam!

He jumped. "Vincent?"

Vincent's hand curled around his amulet. "Yes?" His voice was a whisper as well.

"Is it a spirit? Not a-a trick, to scare us?"

Vincent nodded slowly. "It's Reyer." He wiped at his mouth with the back of his hand as if wanting to scrub away the taste.

"Oh." Henry slid off the bed. His hand found Vincent's just in time for another blow to strike the wall, just beside the door.

The light of their candle flickered, the flame guttering in a sea of melted wax, making the shadows shift and dance. His gaze was drawn to the line of salt across the doorway, searching for any break. Or for a shadow sliding in, heedless of their feeble defense. But the salt line was solid—Vincent had done his work well.

The door latch rattled.

Henry's breath caught in his throat, and he took an instinctive step back. The floor felt like ice beneath his bare feet.

Another try at the door.

All the hairs along the back of Henry's neck stood up straight. What if the ghost managed to force open the door? Would it disrupt the line of salt? Or did the salt somehow keep it from opening the door in the first place?

Silence. Henry breathed in the cold air—was the chill caused by the spirit, or the natural consequence of a winter night? He should have brought his thermometer, taken readings.

Still quiet. Had it given up?

"Do you think—" he began.

There came a pounding on the door, over and over, a rain of blows shaking it in its frame. Henry cried out in shock at the suddenness of it. Vincent's arms slid around him, pulling him close. They clung to one another, shivering from the intense cold, barefoot and in their nightshirts, while the door shook and rattled and quaked.

The blows ended as abruptly as they'd begun. Henry took a deep breath and braced himself for them to begin again.

Another strike against the wall—but not outside their room.

A series of knocks sounded. Moving away, growing fainter as the spirit stalked the balcony.

"Thank God," Henry whispered, and some of the tension eased from his muscles.

There came another storm of pounding, the spirit trying another door. If everyone just did as he and Vincent had, stayed put, surely everything would be all right.

A feminine scream cut through the air even as the ghost's assault intensified.

Oh God. Jo.

"No!" Henry shouted and lunged for the door.

Vincent grabbed his arm, pulling him back before he grasped the latch. "Henry, stop! If they stay inside the room, if they put the salt down, they'll be fine."

Both women screamed now. Their cries seemed to incite more pounding, as if Reyer's ghost delighted in their terror.

"You don't understand!" Henry pulled free of Vincent's grasp. "I have to help her!"

"She's safe, and if you go out—damn it, Henry!"

Henry flung open the door and ran into the hall.

The only light on the balcony came from a single gas lamp, its flame gone cold blue in the presence of the ghost. A dark shape roiled like thick smoke in front of the door leading to Miss Prandle's room. As Henry stepped out into the hall, he felt its attention turn to him.

He staggered, as if at a physical blow, a sense of utter malevolence washing over him. Sickly spots of greenish-white glowed amidst the darkness, like hateful eyes. They transfixed him—he stood in place, swaying weakly. As if sensing it had him pinned, the spirit abandoned its assault on the door and moved toward him. Henry's breath turned to frost, and his legs refused to respond even though he knew he had to run, to hide, to get away…

A hot brand in the shape of a hand wrapped around his arm. "Run!" Vincent snarled. "Run, now!"

The taste of rusty nails and old blood filled Vincent's mouth. Anger beat at him like a physical force, and the amulet around his neck flashed cold.

Henry at least started moving again, broken from the paralysis of terror. His skin felt like ice, even through the cloth of his nightshirt, and their breath steamed in the air.

"Back to the room—we have to get the salt down again before it's too late," Vincent said through chattering teeth.

A painting depicting a hunting scene flew off the wall. Vincent barely had time to duck; the wooden frame caught his temple with its edge, sending a spark of pain through him. An instant later, a trickle of blood made its way down his face, hot against his chilled skin.

"Vincent!" Henry cried. In the ghastly blue light, his pale skin took on the unnatural hue of a corpse.

"I'm all right—keep going."

They'd only ventured a few feet from their door, and yet the distance back to the bedroom seemed to elongate. Was the ghost warping their perception of reality? Or doing something to the house itself? Reyer had built the place, had laid out the plans, had died here. Did he have an element of control over his environment far past that of an ordinary ghost?

Vincent gritted his teeth. Reyer might be able to play tricks on someone like Henry, but Vincent was a medium. Dunne hadn't spent years training him to hone his will against ghostly influence just for him to die a few inches from a door he couldn't quite reach.

The air had grown thick, a tangible wall of hate and blind rage, underlaid by something far worse. A sort of possessiveness, almost, as if the thing chasing them wanted far more than their lives.

It wanted their very souls.

No. He couldn't succumb to the ghost's influence. Vincent breathed deep, centering himself, pushing back against the pressure squeezing his mind. The tang of old iron flooded his mouth, and he spat.

Reality snapped back into place, and he lunged for the door, dragging Henry behind him. The salt was helplessly scattered. "Henry—grab the bag of salt!"

Henry snatched the bag up, but it was already too late.

A low growl sounded from inside the wardrobe an instant before the contents exploded out. A loud rip announced the shredding of Vincent's velvet coat. The bed curtains tore free an instant later, a violent wind blowing out the candle and leaving the two men in darkness, save for the bluish glow from the balcony lights.

If it slammed the door and trapped them in here, in the dark—

"Henry, get out!" Vincent ordered. "I'll stay and try to keep it from following you."

The room erupted in a whirlwind, furniture hurled about, the blankets ripped from the bed. The pitcher on the washstand exploded, and chunks of either glass or ice peppered Vincent's skin.

"I'm not leaving you," Henry said.

Their refuge had become a trap. There had to be some way of getting out without them both dying here, torn apart by wood and metal and glass.

Lavender, sweet and just a touch astringent, joined the sour tang of rusted iron on his tongue.

Another ghost?

Vincent's heart clenched. They were well and truly done for now. Just one spirit had enough energy to kill them, but a second…he didn't know how to even begin to fight back against both at once.

The crashing sounds died away, and the growls rose in pitch. Bedding crumpled to the floor, and the whirlwind keeping the fragments of pitcher aloft died abruptly. The taste of lavender grew stronger.

"Vincent?" Henry's hands tugged on his arms now. "Hurry—we have to get out—something is happening."

"Martha Reyer." It must be her.

There was no time to wonder. They ran, plunging out the door and onto the balcony. Vincent slammed the door behind them. Despite all the crashes and shouts, no one else had come out onto the balcony to help them.

Even if everyone else cowered in terror, Lizzie wouldn't leave him to face the ghost alone. Reyer must be muffling the sounds somehow.

Cutting them off from one another. The whole performance in front of Miss Prandle's door had been nothing more than a trap to lure one set of victims out where Reyer could reach them.

"Where can we go?" Henry asked, his voice trembling. "One of the other rooms? Or—"

Martha Reyer had tried to warn them. Perhaps had even come to their assistance just now. "The schoolroom."

"Of course—my equipment—do you think we have time to put up the fence?"

"That isn't why." Vincent wrapped his cold fingers around Henry's, tugging him along the balcony. "I'll explain in a minute, just—"

The bedroom door crashed against the wall, and the flavor of iron sharpened, overriding lavender. They bolted, making for the stairs, which would take them to the second floor and the schoolroom.

The spirit howled after them, all glowing eyes and rage. They reached the second floor ahead of it, bare feet drumming on the rat-chewed carpet. As they ran past the mirror hanging near the servants' stair, it exploded in a shower of glass.

Henry cried out and began to limp. "Curse it—I've got glass in my foot—"

Vincent hauled Henry's arm over his shoulders, all but carrying the other man along. His heart pounded madly in his chest, and the freezing air seemed to strip both throat and lungs, but he kept going. The schoolroom door waited open for them, darkness and silence on the other side.

A hard blow struck Vincent in the center of the back, sending them both sprawling. He rolled over, clutching at his amulet, swearing furiously. The spirit loomed over him, all churning hate and corrupted ectoplasm, its greenish-white eyes fixed on his.

"No!" Henry exclaimed, and he flung the bag of salt he still clutched directly at the ghost.

The writhing mass of darkness came apart at the impact, falling into misty tatters. The pungency of iron told Vincent it was still there, but for the moment the ghost's energy had been dissipated.

He stumbled to his feet. Henry stood on one leg, blood dripping onto the boards from his other foot. "Lean on me," Vincent ordered.

Behind them, the darkness started to thicken once more.

Vincent wrapped his arm around Henry's waist, practically dragging him the final few feet to the schoolroom doors. The instant they were inside, he slammed them shut.

The room was utterly black. Rather than let go of Henry, Vincent wrapped his other arm around him, holding him close. Henry clung to him in return, and they both stood frozen. Listening.

A low growl came from the other side of the doors. A soft scratching followed, accompanied by a louder growl, this one sounding almost frustrated.

Then nothing. Vincent swallowed and realized only the faint essence of lavender remained.

"Reyer's gone," he said, although he kept his voice at a whisper. It was foolish, but he couldn't shake the feeling that speaking too loudly might draw the spirit back.

Henry began to shiver in his arms. "What happened? Why did it stop attacking us in the bedroom? And why did you say to come here, if not for my equipment?"

"Martha Reyer."

Henry drew back slightly, as if to look at him, but without either candle or moonlight, it was a futile gesture. "Martha Reyer? The wife he murdered?"

Vincent nodded. "I sensed her in the bedroom. It would seem she bears no love for the husband who killed her and their children."

"Hardly a surprise." Henry rested his head against Vincent's shoulder. "You're saying she fought him?"

"It's the day of her death as well. He might be stronger than usual… but so is she."

"And the schoolroom?"

Vincent pressed his lips against Henry's hair. "She gave her life trying to keep him out of here. The atmosphere has always been lighter than anywhere else in the house. I thought her influence here might be strong enough to overcome him."

"Well. It seems you were right." Henry shifted. "Can we sit down? My foot hurts."

Vincent winced. "Of course. If we had some light—"

"I think there might be some matches with the tools."

"Good." He gave Henry a quick squeeze. "Just don't move until I get some light. I'll tend to your foot, and we'll spend the rest of the night here. Not as comfortable as a bed, but I for one don't want to venture out onto the balcony again until dawn."

CHAPTER 17

HENRY SPENT the rest of the night drifting in and out of sleep, stretched out on the floor with his head pillowed on Vincent's shoulder. When dawn finally struggled through the heavy clouds outside, he awoke to an aching foot, sore neck, and stiff back from the hard floor.

"Do you think it's safe to go out?" he asked.

"I hope so." Vincent's face was drawn, and the flesh beneath his eyes looked bruised.

Henry sat up, wincing at his many pains. "Did you sleep at all?"

"I thought it better to keep watch. Just in case. How is your foot?"

Henry unwrapped the makeshift bandage Vincent had put on it last night, made from the bottom three inches of his nightshirt. Thankfully the shard hadn't been too large, and although the wound hurt, it didn't appear serious. "It won't be comfortable to walk on, but I'll manage."

"Good." Vincent sat up as well.

Henry turned to him. "Vincent…thank you. For everything. You saved my life last night. I shouldn't have run out of the bedroom, I know, but…"

Vincent smiled at him, wry and affectionate all at once. "It's not in your nature to let anything bad happen to Jo if you can help it." He reached out and gently brushed a strand of hair from Henry's forehead. "It's one of the things I like about you."

Henry swallowed against a sudden constriction in his throat. Not certain what he could say—what he *should* say, or not say, really—he leaned in and kissed Vincent with all the tenderness he could muster. "I don't want this to end," he admitted.

Surprise flashed across Vincent's features before they eased into a grin. "Neither do I. After we finish things here at Reyhome Castle, we'll talk."

"Agreed." Henry sat back. "So how are we to finish things here, as you put it?"

Vincent sighed. "I don't know."

"I expected you to suggest we leave."

"I've changed my mind."

"What?" Henry turned to him in shock. "Do you exist just to be contrary? You've been arguing for us to leave the whole time, and now—*now*—you argue for the opposite?"

"I know, I know." Vincent held up his hands for peace. "Hear me out. The night before last, when Lizzie used psychometry on the maid's hairbrush, we came up with a theory about Reyer and the house."

"What theory?"

Vincent wrapped his arms around his knees. "He built Reyhome Castle as a prison for his wife and children. We think it's become a literal prison, not only for them, but for the spirit of anyone else who dies here."

A chill having nothing to do with the cold air walked up Henry's spine. "Explain."

"The spirit of the maid seemed trapped. Lizzie and I think Reyer is keeping her—and presumably his wife—from moving on." He looked around the room. "I'm not sure about the children—I haven't sensed them, but it's possible Martha is keeping them hidden somewhere, masking their energy with her own. I hope not, but I can't discount it."

Henry's heart sank. "And you want to free them."

Vincent rubbed tiredly at his eyes. "Martha saved us from severe injury last night. Possibly death. I can't abandon her—abandon any of them—knowing they're still trapped here by the ghost of a madman."

"Does it have to be today, though?" A sudden thought occurred to Henry. "What if we both refuse to continue? We'll tell Gladfield we're willing to return in a month, when things have settled down and it isn't the anniversary of the murders. If we insist, there's not much he can do. We'll regroup, decide what to do, and return ready to finally put the ghosts to rest."

"You have a point." Vincent grinned suddenly. "And if Gladfield agrees, you'll have your excuse to see me again."

"Do I need one?" Henry asked a bit archly. Was that what he wanted—to be constantly looking for some reason, some excuse, to see Vincent? True, they lived in different cities, but the railroad made visits practical, at least on occasion.

Could such an arrangement even work, or was he fooling himself? Was it better to agree that they'd enjoyed one another's company, then part ways? He'd worried before about what people would think if he associated with a medium, but…

But to hell with them. Had he worried what others would say when he'd agreed to let Jo stay with him, when he'd openly acknowledged their relation? Devil take anyone who thought to tell him who he could associate with.

"I thought you might require one," Vincent said. "For your own conscience." There was something tentative, hopeful, in his dark eyes. "I'm glad to hear otherwise."

An odd warmth settled into Henry's chest. He leaned in to kiss Vincent.

"Henry!" Jo cried, her voice muffled. "Where are you?"

They jerked apart. Vincent rose to his feet and went to the doors just as Miss Prandle's voice joined Jo's. "Mr. Strauss? Mr. Night?"

"We're in the schoolroom!" Vincent called up. There came the sound of running feet on the stairs. A moment later, the door opened and Jo came in. "We had a bit of a difficult night, as you see, and were forced to take refuge here. Mr. Strauss injured his foot, and—"

"Henry!" Jo shoved past Vincent and ran to his side, dropping onto her knees. Her brown eyes were wide. "The ghost scared us—banging on the door—but it went away. We didn't hear anything after, not the mirror breaking or you calling for help or—"

"It's all right, Jo." Henry patted her shoulder. "I've only a small gash on my foot, which Mr. Night tended to already."

She stood by anxiously while he climbed to his feet. A sharp pain radiated from the wound when he put his weight on it, but he thought he could at least hobble about. "Now, if you'll excuse me, I'd like to dress a bit more properly for company."

While everyone else retreated downstairs to breakfast, Henry and Vincent went to their rooms to dress and shave. "Do you need to borrow anything?" Henry asked as Vincent sorted through the wreckage of his wardrobe.

Vincent tossed his torn velvet coat aside with a sigh. "No. The rest of my things are intact, just creased from spending the night on the floor. Hopefully our company will be forgiving of my disreputable looks."

"I'm sure it will be fine."

"Perhaps." Vincent held up a wrinkled shirt and made a face. "The clothes are armor, you know."

Henry cocked his head. He knew he should go back to his own room—he was standing in the doorway in his nightshirt, without so much as a robe, but he couldn't leave without asking. "What do you mean?"

Vincent pulled a tie from the mess and tossed it over the back of a chair. "Clothes make the man, as they say. If I dress to a high enough standard, those around me see…well, they still see a savage, but a tame one. Depart too far from that standard, and things become, shall we say, problematic."

"Dress respectably, and one becomes respectable," Henry murmured. It was something Isaac had said once, in passing. Henry had been too dazed with lust to understand until far too late.

"Precisely." Vincent turned to him. "Now, if you'll excuse me?"

"Oh, yes. I'm sorry." Henry quickly stepped back to let Vincent shut the door. "I'll see you at breakfast."

He returned to his room and opened the wardrobe, pulling out his own clothing for the day. Still, what Vincent had said—what Isaac had said—itched at the back of his mind. Obviously he didn't like how people judged Vincent by his skin the same way they did Jo, but there was more to it.

Perhaps it was just the memory of Isaac. Someone who had pretended to be something he wasn't. Not at all the same as what Vincent was doing.

But someone in this house had tried to kill Henry. Unless Reyer had dispatched some unknown squatter in the walls, one of their company was also pretending to be what they weren't.

Vincent said Miss Devereaux had valid reasons for not wishing to share a room with the other two ladies. And true, there hadn't been any attempts at trickery last night, but perhaps she'd sensed the ghost was active and wisely chose to stay her hand.

The packet the detective had sent him. Henry had forgotten all about it in the chaos following the Electro-Séance.

When he'd engaged the detective, he'd been certain he was coming here to meet a pair of frauds no better than Isaac. He'd hoped to show up on the doorstep, brandishing proof and clearing the way for his own triumph.

Instead, Vincent had ended up saving him from injury or even death. Had become a friend, and…well. Maybe more. A lover, certainly.

But it would do no harm to look at what the detective had sent. Despite their long friendship, Miss Devereaux might still have tricked Vincent. Henry would be doing Vincent a favor if the detective had indeed uncovered something questionable about her.

Henry retrieved the sealed packet from the bottom of the wardrobe. Sinking down on the edge of the bed, he tore open the envelope and shook out the contents.

When he read the first lines, he wished he'd never remembered the packet at all.

Thanks to the destruction of the dining room, breakfast was served around the fireplace in the grand hall. Vincent accepted coffee and a few slices of toast from Bamforth, but found himself too tired to have much in the way of appetite.

"Bamforth and I had quite the restful night," Gladfield said, spooning jam liberally onto his toast. "Fascinating how the ghost isolated the sound of your troubles from the rest of us, Mr. Night."

Vincent glanced automatically at the stairs. Where the devil was Henry? He didn't seem like a man to spend a great deal of time on his toilette. What could be keeping him in his room? "I would call it troubling, rather," Vincent said.

"Agreed." Lizzie held out her cup for Bamforth to refill. "For a spirit to have such control over its environment is highly unusual."

"Mr. Strauss and I discussed the matter." Vincent set aside his untouched toast. "We feel—"

The sound of slow, measured steps on the stairs distracted him. Vincent rose to greet Henry, then stopped. Henry's face was deathly pale, and he clutched a sheaf of papers in his hands.

"Henry? I was just telling Mr. Gladfield about our discussion." When Henry made no reply, he asked, "Is everything all right?"

"No. No, it isn't." Henry finally met Vincent's gaze, and his eyes were hard and cold as the glass lenses of his spectacles. "Mr. Gladfield, I'm afraid we've been taken in."

What was Henry talking about? Vincent took a step toward him, hand lifted. "Henry, what—"

"Don't touch me." The vitriol in Henry's voice hit Vincent like thrown acid. "I know. I know everything. All your lies."

"Explain yourself, Mr. Strauss," Lizzie ordered, rising to her feet.

Henry's grin was a ghastly thing, without humor at all. "Was it you who tried to kill me with the chandelier? It was, wasn't it? And if I'd died, Mr. Night would have claimed it the work of a spirit. Since I didn't, some other lie was necessary."

"What the devil?" Vincent exclaimed. "Henry, you're talking nonsense."

"Am I? Why should I listen to a word you have to say, liar?" Henry clutched at the sheaf of papers like a man clinging to flotsam in a storm. "When Mr. Gladfield arranged our little contest, I asked him for the identity of the medium I would face. He told me there would be two and gave me your names. I assumed you were frauds, so I hired a detective to find you out even before we came here."

No. Oh no. "Henry," Vincent started.

"Shut up." Henry didn't even look at him now, all his attention focused on Gladfield. "The information didn't come in time, and when Bamforth so kindly brought my mail from the station, I thought it unnecessary. I thought *Mr. Night* and *Miss Devereaux* had proven they possessed real psychical talents, and didn't bother to look through the detective's findings."

No. No, no, no.

Gladfield's brows drew together. "What do you mean, man?"

Henry swallowed, his throat working hard. "Everything they've told us has been a lie."

God. Oh God. He'd been going to tell Henry the truth last night. Just before the damned spirit started pounding on the wall. "Th-that isn't so."

"Isn't it, Mr. Night?" Henry brandished the papers. "Oh, but wait, Night isn't even your name, is it?"

It was, though. One paid for and hard-won. But even a glance at Henry's face killed any hope Vincent might be allowed to explain.

Henry made a show of adjusting his spectacles. "Vincent Watkins, alias Fast Vinnie, alias Red Knife, alias Vincent Night. No record of birth, but the police first came across you in the Bowery, age seven. They encountered you again, I see, and again—petty theft, pickpocketing, and my favorite, 'solicitation of unnatural acts.'"

Vincent wanted to close his eyes and hide. Or maybe the opposite—maybe he wanted to scream it didn't matter, none of it mattered. Because Dunne had come along and taken him away from it all, made him whole.

Let him become the person he'd been meant to be.

Henry pushed on. Relentless. Digging the blade in farther. "Apparently, by age fifteen, you were part of a group conducting fake séances. You would cover yourself in starch powder and appear as the 'spirit guide' Red Knife."

"Henry," he tried again, but his voice cracked helplessly.

"You're a fraud." Henry's tone left no hope of reprieve. Vincent had been judged and found wanting. "None of your so-called 'clairgustance,' or whatever ability you claim, can be trusted. All of which puts a very different aspect on this haunting, wouldn't you say?"

"Henry, no!" Vincent's eyes widened. "This house is dangerous! You've seen it yourself—"

"In your company, Mr.…Watkins, was it?" Gladfield asked, and the edge to his voice might have cut glass. "Who is to say what was part of your act or sleight of hand, and what wasn't?"

God. This couldn't be happening. Vincent held up his hands. "Please…be reasonable. Just listen for a few moments."

"I think we've heard enough out of you," Henry replied. "And your partner as well."

Vincent's heart contracted, and he exchanged a quick, panicked look with Lizzie. "Please," he said to Henry. "I'm begging you. Don't do this. I'll go. I'll leave right now, and—"

"Your partner." There was no mercy in Henry's eyes, only hurt. Betrayal. "Elizabeth Devereaux. Or should I say Edward Dabkowski?"

Vincent closed his eyes, heard hisses of indrawn breath all around.

"What?" Gladfield demanded, the word cracking like a whip.

"See for yourself," Henry said. "Or, if the detective's word isn't good enough, perhaps one of us could make an examination…"

"Go to hell," Lizzie snarled. Vincent opened his eyes, saw she'd risen to her feet, eyes wild with fury.

Silence. Utter, shocked silence. On the outside, anyway. Inside Vincent's head, there was nothing but the crash of their lives coming apart, the pieces raining down around them. Nausea clenched his gut, and he swallowed against bile.

Bamforth had gone pale, and Miss Prandle looked both revolted and shocked. Miss Strauss didn't seem to know what to think, looking between Henry, Lizzie, and Vincent. But Gladfield's face had flushed a deep, ugly shade of red, and his hands clenched into fists.

"What *depravity* is this?" Gladfield growled.

"Did you disguise yourself as a woman, hoping no one would

suspect you of attempted murder?" Henry asked. "Or did you have some other motive?"

Lizzie's lip curled in disgust. "You overestimate your importance to me, Mr. Strauss."

Gladfield took a threatening step toward Lizzie. "I ought to thrash you for exposing my niece to your—your filth!"

Vincent moved between them. "Mr. Gladfield—"

Gladfield struck him, a hard blow to the face which left him reeling. Blood filled his mouth where the corner of his lip had split against his teeth, but he swallowed it, afraid spitting would be seen as a challenge. Henry let out a startled cry, and Lizzie shouted, "Don't! We'll leave; we'll leave!"

"Uncle, stop." Miss Prandle caught Gladfield's upraised hand before he struck Vincent again. "Let them go. They aren't worth sullying your hands."

Gladfield slowly lowered his fist. "You're right, Wilma." Casting a glance of searing hatred at Lizzie, he said, "Get your things, and leave this house, right now. The both of you. And if I find you're still in your shop when I return to New York, I'll have you before the magistrate."

God. They weren't just going to lose the contest. They were going to lose everything.

Lizzie made for the stairs, her head held high like a queen's. She didn't bother to glance in Henry's direction. Vincent did though, and for a moment their eyes met. Hurt and grief filled those blue eyes along with a little bit of shock, as if he couldn't believe Gladfield had actually struck Vincent.

How naïve. Almost as naïve as Vincent had been, thinking they might have had a chance for something more.

"Congratulations, Mr. Strauss," he said as he passed by. "You've won. How very pleased you must be with your victory."

Then he was past and up the stairs, and anything Henry might have said in return was lost behind him.

CHAPTER 18

HENRY STOOD at the door to the schoolroom, feeling utterly, wretchedly miserable.

He'd let himself be taken in by a medium a second time. Isaac had been bad enough, though at least Henry could blame his former gullibility on the inexperience of youth. But now he had no excuse save for his own stupidity.

Vincent and Miss D—Mr. Dabkowski, had pretended to be everything they weren't, and Henry had accepted the illusion without question.

Still, he wished Gladfield hadn't hit Vincent. Or chosen to throw them out. The snow had begun to fall in earnest, and it was a long walk back to the rail station on foot.

Then again, they'd likely conspired to murder Henry. Although why Vincent would have brought up the secret passages and helped Henry map them if he truly was in on the scheme…

No. So what if it made no sense? Who could fathom the motives of such twisted liars? If the facts didn't quite fit his theory, well, it simply meant he'd been duped even more thoroughly than he realized. Had there really even been a ghost on the stairs with them, or had Vincent used some trick to turn the lantern flame blue? A pinch of chemicals would suffice. "Ghosts" had been created through use of muslin and phosphorescent paint before—perhaps that's all Henry had ever seen, and his imagination had supplied the rest.

What had happened during the Electro-Séance had been real. But anything else—everything else—could have been nothing more than a bit of clever trickery and playacting meant to humiliate him.

Henry's throat ached and his eyes burned. Stupid. He couldn't waste time thinking about this. He had to focus on using his equipment to remove the ghosts as quickly as possible, so he and Jo could get out of this house and back to Baltimore. Put it all behind them.

Jo's skirts rustled as she entered. He forced himself straight and turned to her. "We should consider…"

"Consider how anyone can be this stupid?" she shot back. Anger gleamed in her brown eyes, but her mouth was set in a look of disappointment. "How could you do that to them? I thought you liked Mr. Night! And Miss Devereaux—"

"Isn't a 'miss' at all," Henry shot back. "It's clear they've been playing us for fools from the start."

Jo shook her head. "No. I don't believe it."

"Believe it. It's all been nothing but lies," Henry replied savagely. "Their names, their pasts, the automatic writing séance 'Miss Devereaux' conducted, every word out of their mouths a falsehood."

Especially what Vincent had said about wanting to see him again. Every smile, every touch, just another way to use and trick. His chest ached with it as if Vincent had taken a knife to him. Perhaps that would have hurt less.

"You could have died last night!" Jo flung her arms out in exasperation. "Now you're pretending it was all—all some sort of trick?"

"The spirit didn't hurt me—hasn't hurt anyone." Henry swallowed against the knot inside his throat. "It was frightening, yes. It threw things around and broke the mirror, yes. But my injury was purely an accident—had I been wearing shoes, it wouldn't have occurred at all. The only 'evidence' we have of real danger is the mediums' claims, which they no doubt made up to make themselves look better."

"How can you be so blind? Just because they lied about—about their pasts—"

"Enough!" Henry slammed his fists on the table. "I have made my decision, and I won't have any more back talk from you, do you understand?"

Jo drew back, blood draining from her face. "You're just going to pretend the thing in the hall last night didn't want to kill us? Just throw two people, whatever their names might be, out in the snow and hope they don't die?"

"What do you want from me?" he demanded.

"A heart? Vincent isn't Isaac."

Something heavy settled into his gut. "You don't know anything about that."

"Yes, I do." Her lower lip trembled, but she stood her ground. "When I told Aunt Emma I wanted to meet you, she said he…and you…"

"I'm not having this conversation with you." Curse Emma. "Not now, not ever. You're too young to understand."

"You're wrong!" Jo's hands balled into angry fists. "I understood. I just didn't care! At first I just wanted to get away from Aunt Emma, but I met you, and I love you, and I don't *care*." She dashed away angry tears. "But now you're going to let Mr. Night get hurt for no better reason than that Isaac hurt you."

"That's it." Hot anger ran through his veins—at himself, at Isaac, at the damned liar Vincent. "I already told you this conversation was over, and you disobeyed me. One more word—one more—and I'm sending you back to Emma."

Her lips parted, but no sound came out. Belatedly, he realized exactly what he'd just said.

"Jo, I'm sorry," he said, reaching for her.

"No." She stepped back, tears spilling over onto her cheeks. "I should've known you didn't really want me."

She turned and ran. Henry followed to the doorway, then stopped and stood alone, wondering how everything had gone so horribly wrong.

Vincent savagely stuffed the last of the things he could easily take with him into his valise. Most of his belongings would have to stay here. The walk would be long and bitter as it was, given they weren't prepared for a hike in such weather.

But he and Lizzie would make it. They'd lived through worse, hadn't they?

And so what if everyone they left behind would be doomed? Henry and Gladfield deserved whatever fate the ghosts had in store for them. Vincent had done everything possible, given every warning. If they chose to ignore him, it was their fault. Their blood certainly wouldn't be on his hands.

As for Miss Prandle, Bamforth, and Miss Strauss…well. You couldn't save everyone. Sometimes, you couldn't save anyone.

Dunne hadn't believed that. But he was dead, killed by the very apprentice he'd taken in. Clearly his judgment had been faulty from the start.

Flinging his bag over his shoulder, Vincent shoved open his door. It nearly collided with Miss Strauss, who stood trembling outside, her face stained with tears.

"Miss Strauss? I didn't realize you were there," he began.

"Take me with you," she blurted out.

What the hell was happening? "I can't," he said automatically. "Why would you even ask such a thing?"

"H-Henry." She scrubbed angrily at her cheeks "He said he'd send me back to my Aunt Emma, and I-I can't go back there, I can't."

Had Henry completely lost his mind? "Your cousin is an idiot," Vincent said. "But he loves you, and he would never send you back. If he threatened otherwise, it's because…well, as I said, he's an idiot."

She shook her head frantically. "He meant it. He was so angry. Please, take me with you."

Damn Henry. Vincent put a hand to her shoulder, feeling her tremble beneath his fingers. "Trust me. Last night, Henry was willing to risk death for your sake."

"He says there isn't any danger." She glanced up at him apologetically. "You made it all up."

God. Maybe he *should* take the girl with him. But it wouldn't be allowed, by Henry or Gladfield or anyone else.

Meaning he had to talk to Henry.

Vincent didn't want to see Henry. Didn't want to look at him and remember those moments over the last few days, when their eyes had met. How Henry's initial shock and annoyance had given way to something softer.

Vincent should have said something last night. No, before last night. The moment Henry told him about Isaac, he should have confessed the truth about his own past. But he hadn't, because he wanted…

Wanted Henry to like him.

"Let me talk to your cousin," Vincent said resignedly. Giving her shoulder a squeeze, he went to the stairs and thence to the schoolroom.

Henry stood in the middle of the room, looking lost. His head snapped up as Vincent stepped in. Miss Strauss lingered outside, unwilling to come too close. Henry's eyes widened, and he opened his mouth to say something—to condemn Vincent, no doubt.

Vincent held up his hand sharply. "Shut up and listen for once in your damned life. You believe I'm a fraud? Go ahead."

"It's more than that." Henry had regained his power of speech a little too quickly for Vincent's liking. "You *are* a fraud. Fake séances. Fake name. Even your partner is nothing but a falsehood."

Vincent's chest grew tight, and his nails cut into his palms. "There are two things you need to understand, right now," he said in a low voice. Henry took a worried step back, but Vincent didn't give a damn and stalked after him. "I am Vincent Night, and Lizzie is a woman. And if you honestly think what someone else might have named me or what Lizzie was born with between her legs defines us, then I'm *ashamed* I ever touched you."

Henry took a quick sip of breath, brows climbing to his hairline, but Vincent wasn't done. "The prize money is gone. The only thing Lizzie and I had left of Dunne's is gone. You've ruined us, Mr. Strauss, and if that makes you happy, so be it. But this spirit is dangerous and it will kill you. And if you think I'm so petty as to want to see such a thing happen, to you or your cousin or anyone else, you've committed almost as grave an error in judgment with me as I did with you."

"Vincent—" Henry started.

The tang of iron and blood bloomed on his tongue.

"Damn it!" Vincent turned his back on Henry, casting about frantically. Miss Strauss hovered by the door, so he yelled, "Reyer's here—get in the schoolroom now, put down salt, and don't come out!"

He ran past her without waiting to see if she obeyed. Footsteps pounded behind him—Henry following, although God only knew why. No doubt the man thought Vincent was making everything up again.

Lizzie's cry of pain sent Vincent's heart jolting against his ribs. Angry voices echoed from the third floor, and the taste in Vincent's mouth grew stronger. He took the stairs two at a time, emerging to see Gladfield strike Lizzie a blow which sent her to the floor.

Gladfield loomed over her on the balcony just outside of the door to her chamber. She'd changed into her most sensible dress for the trek through the snow. A single bag lay on the floor beside her, its contents spilling out onto the wooden boards. Miss Prandle and Bamforth both hovered not far away, Bamforth with his hand on Miss Prandle's arm as if he'd tried to restrain her.

"How dare you?" Gladfield roared. "To continue to dress in such a fashion?"

"Please—I don't have anything else to wear," Lizzie protested.

"I should burn it, with you in it," Gladfield shouted and drew back his foot to kick her.

"No!" Vincent didn't even remember crossing the distance between stairs and balcony. The taste of rusted nails grew strong enough to gag him, and the air went from cold to freezing. Gladfield's rage, Lizzie's pain and misery—Reyer was feeding off it, growing stronger by the instant.

Vincent fell to his knees and hunched over Lizzie in an attempt to protect her. Gladfield's kick landed on his thigh, and he bit back a cry of pain. Then Henry was shouting, and Gladfield shouting back, and the malevolence in the air coalesced thick on Vincent's tongue.

He spun and grabbed blindly for Henry, pulling him to the floor just as the world around them exploded into fury.

Every picture on the wall tore free in a shower of wood and canvas. The gaslight burned blue. Miss Prandle screamed, and Bamforth dragged her back, his arm up to shield them both from the flying debris.

Gladfield was hurled like a doll into the balcony's railing. The old wood, weakened from years of neglect, shattered like kindling. For a moment he seemed to hang in space, arms reaching, legs flailing. Eyes wide with shock and terror.

Then he fell. The sound of his body smashing into the flagstones two stories down echoed in the sudden silence.

Henry dragged one of the rugs from near the great hearth and flung it over Gladfield's broken body. Everything had happened so fast. Gladfield beating Miss Dev—Mr. Dabkowski, Vincent's intervention, the ghost…he felt in shock, as if he clung to the back of a galloping horse, able only to hang on and hope he would make it to the end of the ride.

The rest made their way down the stairs, Miss Prandle leaning heavily on Bamforth's arm. "Uncle," she sobbed. "Mr. Strauss, is he…?"

"I'm afraid so."

Jo made a small, scared sound in the back of her throat. Henry moved to her side and put an arm around her. A moment later, she pressed her face into his shoulder, her entire body shivering.

Vincent stared at the rug and the body it concealed. When he lifted his gaze, he met Henry's unflinchingly. His eyes were dark and cold as the night sky, and Henry had to look away.

"Well, Mr. Strauss?" The snow falling past the window couldn't compete with the chill in Vincent's voice. "Aren't you going to accuse us of murdering him through some use of sleight of hand? Or perhaps we simply lied him to death."

"Don't, please," Miss Prandle begged. She wiped away tears and straightened. "What—how did this happen? In the middle of the day?"

"It's the anniversary of Reyer's death, and Mr. Gladfield's attack just gave the spirit more energy to feed on." Vincent's lips formed a hard line. "Reyer seems to have expended his reserves for the moment, but it won't take long for him to regather strength. We must leave the house before that happens." He glanced at Henry. "Unless you actually believe Lizzie and I conspired to kill you."

"What did you mean?" Jo asked Henry, looking up from the shelter of his arm. "You said something about the chandelier earlier."

Henry shook his head. "There are secret passages in the walls. The chandelier was rigged to fall."

"What does it matter now?" Bamforth cut in. "We must get Miss Prandle to safety."

Miss Prandle said nothing, tears streaking her face. Henry stared down at the rug concealing Gladfield's body, feeling numb. This was his fault. If he'd just done as they'd agreed this morning, told Gladfield they had to leave…

But he'd suspected that Vincent's partner was a potential murderer. And after learning the truth about them, he'd been sure of it.

Hadn't he? Maybe he hadn't been sure at all. Maybe he'd just been angry.

And now Gladfield was dead.

"Very well." Vincent looked around at them all. "This is what we'll do. I don't want anyone wandering about alone. Bamforth and I will bring the wagon around to the front of the house. The rest of you go upstairs and pack whatever you need. Don't split up even for a moment." His gaze first met first Henry's, very deliberately, then Miss Prandle's. "And if Lizzie tells you to do something, do it. Don't ask questions, don't dither as to whether or not you can trust her. If you do, you'll end up like Mr. Gladfield here. Do you understand?"

Miss Prandle nodded shakily. "Yes, Mr. Night. I'm sorry, I…yes. We'll do whatever he says."

"You'd better." He turned to Bamforth. "I'll get my bag and Lizzie's and rejoin you in a moment. Wait here."

The man nodded. "I understand, sir."

Vincent started for the stairs without another word. As he brushed past, Henry put out his hand. "Vincent—"

"Excuse me, Mr. Strauss." Vincent evaded his grasp easily. "We really do need to move quickly."

Henry's hand fell to his side, and he fought back a surge of disappointment. “Yes, of course,” he said, but Vincent had already started up the stairs and didn’t look back.

CHAPTER 19

THE AIR outside the house was bitterly cold, and the snow piled worrisomely deep. Vincent trudged after Bamforth toward the makeshift stables, carrying both his own bag and Lizzie's. Bamforth carried the tack and harness for the horses.

The grounds had once boasted a large stable, of course. At some point in the last thirty years, the structure had burned down. For lack of any other options, a small garden shed had been hastily fitted to hold the two horses and their food. Even the tack had to be stored in the house.

"Do you think we'll have any trouble getting through?" Vincent asked, looking around at the drifts. The gray sky continued to relentlessly spit snow: big, fat flakes caught in their hair and dusted their shoulders briefly before melting. The trip back to the rail station wouldn't be pleasant, even with the wagon.

Far better than going without it, though. If Gladfield had lived long enough to have his way…

The man was dead, but it didn't blunt Vincent's anger at either him or Henry. Yes, Henry had seemed shocked and distressed when Gladfield attacked Lizzie, but what the devil had he expected to happen? Was the fool really so coddled he didn't realize he'd exposed Lizzie to the threat of violence?

Well. Henry had shown his true colors. And if the thought of the other man still made Vincent's chest ache, it said more about Vincent's own stupidity than Henry's worth.

"I hope not," Bamforth replied. He stopped at the door to the stable, clearing away snow with his boot in order to drag it open. "But if it keeps on like this…well, best we don't dawdle."

"Agreed." Vincent waited outside—there wasn't enough space for them both within. While Bamforth led the first horse out, Vincent pulled the cover from the wagon and tossed their bags into the back.

"Do you think the house will ever be safe again?" Bamforth asked as they hitched the horses to the wagon. "I don't mean perfectly, but once we're gone, will things settle down?"

Vincent nodded. "They should. Without our presence adding energy to the house, and with the anniversary of the murders past, the ghosts will eventually become quiet again."

"Good. I was thinking…well. Mr. Gladfield's things, his family will surely want them, and we can't bring everything in the wagon with us. I'd hate for them not to be able to return and fetch anything."

A kind thought. "They should be able to in a few months, especially if they don't linger in the house any longer than necessary." Henry would probably need to return as well—his equipment wouldn't possibly all fit in the wagon along with six living people and a dead body. "Did you work with Mr. Gladfield long?"

"All my life," Bamforth said regretfully. "Not him in particular, but my father was his father's valet, and my aunt worked here as the tutor."

Vincent climbed into the wagon as Bamforth took the drivers seat. "The tutor? The one Reyer injured?"

Bamforth nodded, and for a moment his expression grew hard with anger. "Yes. She lost three fingers—the cuts from the knife were too deep to save them. Drank herself to death, she did. I suppose she couldn't forget what she'd seen him do to the children."

"I'm sorry." The wagon lurched into motion, horses straining to drag it through the thick snow. "Coming here must have been difficult for you."

Bamforth shrugged. "In a way. But it was a long time ago, and I was more curious than upset, if you understand. This house was a part of my family's history just as much as Mr. Gladfield's."

"I'm sorry it had to end this way."

Bamforth looked sad for a moment before shaking himself. "So am I."

The horses dragged the wagon through the piling snow, making something of an effort—and this was over level ground, not the rutted, overgrown track leading back to the town. Bamforth's expression became worried, but neither of them spoke their fears aloud. After all, what choice did they have? Staying in the house was out of the question.

When the wagon finally creaked to a halt in front of the door, Vincent swung down. "I'll see how the others are coming and assist if necessary," he said. "It's probably safer if you stay out here with the horses in the meantime."

Knocking the snow from his shoes, he went to the door. It refused to open.

"The devil?" he muttered and shoved harder.

"It can't be locked," Bamforth said. He dismounted from the wagon and came up to try the latch himself. "We just came out ourselves."

Vincent rattled the door, then threw his weight against it. It didn't budge, but he caught the lingering taste of rusted iron nails.

"Damn it." He stepped back and stared at the heavy oaken panels. "It's not locked. It's Reyer. He's keeping us out."

"Mr. Dabkowski," Henry began uncertainly as they started up the stair.

The medium spun on him, her—his—face drawn into a furious glare. "Let us get one thing straight, Mr. Strauss. I'm here to keep Reyer's ghost from hurting anyone else before we leave. I could, if I wished, walk out the front door this moment and abandon you to your own devices—as you have repeatedly wished me to from the beginning, I might add."

Taken aback, Henry held up his hands. "Of course. I understand—"

"Good. And in return for my services, which I am doing purely from a sense of honor and obligation, you will refer to me by my name. Elizabeth Devereaux."

His green eyes flashed angry fire, and Henry took a half step back. What was it Vincent had said? About letting others define both himself and his partner?

But Dabkowski *wasn't* a woman. He couldn't be, with male anatomy. The thick chokers she—he—wore concealed his Adam's apple, and the flowing gowns covered a frame that was decidedly delicate for a man's. His features would be sneeringly called pretty on a man, but the line of the jaw was rather rugged for a woman, although the long golden curls distracted from it. Dabkowski must either have an exceptionally light beard or spent hours each day skillfully plucking away any offending hair. The mimicry was masterful—other than his height, which could hardly be altered downwards, everything from gesture to dress to soft voice would lull an observer into assuming him female.

An involved performance indeed. Too involved to be part of a single, bizarre scam, as Henry had earlier accused. Dabkowski obviously spent his everyday life as a woman. But that didn't make him one the way Vincent seemed to think it did.

There were people who said Jo wasn't a person. She couldn't be, with her skin color.

It wasn't the same, though…was it?

God, he didn't know. But it seemed Dabkowski, or Deveraux, or whatever he—or she—wanted to be called was trying to save them. And it would hardly cost Henry anything to agree to his—her—demand. "I… yes. Please, forgive my poor manners, Miss Devereaux."

"Apology accepted." She turned back to the fore and started up the stairs again. Henry had the distinct impression that the apology was only understood to cover his latest faux pas.

"We'll go to Miss Prandle's room first," Miss Devereaux said as they gained the third-floor landing. Her skirts rustled as she strode before them, her head held at an imperious angle proclaiming nothing would break her spirit, their opinions least of all. "Miss Prandle, please gather only what you absolutely need. I'll remain outside and attempt to sense the ghost."

"Attempt?" Henry asked.

"Vincent is far better at such things than I. It's what makes him such an extraordinary medium." She cast him a glance edged with scorn.

If only he had his galvanometer. Or anything, even…

"Do you have a hair pin, Miss Devereaux?" he asked.

The look she shot him could have frozen lava. "Yes."

"If it's steel, may I borrow it? If the electrical charge of the air shifts, it might give us a small amount of warning."

They'd come to Miss Prandle's door. Miss Devereaux's look didn't warm, but she pulled free a hair pin, leaving a blonde lock to tumble over the shoulder of her dark dress. Henry pulled a bit of string from his pocket and used it to hang the pin from the balcony railing. It swung gently in the air currents, and he wondered if his makeshift galvanometer would really do anything to alert them or not.

"Shall I help?" Jo offered. "To make the packing go quicker?"

"Thank you," Miss Prandle said and led the way inside the room.

Henry remained on the balcony with Miss Devereaux. The medium stepped a few paces from the door, her head cocked as if trying to hear a conversation just out of reach.

It seemed as good an opportunity as any. "Miss Devereaux?" he asked, pitching his voice too low for the ladies to hear in Miss Prandle's room.

"What is it now?" she asked impatiently.

He winced. "You have good reason to be angry with me. I only wanted to say I'm sorry. I didn't realize Mr. Gladfield would react with such violence."

"How nice for you." Her eyes narrowed, and she touched the bruise beneath one. "This isn't the first—or the worst—time I've been beaten for the simple crime of living as a woman."

"Then why do you do it?"

She arched a brow. "Why do you do any of the things you do, Mr. Strauss? Surely you have some behaviors upon which society frowns."

Heat crept up Henry's neck. No doubt she guessed what he and Vincent had done together…was it just last night? "Yes, but…"

"But why not stop?" she challenged. "Change yourself. Become someone else. You can't, can you?" She turned away from him. "Neither can I. I am what you see before you, and I will not be less simply because other people wish me to be. Even if it costs me everything."

Henry took a deep breath and let it out slowly. Could he be so brave? True, he'd found himself unable to conform to a world which said he should desire women, but it wasn't as if he'd even considered living openly with another man.

"I'm sorry," he said at last. "If Vincent had just told the truth from the beginning…"

"And what lie did he tell which did you such injury?" Her lip curled. "Should he, upon meeting you, have given you every detail of his life, including episodes from long in the past, of which he is justly ashamed?"

"He didn't have to make up everything from whole cloth," Henry hedged.

"Because men like Gladfield can't wait to invite former street rats into their homes. How charmingly naïve you are, Mr. Strauss."

Henry wanted to protest. To say Vincent was no better than Isaac, using lies and tricks to work his way into a man's heart.

But his mentor's death hadn't been a lie; that at least the detective had confirmed. The bravery it must have taken to come here, even after seeing the worst that could happen, was genuine. All of the soft smiles and small kindnesses, admiring Henry's ingenuity even when disagreeing with the use he put it to…it had all felt real.

Should Henry judge Vincent on the circumstances of his life, on whatever lies he'd felt the need to tell about his background…or on the fact that Vincent had stayed behind and vowed to help them all get away from Reyhome Castle alive even after the way they—the way Henry—had treated him?

"You're probably right," Henry said. He turned back toward the door to Miss Prandle's room. "I should—"

The pin suddenly jerked and danced madly on its string. An instant later, the temperature plunged around them. "Jo!" he shouted and lunged instinctively for the door.

It slammed in his face. He jerked back—then gasped.

The wall in front of him was completely smooth, without trace or sign the door had ever existed.

"Damn it!" Vincent struck the front door with his fist, but the heavy oak remained unmoved.

This was bad. Reyer had regathered his power far more quickly than Vincent had expected. The amulet around his neck burned cold, and he shuddered. Lizzie had no such protection—what if Reyer tried to possess her? Or what if he simply decided to kill everyone in the house?

Was Lizzie all right? Henry?

"We have to do something!" Bamforth exclaimed. His face had gone pale, and Vincent remembered how solicitously he'd behaved toward Miss Prandle.

"We will," Vincent reassured him, although what exactly they would do, he didn't know. "The ghost wants to divide our forces. Weaken us. At a guess, once he's done toying with those still inside, he'll let us enter."

Toying with—or murdering?

He closed his eyes, saw a body lying dead on the floor. Only this time, the body didn't have Dunne's face, but Henry's.

No. He'd lost too much already.

"We must get inside now," Vincent went on, blinking rapidly. "And do whatever we can."

"How?" Bamforth asked. "Through the servants' entrance, maybe? It's over off the kitchen, not too far from the patio."

"Reyer will have it blocked," Vincent said with grim certainty. They might be able to smash a window, although with the ghost so strong, he wasn't even certain of that.

"What about the root cellar entrance?" Bamforth suggested. "There's a door connecting it with the main basement. We can go through there."

Going into a basement, where it was completely dark, in a house possessed by a ghost, was madness. Utter madness.

"Stay here," Vincent ordered and hoped Bamforth put any quiver in his voice to the cold air. "I'll try the root cellar."

"But—"

"No. It's too dangerous." Vincent's heart had climbed up into his throat, and he tried to swallow it back into position. "Remain here, in case the others manage to escape. If they do, don't let Lizzie go back inside after me."

Bamforth nodded. "I understand."

Vincent went to his bag in the back of the wagon. The last of his stockpile of salt was within, and he hurriedly stuffed as much of it as possible into his pockets. The cellar would be unlit, so he took one of the wagon's lanterns and a packet of matches. Hunching his shoulders against the cold, he made his way around the west side of the house to where the cellar door lay.

Away from the portico, the drifts came above his knees in places. If they didn't leave soon, they'd be trapped here.

It didn't matter at the moment, so Vincent put the thought from his mind. He located the cellar door, shoved accumulated snow from it, then braced himself and tugged on the handle, half expecting it not to open.

The wooden door swung back with a squeal of rusted hinges. Either the ghost's power didn't extend out this far or it wanted someone to come in through this entrance. If the latter, he'd best be on his guard.

Lighting the lantern, Vincent climbed down the wooden steps. Wooden boards groaned beneath his weight, but thankfully held. The pale flame of the lantern barely penetrated the gloom. Stone walls seeped moisture, and the air was only slightly warmer than the freezing temperatures outside. The remains of old shelves lined the walls, along with barrels covered in mold. Thankfully any foodstuffs inside had rotted away too long ago to leave anything in the way of a smell.

At the far end of the root cellar, beneath the house, stood a door set into the stone foundation. Vincent tried the latch, and his heart sank when it opened easily.

A trap. How nice to be expected.

Holding the lantern aloft, he stepped into the basement proper. He'd investigated it with Miss Prandle two days ago and found no trace of spirit activity. Of course, at the time, Reyer hadn't possessed the entire house. The lack of any cold spots or activity before meant nothing today.

The first part of the basement had been used as a wine cellar, and racks filled with dusty bottles turned it into a bit of a maze. Vincent walked slowly, his gaze tracing the shadows, making sure they stayed put or moved as they were supposed to. The hair on the back of his neck pricked, and there came a faint scrape behind him, as if he were being followed.

Rusty nails and blood on the edge of a razor slid across his tongue.

His heart quickened, and he began to walk faster, determinedly fixing his eyes ahead. The basement stair wasn't far, if he could just get through the cellar—

A bottle smashed against the floor behind him. Vincent spun around. The flavor of iron grew stronger in his mouth, and the lantern flame turned sickly blue.

Something flickered in the shadows behind him. A man-shaped blot of darkness not dispersed by the lantern's light as it should have been.

Flicker—it was at the end of the row.

Flicker—it was halfway up the row.

Flicker—almost on him.

Vincent turned and ran.

CHAPTER 20

"JO!" HENRY shouted. "Jo, can you hear me?"

Muffled cries came from behind the featureless wall, followed by the sound of hands pounding frantically.

"Miss Devereaux, help!" Henry called over his shoulder. "They're trapped!"

The gaslight faded from soft yellow to ghastly blue, and the air grew colder by the second. Henry ran his hands over the wall, searching for some catch, some indicator there had ever been a door. "We have to get them out!"

"Stop shouting at me, Mr. Strauss. I can see the situation." Miss Devereaux stepped up to the wall, staring at it with narrowed eyes. "He's strong," she murmured. "To be able to do this, to fool our senses in such a way…it's almost unheard of."

The pounding on the wall increased. "Henry!" came Jo's muffled voice. "Henry, help!"

"I'm coming! Hold on!" He took a step back, casting around frantically. "An ax—there must be an ax or something about. We'll chop through the wall—"

"No need." Miss Devereaux closed her eyes and slid her fingers over the paneling. "The door is still here, even if we can't see it."

"I don't see what good it does us."

"Have you forgotten my talent? Objects speak to me, Mr. Strauss.

And doorways are powerful things." Her hand stilled. "Here."

The spot looked no different than the rest of the wall. "What good does it do to have a door in front of me that I can't open?" he demanded.

"Close your eyes. The door is there, but you can't believe it, because your eyes are lying." She leveled a glare at him. "Do it, Mr. Strauss. Close your eyes, believe the door exists, and break through it if Reyer is holding it shut. It's the only way we'll get them out of there."

For just an instant, he hesitated. He was putting Jo's life in the hands of someone he'd wronged just hours ago, someone he'd caused to receive threats and cruel blows.

Logic, now that he was ready to listen to it, assured him Vincent couldn't have been in on some scheme to trick everyone and kill him with the chandelier. But he still couldn't be sure of Miss Devereaux's innocence in the matter. What if—?

No. He had to trust her. There was no other option if he was to save Jo.

Closing his eyes, he took a step back before kicking the wall as hard as possible.

It didn't open, but something gave beneath the blow. Encouraged, he kicked again and again, agony shooting up his foot as the wound on the sole reopened.

With a loud crash of splintered wood, the door flew open. Jo and Miss Prandle stumbled out into the hall.

Henry pulled his cousin into his arms, holding her tight. She shook against him, and he pressed a kiss into her hair. "It's all right, Jo. You're safe."

"Are you hurt? Either of you?" Miss Devereaux asked.

"N-no. Just frightened." Miss Prandle shivered. "It was toying with us—throwing things."

"Gathering its strength," the medium said. She shook her head. "Our plan has changed. We leave everything here. Nothing in this house is worth our lives."

"Agreed," Henry said. He gave Jo a last squeeze and let her go. "Come—let's meet Vincent and Bamforth out front."

He turned and began to retrace their steps along the balcony, back to the stairs, moving at a quick walk. His nerves pulled tight—if only there was some way to know if the spirit was nearby. But all his equipment was in the schoolroom.

If he survived this, perhaps there was a way to make some sort of portable device…

No. He was done with this madness. Best just to leave and forget it all.

Shouldn't they have reached the stairs by now?

He stopped. They were back by Miss Prandle's door.

"The devil?" Surely he hadn't been so intent he'd missed the stair and walked all the way around the floor? And even if he had, someone else would surely have noticed.

Miss Prandle let out a gasp. "Oh God! It's keeping us here! It's not going to let us go."

She was right. They were trapped on the third floor, with an angry ghost at their backs.

Vincent's shoulder struck one of the wine shelves, sending more bottles crashing to the floor. The smell of spilled wine rose up around him, almost strong enough to mask the flavor of rust. The soaked legs of his trousers adhered to his skin in the freezing air.

His shoes slipped in the spill, and he swore. The flickering shape of Reyer would be on him any instant. He stretched his legs, praying he could run faster than the ghost could siphon energy out of the atmosphere to attack him. The basement stairs appeared at the end of the row, and with a glad cry he made for them. The amulet burned cold against his neck, and every breath excoriated his lungs. His limbs felt heavy, mired in treacle, and the basement seemed to stretch impossibly far in front of him.

Reyer played his tricks again. Vincent firmed his will, whispering a mantra in his mind, the way Dunne had taught him. He wouldn't let the spirit alter his perception, wouldn't let it drag him down into madness and death with it.

The world snapped back into place, the stairs only feet away now.

A flickering shadow shape appeared just in front of them, blocking his path.

Vincent skidded to a halt just as it reached out for him. One shadow hand brushed his right arm, and it was as if he'd plunged the limb up to the elbow into a snow bank. All sensation vanished, replaced by cold that seeped deeper and deeper, creeping into his chest and making for his heart.

He thrust his left hand into his pocket, dug out a handful of salt, and hurled it into the ghost's face.

The apparition stuttered, the pure crystals tearing tiny holes in its ectoplasmic body. Forcing life back into his numb right hand, Vincent dug through both pockets, hurling more salt directly at it.

The apparition vanished in a cloud of smoke smelling of something long dead. Vincent scrambled up the stairs. Reyer's apparition might have been forced to dissipate, but the ghost still controlled the house.

He hurled the last grains of salt at the door, then yanked it open. As he lunged into the kitchen, some force tried to slam the door shut on him. It cracked hard against his hip, but he was already halfway through, and the ghost's attempt to trap him in the basement failed.

He staggered further into the kitchen, rubbing his hip. He'd made it back in the house. Now all he had to do was find the others and get them to the front door.

There came the scrape of a drawer opening. Startled, he turned just in time to see the gleam of a knife blade lifting from the now-open cutlery drawer.

Vincent ducked. The blade thudded into the wall over his head. Crouching low to make himself less of a target, he ran for the door.

A meat cleaver thunked into the floor just in front of him while three knives buried themselves in the huge butcher's block in the center of the kitchen. He ducked out from behind its cover, and pain bloomed as a serving fork stabbed into his shoulder with enough force for the tines to pierce his heavy coat all the way to his skin. He yanked it free and flung it blindly behind him.

More drawers tore open, and he didn't wait to see what they might hold. Gaining the door, he slammed it shut behind him just in time to hear more objects hitting the wood.

Close. And the butler's pantry, with all the china, was between him and the main hall.

He ran flat out, pain stitching up his side, his bruised hip screaming a protest. The sound of exploding glass came from the butler's pantry, but he didn't let it distract him, and an instant later, he burst out into the grand hall.

And collided with someone, sending them both tumbling to the floor.

"Perhaps if we run," Jo suggested.

Ice seemed to wrap around Henry's heart, packing against his ribs with every beat. The ghost was indeed toying with them, like a malicious child ripping the wings from a fly.

"Can we close our eyes, as with the door?" he asked Miss

Devereaux.

She nodded, her loose coil of hair whispering over her shoulder. She looked pale—did her efforts to see through the ghost's lies take some toll from her? "Yes. At least, I think so." She straightened with apparent effort. "Join hands and form a line. I'll lead us out of here."

Henry grasped Jo's hand in his, and she took Miss Prandle's. "Close your eyes, and whatever you do, don't let go," Miss Devereaux ordered as she took Henry's free hand. "If you do, you'll be lost. I have no doubt the ghost is more than capable of separating us from one another."

Henry nodded and closed his eyes. Jo shivered beside him, and he gave her hand a tight squeeze. "We're ready when you are, Miss Devereaux."

It was hard, letting her lead him, trusting his feet not to trip. With no sight to distract him, he became painfully aware of the freezing air on his skin, burning in his nose with every breath. Jo's hand was a like a brand in his, but Miss Devereaux's fingers felt like ice.

His foot caught on something—probably the edge of the carpet runner—and he nearly fell. The medium's hand tightened on his convulsively, but she didn't say anything. Her breathing grew rapid, labored, as if she hauled them behind her up a steep hill.

A finger ran slowly along his cheek.

Henry gasped sharply. "Did—did one of you touch me?"

"No," Jo said, and an instant later, Miss Prandle let out a gasp of her own.

"There's something behind us!"

"Keep going," Miss Devereaux grated out. Her voice was thicker, lower, closer to what Henry supposed her natural tones must be. "It's trying to trick you into letting go."

Fingers pinched Henry's side viciously, even through the layers of his clothing. He winced and tried to ignore the touch.

Nails now. Scraping along the back of his neck. A breath in his ear.

There was something beside him in the hall. Right beside him; he sensed its presence, and if he just opened his eyes, he'd see it looming only inches from his face.

"D-don't look, Jo," he ordered. "Keep going!"

It exhaled again, breath fetid, like a beast's. Maybe it was a beast. A monster, meaning to kill him, and oh God he was going to die, he had to look—

"We're at the stairs," Miss Devereaux said. "Just a few moments longer. Henry, the step is right in front of you."

Gritting his teeth, he fought against the overwhelming sense of menace commanding him to freeze, to look. He felt carefully with his foot, found only air instead of floor, and stepped down.

His ears popped, and warmth flooded back into his limbs. Opening his eyes, he beheld the sweep of stair, the grand hall far below.

"To the door, now," Miss Devereaux said. Ignoring the pain in his foot, Henry pelted down the stairs after her, pulling Jo and Miss Prandle behind him. They reached the grand hall, and Henry let go of their hands.

A dark shape, moving fast, caught the corner of his eye. He didn't even have time to turn before it collided with him.

He struck the floor, sending a jolt of pain through his elbow. Whatever had attacked him was heavy and surprisingly solid, and he managed to throw a glancing blow.

"Henry!" Vincent exclaimed. "Stop, it's me."

Henry blinked stupidly. Vincent lay atop him, their faces only inches apart. His dark hair was in disarray, and he reeked of wine. "Vincent? What are you doing in here?"

Vincent rolled off and staggered to his feet with a wince. "Reyer held the front door closed. I came in through the basement to find you."

Even though Henry knew Vincent didn't mean him in particular, it still warmed his chest foolishly. "Thank you. The spirit tried to trap us on the third floor—we're abandoning our things and meant to leave immediately."

Vincent nodded. "Good idea. Come along."

They made their way toward the vestibule, both Vincent and Henry limping. As they approached, the front door swung open, and Bamforth ducked inside.

"Bamforth?" Miss Prandle asked in surprise. "But the door—"

"It just suddenly opened," he said.

"Reyer must have exhausted himself, at least for the moment," Vincent said. "Working against both me and your group, and holding the house sealed, drained his energies."

"For how long?" Henry asked.

Vincent shrugged, then winced yet again. Blood showed through a small tear in his coat. "Impossible to say. If we're lucky, he won't be able to do anything further in the daylight. Nonetheless, I wouldn't suggest trying to gather our things, just in case. It's not worth the risk."

"Agreed," Miss Prandle said, starting for the door. "Let's be off."

"Forgive me, miss, but I came in to tell you." Bamforth took off his cap and crushed it worriedly between his fingers. "The snow's gotten worse. It's…well, see for yourself."

He swung the door open. Outside, past the edge of the portico, the snow came down in a blinding torrent, so thick and heavy Henry couldn't even see the woods beyond the drive. "It's a blizzard," he said.

"And accumulating fast." Bamforth's face had gone pale. "Unless it stops soon, we'll never make it through to the rail station."

"Then that's it." Vincent exchanged a look with Miss Devereaux. "We're trapped."

Vincent sat in one of the chairs near the great hearth while Lizzie tended the punctures the fork had left in his shoulder. Miss Prandle wept quietly across from them, her arms wrapped around her stomach. Bamforth stood nearby, looking helpless, while Miss Strauss huddled near the fire. Henry had left a short time ago, saying he wanted to look over his equipment in the schoolroom. As if he thought there still might be some chance of saving them.

Outside, the storm continued to rage, snow piling high against the doors and windows. Soon the sun would set, and Reyer would return. Would the ghost take him first, or would he have to see Lizzie and Henry lying dead, just as he'd seen Dunne?

If only that would be the end of it. But even death wouldn't free them from this place. Because there was a new taste on his tongue, of damp cigars. Gladfield's spirit, trapped in the hall where he had died, unable to move on thanks to Reyer.

"There." Lizzie stepped back. "At least you won't be bleeding everywhere now."

Vincent pulled his coat back on, glad for its warmth. Should he tell her? Wouldn't it only make things worse?

But Lizzie deserved his honesty. He indicated the other end of the hall with a nod before standing up and making his way past their silent companions. Gladfield's rug-covered body laid against the wall now, a grim reminder of the fate awaiting them all.

When they were far enough away to have a private conversation, Vincent came to a halt. "I'm sorry," he said, because he didn't know what else to say. "I'm sorry I failed you. If I hadn't let fear get the best of me, the shop wouldn't have foundered, and we wouldn't have been forced to take up Gladfield's ridiculous challenge. And now we're going to die here, and…and I'm sorry."

Lizzie sighed. After a moment, her hand came to rest on his good shoulder. "There's more than enough blame to go around. I clung to the shop as if it would bring Dunne back somehow. As if keeping it meant he wasn't really gone. But the shop isn't him, or us. It's just a place."

"We won't escape, you know. Even after…" Vincent swallowed convulsively. "Gladfield is here. Trapped."

Lizzie closed her eyes and swayed slightly. "Reyer wants not just our lives, but our very souls. And he has the ability to keep us here, with him, forever."

"Yes."

"I see." Lizzie tipped her head back, staring up at the rafters above them. "One of us should see to Mr. Strauss. It isn't safe for him to be alone upstairs."

The anger Vincent had harbored toward Henry had drained away, leaving behind only weariness and a sort of grief for all the things which might have been. "I'll do it."

As he started to turn to the stairs, Lizzie touched his arm, staying him. "Mr. Strauss tried to make amends," she said. "For whatever it may be worth. I will admit I'm not pleased with his actions, but at least he's apologized. I believe he acted out of anger and stupidity, rather than malice."

Vincent frowned. "Why are you telling me this?"

"I just wanted you to know, I think there's hope for him. Or there would have been." She let her hand fall. "He's proud and stubborn to the point of foolishness, yes. But he can learn."

Vincent glanced past Lizzie to where Miss Strauss sat miserably in front of the fireplace. "Thank you, Lizzie." Turning away, he made for the stairs.

CHAPTER 21

"YOU NEVER give up, do you?" Vincent asked.

Startled, Henry turned from where he'd been bent over the equipment, reconnecting the last wires of the phantom fence. Vincent stood in the doorway, his head cocked to one side. A tuft of black hair spilled across his forehead, and his clothing was covered in wine stains, blood, and cobwebs. A bruise darkened one cheek, and his stance favored one leg. And yet somehow Henry found him even more beautiful than before.

Henry gestured vaguely at the table holding the remaining fragments of what had been the work of years. "I have to do something. Have to try."

A tiny smile flexed the corner of Vincent's mouth. "I don't know whether to admire you or think you mad."

"Mad, then. Certainly I've done nothing to admire." Henry turned to the window, unable to look at Vincent as he spoke. Wind whipped the snow into a frenzy, turning the world beyond perfectly white, as if nothing really existed beyond these walls. "We're trapped here, thanks in part to my actions. We can't leave until the storm ends. And it's far more likely Reyer will end us first."

Vincent's soft sigh was barely audible over the groan of the wind around the cornices. "Henry…"

Henry held up his hand. "Don't. I know what I've done. I only…"

"What?" Vincent prompted when he lapsed into silence.

"I just wanted to help people." Henry shook his head miserably. "I wanted to keep anyone else from being taken advantage of, the way my family had been. I wanted to make the world a better place. And now it's all gone wrong." He wrapped his arms around his chest, feeling as if the blizzard outside had crept within. "You say I never give up, but you're wrong. I did give up. On people. On hope." Henry glanced over his shoulder and found Vincent watching him. "On you."

"You had good reason."

"Did I? Clinging to old hurt, like a jilted bride to the gown she never wore." He crossed the room to the window and stared out into the streaming snow. How long did they have until sundown? "When I found out you'd lied about your origins…it was like Isaac all over again."

"I know." The floorboards creaked beneath Vincent's weight as he drew closer. "I should have told you. I intended to last night, after we made love."

No one had ever called it that before, not with him, at any rate. "Oh." Would it have changed things? Henry would still have been hurt, but if they'd had a chance to talk before dawn…

It didn't matter. He'd never know. "Why did you do it?" he asked. "Miss Devereaux said your background wasn't the sort to inspire confidence in men like Mr. Gladfield, but why make up some fairy tale of Indian princesses and medicine men?"

"Why do you think?" Vincent's voice held a bitter edge. "People who look like me are still being killed every day in the West. But here in the East, with the tribes safely dead or contained, we've become 'noble savages.' Magical spirit guides. Fairy tales, as you said, instead of people. Why not take advantage of it? I don't know if I'm Mohican or Iroquois or even Comanche. I don't even know if I have a drop of white blood in my veins. Given my looks, I doubt it, but I suppose it's possible. What choice do I really have but to weave the fantasy my clients want to hear? If saying my father was white, if claiming good missionary folk raised me, it harms no one and allows me to do the work I'm called to do."

"It does hurt someone, though," Henry said. "It hurts you."

"Perhaps." Vincent sighed. "The truth—the entire truth—is that I never knew my parents. At least, as far as I know. There was a young woman—a girl, really—who might have been my mother. Or my older sister, perhaps. She died when I was very young. After, I was on my own. I did whatever it took to survive, from selling newspapers on the corner, to scavenging scrap out of middens, to letting men fuck me for money.

And in the end, yes, I did run a scam, just as your detective found out."

Henry's throat felt tight. No wonder Vincent had invented a happy childhood, safe and cared for. "Vincent, I—"

"Just let me finish." The boards creaked again as Vincent shifted his weight. "I know the scam was wrong. But at the time, it seemed easy. A safe way to make money. A…well, I wouldn't really call him a friend, I suppose. An acquaintance came up with the idea. He pretended to be a medium. I was his 'Indian spirit guide.' During the séance, I'd come out dressed in a loincloth and covered in starch. Say a few sentences in the sort of broken English the audience expected an Indian to use. Then retreat back behind the curtain. Until the day I ended up channeling an actual spirit."

Henry finally found the courage to turn and face Vincent. "That must have been frightening."

Vincent laughed tiredly. "To say the least. But it brought me to Dunne's attention, and despite everything, I can't regret it. He was the first person who really saw me for who I was deep inside."

The ache of raw grief in Vincent's voice drew tears to Henry's own eyes. "You loved him a great deal."

"He was the closest thing I ever had to a father." Vincent's gaze went past him, focusing on the curtain of white beyond the windowpanes. "The first night in his house, I assumed he wanted…what any man who showed interest in a scrawny boy from the streets wanted. But he didn't. He told me I was there to learn, to become the person I was meant to be, not to repeat the past. He said I could be anyone I wanted to." Vincent bowed his head. "I kept my first name, but I chose Night because he always said mediums like us lived on the night side of nature."

God. Henry had made so many mistakes over the last few days, but somehow this cut most deeply of all. He'd hurt Vincent without just cause, as if spreading pain to another would somehow lessen his own. "It's a good name," he said quietly.

"Thank you."

Henry took a step forward, even though his knees trembled. Vincent's gaze slipped from the window and met his, and Henry found he couldn't have looked away even if he'd wished to. "There's nothing I can say to express how terrible I feel about everything," he said. "Please, Vincent. Let me make it up to you. I'll do anything it takes to earn your forgiveness."

Vincent's black eyes seemed to bore into his, to peel back all the protective layers and peer at what lay beneath. For a long moment, he didn't respond, and Henry's heart sank.

Then Vincent stepped forward until they were only inches apart. Lifting his hand, he traced the line of Henry's jaw slowly with his thumb. "Anything?"

Henry's heart beat so hard his hands shook. He licked dry lips, saw Vincent's gaze shift to track his tongue. "Anything."

A slow smile bloomed over Vincent's mouth. "Well. Perhaps I'll take you up on your offer, Mr. Strauss."

The kiss was tender, slow. A gentle caress of lips, followed by tongues and heat. Henry's hands threaded through Vincent's hair, and Vincent slid his arms around Henry in return.

When they finally parted, Vincent drew back only far enough to rest his forehead against Henry's. "That felt like a promise," he whispered.

Henry drew in a deep, trembling breath. "It was." With a sigh, he stepped back reluctantly. "You've given me a second chance. I'm not going to die here and miss out on it, Reyer be damned." He gestured to his equipment. "There must be something we can do—some vulnerability we can exploit."

Vincent tossed back his head and laughed. "You really *don't* give up, do you? Very well—you've convinced me. What do we have available to us?"

Henry contemplated the equipment. "The Wimshurst machine is destroyed, but it isn't as if we wanted to give Reyer more energy anyway. The dispeller is also beyond all hope of repair. Leaving us with the phantom fence, Franklin bells, and the ghost grounder." He glanced at Vincent. "And of course you and Miss Devereaux."

"So you admit a medium may have his or her use after all?" Vincent asked archly.

The memory of the distorted hallway, the blank wall, the unfindable stairs, came forcefully back. "Yes," Henry said, though the word stuck in his throat. "Whatever my theories may have been before coming here, I think I can safely say that mediums are indeed needed."

Vincent offered him a small bow. "And I shall admit your science has things to offer as well." His expression sobered. "If something like the ghost grounder had been available to Dunne when the spirit possessed me last summer…"

"There's no knowing, either way," Henry said softly. "But if it helps, this time we do have options."

"Yes." Vincent's expression firmed. "Reyer died in the tower, I'm almost certain of it. It's his point of greatest connection to this side of the veil. He'll be at his strongest there…but possibly his most vulnerable as well."

"Perhaps we can drain him there?" Henry suggested. "Take the grounder to the top of the tower, secure it to the lightning rod on the roof?"

"How do we get him to manifest at the top of the tower?"

"Remove all his other choices?" Henry suggested. He gestured at the room. "He couldn't reach us in here, thanks to Martha. If we put Jo, Miss Prandle, and Bamforth here, surely Reyer will come to us at the top of the tower as the easier target."

"Perhaps." Vincent touched the front of his shirt, over where the amulet lay. "I want you and Lizzie to stay here with them."

"What?" Henry's brows snapped together. "Why would you suggest such a thing? Don't you trust me?"

"I do." Vincent looked away. "But I had to watch Dunne die already. If I had to watch you die as well…I can't. I won't."

"I'm not going to die," Henry said firmly. "I know you're afraid, but I'm coming with you, and that's the end of it."

"Henry—"

"So you propose to use your talents against Reyer *and* wield the ghost grounder at the same time?" Henry arched a brow. "That will be an interesting trick. I'd like to see it for myself."

Vincent glared at him. "Stop being logical. It's distracting."

"Admit it. We're going to have to work together if we're to have any chance of success." Moving closer, Henry laid a hand on Vincent's chest. He felt the other man's heartbeat, steady beneath layers of cloth and skin, muscle and bone. "I know you want to protect me. But do you really think I'm going to cower here while you go off to almost certain death in an attempt to fix the problem I helped create? We *have* met, haven't we?"

Vincent snorted, but the smile was back. "Point taken. But I want you to set up the phantom fence. If I tell you to retreat inside its protection, do it. No arguments."

Henry nodded reluctantly. "Agreed. We still haven't come up with a way to keep the ghost from draining the batteries, though."

"Dump salt over their container." Vincent shrugged. "Reyer won't be able to reach them, and we'll still have a protective circle which can't be blown away or dissolved by the blizzard."

A slow smile spread over Henry's face. "Brilliant."

"I have my moments."

Henry tipped back his head for a kiss. "Indeed you do."

Only a short time later, Henry stood at the base of the tower stairs, the pieces of the phantom fence held loosely in his arms.

They'd moved as quickly as possible given the sun was slipping rapidly toward the horizon, somewhere on the other side of the heavy snow clouds. Once it set, Reyer's full wrath would be unleashed at last.

Miss Devereaux had made a single alteration to their plan when they explained it to her. "We can't leave everyone else unprotected," she'd said. "If you fail to remove Reyer, or if Martha can't hold him back from the schoolroom, they'll be in desperate straits."

Henry put one arm around Jo's shoulders and hugged her. "What do you suggest?"

"Either Vincent or I have to stay here."

"You," Vincent said. When she started to protest, he added, "If Reyer starts playing tricks with the house again, you're better able to lead everyone else outside."

Where they would most likely perish in the blizzard anyway. But no one pointed that out.

Miss Devereaux sighed and pinched the bridge of her nose. "You're right," she said grudgingly. "But you'd better not get yourself killed, Vincent."

He smiled wryly. "Trust me, I have no desire to end up trapped here with the rest of the dead. We'd best get started."

"Henry…" Jo clung to him, her eyes wide.

God. What would happen to her if he died here? "The shop is yours if I don't return," he said rapidly. "Don't let anyone tell you otherwise. Hire a lawyer if need be, because my will is absolutely clear."

"No, don't." Her fingers gripped his arm hard enough to leave bruises. "Please—maybe we can—can stay in the schoolroom, all of us, together."

"I don't think Martha Reyer's spirit is strong enough to hold against the ghost until midnight," Vincent said, but his voice was gentle.

"I'll be all right, Jo." Henry hoped it wasn't a lie. He pulled her to him and kissed her forehead. "I love you. I'm sorry I said what I did, about sending you to Emma. I'd never do that, no matter what."

She smiled wanly. "That's what Mr. Night said."

"Mr. Night is a smart man." He let go of her. "Do what Miss Devereaux tells you, without question."

She wiped her eyes with the back of her hand as she drew back. "I-I will. I promise."

"Good girl."

Still, it was hard turning his back and leaving her there. Not knowing if it was the last time he'd ever set eyes on her. Trusting her safety to a ghost, of all things.

A ghost he'd weakened by draining the cold spot outside the schoolroom. There might have been some mistake Henry hadn't made over the last few days, but the list of those he had was depressingly thorough.

Except for kissing Vincent. That at least hadn't been an error.

Now he joined Vincent at the base of the tower stair. Icy air poured down from above, along with stray flakes of snow fluttering down from the open room at the top of the tower. The blizzard's bite was keen enough to penetrate even Henry's thick coat and scarf, let alone his gloves and hat. "Reyer can just stay back and let us freeze to death," he muttered.

"You have a point," Vincent agreed. His breath smoked like a dragon's. "Come on—and let's try not to slip on an icy stair and break our necks."

"Do you really think Gladfield's spirit is trapped here now?" Henry asked as they started up.

"I know it." Vincent said over his shoulder. "He tastes like a damp cigar."

"Wonderful. If we die…"

"Yes." Vincent paused and glanced down. "We'll be trapped here, on this side of the veil, until someone else comes along to deal with Reyer. Or the house is torn down or disintegrates. Possibly not even then—there are plenty of accounts of spirits associated with structures which no longer exist."

A shudder ran through Henry. What would it be like? What *had* it been like, for Martha Reyer and the poor maid and possibly Reyer's children as well? Year after year, trapped with the madman who had killed them…

It couldn't happen to Jo. He wouldn't allow it.

The structure of the tower meant the steps remained clear of snow until they were almost at the top. Henry moved cautiously as possible, making certain of his footing until the stairs finally yielded to the uppermost floor of the tower.

A waist-high balustrade encircled the room. Above, heavy beams groaned in the wind, and Henry fancied the sound echoed the creak of the rope Reyer had used to hang himself. The sky beyond the eaves was dark with clouds and the fading sunlight, and snow still poured thickly down.

They attached the wires of the ghost grounder to the lightning rod affixed to outermost point of the tower. Once it was in place, Vincent hurriedly began to scoop the drifts of snow from the tower floor, flinging them over the side. Henry put down his equipment and did the same, and soon they had a space cleared. Thanks to the broken posts, the phantom fence wouldn't be level—but with any luck it wouldn't matter.

While Henry began to set up the fence, Vincent took a step toward the lone solid wall, where the tower abutted the steeply pitched roof.

"Do you think the secret passage lets out here?" he asked. "Because if so, I'd like to find it. I don't want to give anything the chance to pop out at our backs."

"You'd best look for it while I finish setting up," Henry said with a shiver.

Vincent pulled his gloves off and trailed his brown hands over the wall, probing the cracks between stones. Henry turned his attention back to the phantom fence. The wires were low enough now in places that it could be stepped over easily, and he hoped it would still work. Perhaps some of the sigils Miss Devereaux had drawn yesterday would have made it more effective…but it was too late to worry about that now.

When he was done, he put the battery in place. It was carefully positioned inside the fence, where the ghost *wouldn't* be. Still, he put a bag of salt down beside it. If the damage to the fence allowed the ghost inside, a quick application of salt would at least prevent Reyer from siphoning energy from the battery again. The wires which would connect the battery to the fence he left unhooked for now.

There came a soft click and the grinding sound of stone on stone. Vincent stepped back from the wall, a grin on his face. "Found it."

The doorway was narrow and irregularly shaped, relying on the crevices between the stones to disguise it. When nothing emerged from the other side, Vincent took a cautious step in. "Huh. There's some sort of chest in here. Several of them."

"What's inside?" Perhaps some clue as to whoever had been using the passageways?

"It looks as though they used to be locked, but someone broke into them. The scratches on the metal are fresh." There came the creak of unoiled hinges. A moment later, Vincent let out a low whistle. "Henry. Light the lantern and come look at this."

Henry joined him in the narrow space. The pale illumination of the lantern gleamed off a mass of gold coins filling the small chest to the brim. Vincent ran his hand through them, letting them fall slowly back into place. "Double eagles."

Henry's heart beat faster at the sight of such wealth, even though he had no claim to it. "I suppose we know what became of the fortune Reyer hid," he said.

From behind him, there came the unmistakable sound of a pistol's hammer clicking back. "Indeed," Bamforth said. "And that's why I have to make certain you die here."

CHAPTER 22

"**TURN AROUND** slowly, with your hands where I can see them," Bamforth ordered.

Henry's heart pounded in his throat as he complied. Bamforth stood at the top of the tower stairs, his pistol trained on them. His face was pale, but his mouth was set in a determined line. Snow swirled around him, clinging to the cold iron of the barrel.

"Move away from the door," Bamforth said, motioning with the gun. Not knowing what else to do, Henry complied. Vincent stood, still in the passage. Was he frozen in shock, or did he weigh his chances of escape?

If the thought had occurred to him, he didn't act on it. He followed Henry, but slowly, putting space between them. Making it harder for Bamforth to aim at them both at once.

"Hurry it up, redskin," Bamforth snapped.

Fear tightened Henry's throat, and his mind raced wildly. Of all those he'd suspected, Bamforth had never been a serious candidate. "Bamforth?" he asked past the icy lump in his chest. "You were the one trying to frighten us? You tried to kill me with the chandelier?"

"Of course. It was your fault Mr. Gladfield wouldn't leave." Bamforth moved to the parapet, where he could more easily train the gun on them both. Snowflakes swirled down, sticking to the shoulders of his coat. "The mediums were done with this place, and if you'd refused to continue, Mr. Gladfield would have had no choice but to give up. A few months from now, I would return, load up the gold, and disappear. But you and your stupid insistence on 'fixing' things wrecked my plan."

"How did you know?" Vincent's voice was almost casual, as if they spoke in front of the fire in the grand hall. "About the passageways, I mean."

Bamforth's attention fixed on Vincent. Hoping he wasn't about to get them both killed, Henry edged slowly to his left. If they could only get into position to flank Bamforth, perhaps they stood a chance.

"I already told you—my aunt was the children's tutor," Bamforth said. "She learned of the secret passages by accident. Reyer would have killed her if she'd spoken of them while he lived, but in later years the bottle loosened her tongue. I was always her favorite, so she told me about them. It didn't take a great leap of reasoning to imagine they might hold the secret to his missing fortune. After coming into Mr. Gladfield's employ, I did my best to encourage him to do something with the property. When he sent me ahead to prepare it for the contest, you can imagine I spent every spare moment searching for the fortune. As soon as I found it, I scared away the silly women I'd hired to help clean, to add to the mystique of the place."

"Why try to frighten us into leaving? Were you afraid one of us would find the treasure as well?" Vincent asked. He didn't glance at Henry, who continued to edge further and further left.

"In part," Bamforth admitted. "And if you succeeded in ridding this place of ghosts, Gladfield would have had a crew here in a matter of days, renovating it for his grand scheme. I needed time to come back and retrieve the gold. Convincing everyone the place wasn't worth the trouble seemed the safest bet. If you had just left…but you didn't, and now I'm forced to kill you."

The gun swung around, and Henry found himself staring into the black bore. A single snowflake clung to the cold metal. "And don't think I haven't noticed what you're doing, Strauss. Hold. Still."

Damn. "What about the others?" Henry asked hurriedly. "How did you get away from them?"

"I didn't." Bamforth smiled grimly. "I served them coffee."

Oh God. "You poisoned them." Not Jo, please, not Jo.

"Damn you," Vincent growled. Bamforth pointed the pistol at him again.

"Don't be dramatic. I sedated them and left them safely in the schoolroom. I'll have plenty of time to see to them once I'm done with the two of you." Bamforth grinned. "Miss Prandle in particular—so high and mighty. She thinks she's above me. Maybe once I'm done with her, I'll have a turn with the nig—"

Henry hurled himself at Bamforth with a howl of rage. His hands closed on Bamforth's arm, yanking it back to keep the gun pointed away from Vincent. Vincent dove at Bamforth as well, and the three of them struggled, feet slipping in the skim of ice and snow on the floor. Henry clung doggedly to Bamforth's wrist. How dare he threaten Jo, how dare —

Bamforth abruptly stopped struggling. As Henry was still tugging on his arm, it had the effect of yanking Bamforth's wrist violently toward him. The butt of the gun impacted his forehead, and Henry's grip loosened.

Just as Bamforth had no doubt intended. Bamforth wrenched his arm free. Vincent grunted as the man kicked him in the belly. The medium's feet slipped, and he went to the floor, crying out. His mouth twisted into an ugly expression, Bamforth brought his gun to bear on Vincent once again.

"Die, you filthy redskin."

Henry caught Bamforth about the waist in a flying tackle. His weight and momentum shoved Bamforth heavily back against the parapet. Bamforth's eyes widened in alarm, arms windmilling to keep himself from going over.

Two things happened at once. Bamforth's foot slipped on the ice, and he toppled back, his body plunging into the swirl of the blizzard with a strangled scream.

And pain exploded in Henry's shoulder as the gun went off.

"Henry!" The scream ripped free of Vincent's throat, competing with the fading roar of the gun as Henry slumped against the parapet. Blood reddened the shoulder of his coat and dripped onto the snow-covered floor.

Vincent went to his knees by Henry, barely catching him from collapsing entirely onto the icy stones. "V-Vincent?" Henry mumbled. His pupils were wide, his gaze unfocused. "It hurts."

"I know." Damn Bamforth. If any soul was doomed to suffer here with Reyer forever, it ought to be his.

But none of it—Reyer or the trapped souls or the coming sunset—seemed half as important as the bleeding man in his arms.

"You have to get up," he said urgently. "We need to get you inside, where we can bind the wound."

Henry moaned, and the sound wrung Vincent's heart. Hoping he wasn't causing Henry even more pain, he managed to get the other man to his feet. "That's it," Vincent murmured, half carrying Henry toward the stairs. "W-we'll get you patched up in no time. You'll be fine."

The last light of the sun vanished, plunging them into darkness except for the lantern.

The flame instantly turned blue. At the same moment, the taste of rusty iron nails flooded Vincent's mouth.

Reyer had come.

They'd lost. There was no time left. Nowhere to flee, and no protection from the evil coming for them.

Vincent's foot connected with something in the rapidly accumulating snow, and he almost fell. Glancing down, he saw a half-buried pole from Henry's phantom fence.

The fence.

Not allowing himself to think, Vincent dragged Henry into the protective circle, hefting him bodily over the wires. As the air around them grew colder and colder, he let Henry slump into the snow while he scrabbled for the ends of the wires. Where were they? The battery?

A dark shape emerged from the open door of the secret passageway.

There—his shaking hands found first one wire, then the other, beneath the snow. Glowing eyes fixed on him, and corrupted ectoplasm coalesced as the ghost rushed toward them.

Vincent hooked the leads to the battery, and the fence came to life.

Reyer's ghost recoiled. A howl of fury echoed in the rafters above them.

"It worked," Vincent gasped through chattering teeth. "Look, Henry—your fence worked."

Henry made no reply. He lay on his side in the gathering snow, skin chalky white and shoulder red with blood.

No. No, this couldn't be happening. Henry would sit up at any moment and laugh, proclaim he'd known all along science would save them at the last.

But he didn't.

Vincent dragged Henry's limp form half into his lap. "Your fence worked," he said again. "I've got you. We're safe in here."

Henry shivered against him, eyes fluttering open. "I'm cold," he whispered.

Vincent swallowed, and his throat ached, from cold or fear or grief, he didn't know. "It's going to be all right," he lied.

Henry licked pale lips. "Do you promise?"

How could he? Reyer prowled just outside the fence. Henry's survival—*their* survival—meant getting back inside. Past the ghost and into the warmth.

But he had no way of accomplishing that.

The astringent taste of lavender joined the tang of rusty nails.

Reyer growled again, a low, animal sound. The snow swirled madly, and in its shifting curtain, Vincent just made out a woman's form standing on the other side of the fence. "I told you to leave," she said to him sadly.

Of course. It wasn't just Reyer's death anniversary, after all. It was Martha's as well.

"I can't defeat him alone," she said as if hearing Vincent's thoughts. "I'm stronger than I have been in a long time, but it isn't enough."

"That's right." Reyer's voice was like the scrape of metal on stone, grating and ugly. "You're mine. All mine. As is everyone in this house."

Including Henry, unless…

Unless Martha had another source of strength to draw from, to give her enough energy to defeat her husband.

Such as the energy of a medium.

For a moment, his entire body felt numb, as if his flesh couldn't bear even the thought. Then Henry shifted slightly in his lap, eyes squinting in confusion behind the lenses of his spectacles. "Vincent?"

"Who are you?" Lizzie had asked him the day she'd received the letter from Gladfield. But he'd been too afraid at the time to answer her.

The numbness faded. He'd failed Dunne. Failed himself.

But he'd be damned if he'd fail Henry.

Vincent gently shifted Henry off his lap. Bending down, he kissed Henry's cold lips with all the tenderness he could muster. "Yes, Henry," he whispered. "I promise."

He stood up and faced the two ghosts. Even as Martha turned toward him, he ripped the amulet free from his neck. For the first time in six months, he let it fall to the floor.

"My name is Vincent Night," he told her. "And I'm the best damned medium on the East Coast."

Vincent stepped over the perimeter of the fence, opening his mental barriers wide. Martha rushed toward him—

And then she *was* him.

~ * ~

Rage and grief swirled through Vincent, but it belonged to someone else.

Martha.

Wasted life. Wasted years of torment in this house, before and after death. Accusations and screams: *"Whose are they? Who have you slept with, whore?"*

"No one, no one! The children are yours!"

"They will be."

Vincent's eyes opened—or rather, Martha opened them. In her sight, Reyer was a blotch of darkness on the world, but no longer featureless as a shadow. He'd not been a handsome man in life, and death had made him into something terrible. His mouth gaped into a maw lined with rusted iron nails, and jagged spikes of metal erupted from his arms and legs. Glass and stone formed both clothing and flesh, the house around them a part of him, or he a part of it.

Hungry, glowing eyes fixed on Vincent—no, on Martha. "You think to hide inside his skin?" her husband asked, nail-teeth clattering. "But in truth, you only make it all the easier to reach you."

Reyer lunged at them, his hands tipped with jagged glass claws, but Martha was ready. Vincent's body was her puppet; as if from a distance, he felt her lift his left hand. Ectoplasm flowed free, leached from his body, coiling in long, sticky strands around Reyer's arms.

The spirit let out a roar of outrage and tried to pull away. Never hesitating, Martha grasped the ghost grounder with Vincent's right hand, bringing it up and stabbing it like a sword directly into her husband's heart.

"Vincent!" Henry cried even as Vincent stepped out over the fence. But his lover was long past hearing him.

Henry hurt, his entire existence centered around the blaze of agony replacing his left shoulder. A terrible thirst gripped him, his mouth and throat parched as a desert. No strength seemed to remain in any limb, and a numb cold had set in, soaking all the way to his bones.

But Vincent was in danger—that much he understood. He forced his head up just in time to see the spirit of Martha Reyer step toward Vincent…and vanish into him.

Vincent's body jerked like a glove with a hand thrust into it. Henry caught sight of his eyes rolled so far back in his head only the whites showed.

"No," Henry whispered and tried to lever himself up out of the snow. But no strength remained in either arm. He collapsed against the icy stones with a whimper.

The writhing black shadow, which must have been Reyer, rushed at Vincent. For a horrible moment Henry wondered if it was possible for both spirits to possess the medium at once. Then Vincent's hand snapped out.

Writhing tendrils of glowing ectoplasm unfurled, lashing around Reyer. Binding him in place just long enough for Vincent to scoop up the ghost grounder from where Henry had left it.

A subsonic roar rattled Henry's teeth as Vincent, or the spirit possessing him, impaled Reyer on the copper rod. The blizzard became a hurricane, wind blasting the snow into icy slivers, scouring flesh and stone alike. Henry fought the urge to curl up on himself, to hoard what little heat he had left in his body.

The ghost grounder seemed to be working, the black mass growing less and less substantial. A shimmering haze sprang up around Vincent. "No," the medium said, not in his voice, but a woman's. "This ends now!"

Her ectoplasmic coils appeared to grow weaker. Was the copper rod draining Martha as well? Not as rapidly, perhaps, if she had Vincent's energy to draw from, but fast enough. If she couldn't hold Reyer, if he escaped again, they would have lost their final chance to stop him.

Henry had to do something. Even his brain felt numb, but he fought against his sluggish thoughts. There had to be some weapon, some tactic. Blinking rapidly, he willed his eyes to focus.

The bag of salt still sat beside the uncovered battery.

Forcing himself to move, even though the pain made him dizzy, Henry fumbled at the wires connecting the battery to the fence. They came loose easily.

The field was down. Nothing now stood between Reyer and the batteries.

Reyer seemed to sense the change. Spotting the same energy source he'd used so easily before, the dark mass tore free of the last coils of ectoplasm and rushed eagerly toward the battery.

Henry used the last of his strength to fling the entire bag of salt onto the ghost.

Reyer's misty form shredded into a dozen strands. Vincent and Martha pounced from behind, taking advantage of the injury the salt had dealt. Ectoplasmic coils caught hold of Reyer's form just as it began to coalesce.

And jerked it back. Into Vincent.

Vincent's body arched, going up on his toes, back curving like a contortionist. There came a flash of light that Henry sensed more than saw with his physical eyes.

Vincent collapsed to the floor and lay there unmoving.

"Vincent?" Henry whispered.

No response. No movement.

It took most of Henry's remaining strength to drag himself to Vincent's side. "Vincent?" he asked, his voice cracking. It couldn't end like this, could it? Dying here together atop the tower?

He touched his fingers to Vincent's cheek, but his own skin was so numb from the cold he couldn't tell whether or not Vincent was warm. "Please don't. Don't leave me here. Not when I've just found you."

Vincent's eyelids fluttered.

Henry gasped, hardly daring to believe his senses. Vincent blinked again and turned his head with a moan. For a moment, his black eyes didn't seem to register Henry at all. Then they widened.

"Henry!" Vincent sat up—or tried to. Bracing himself on one elbow, he winced. "I'm a bit on the weak side. Just give me a moment. Are you all right?"

Henry laughed even though it wasn't funny. "Do you mean other than having a hole through my shoulder and being scared to death for you?"

"We have to get you inside immediately." This time, Vincent managed to get to his feet. "Here. Let me help you."

Vincent more carried him than anything else, but somehow, they made it to the stairwell. "Is Reyer gone?" Henry asked to distract himself from the pain in his shoulder. "Truly gone?"

"Yes. Martha weakened him enough to drag him into the otherworld with her. Without a summoning from this side, he's gone for good." Vincent pressed a kiss to the side of Henry's face, his lips hot against Henry's chilled skin. "The spirits he kept trapped here will be able to move on as well. Thanks to you. If you hadn't thought to use the salt, I don't think we could have defeated him."

Despite everything, a certain warmth fought its way through the haze of exhaustion and pain. "I'm just glad it worked," Henry said, leaning his head against the solidity of Vincent's shoulder. "Now let's get down the stairs before I pass out."

CHAPTER 23

HENRY CHECKED the address one final time before entering the apartment building. As he'd committed it to memory days ago, the recheck was more a delaying tactic than anything. Even though he and Vincent had parted on civil terms, after everything that had happened at Reyhome Castle, he wasn't certain of his reception.

A month had passed since that dark night. Fortunately the blizzard had ceased the next day, and a spell of warm weather meant Jo and Lizzie had gone for help shortly thereafter. By then, Henry had grown feverish from the wound in his shoulder. The prodding of the doctors from town, the journey back to the railway station, had all passed in a haze.

The bullet had broken his collarbone, but fortunately missed the great artery. He still wore a sling to keep his shoulder as immobile as possible, and the journey to New York from Baltimore had left him with a dull, throbbing pain in the healing wound. But he hadn't dared to put off the trip any longer.

Of course, he could have wired instead. Except he'd been too afraid of receiving only silence as an answer.

Taking a deep breath, he forced his feet to carry him into the apartment building. Although not one of the slum tenements, it was clear the building's occupants weren't precisely well-to-do, either. The scent of sauerkraut and boiled greens drifted from the communal kitchen, and a polyglot of accents and languages streamed through the thin walls.

Vincent's apartment lay on the third floor, at least according to the information the detective had sent. Henry stopped outside the door, heart pounding from more than the climb.

What if Vincent had moved? What if he wasn't in? What if he was in, but slammed the door in Henry's face?

What if he was in, but had someone else with him?

"Go see him," Jo had said two days ago when Henry had been dithering yet again as to whether he should buy a train ticket. "I'll stay with my friend Millie for a few days. Her mother won't mind. Anything to get you to stop moping."

"I'm not moping."

"Pining, then." Jo had rolled her eyes. "You miss him. I'm sure he misses you. So stop being such a coward and *go*."

"I'm not a coward," Henry muttered to himself now. Except the fact that he was still standing in the hall, afraid of facing the worst, said otherwise.

Only one thing for it. Squaring his shoulders—and wincing at the resulting flash of pain in the left—Henry knocked sharply on the door.

For a long moment, he thought no one was home. Then the sound of footsteps approached from inside the apartment. The door swung open, and there stood Vincent, in his shirtsleeves and vest, looking just as he had when they'd parted a month ago.

"Henry?" Vincent asked in surprise. "What the devil are you doing here?"

Every suave answer he'd come up with on the train ride deserted him. "Please, don't slam the door in my face," Henry blurted out. "I have a proposal for you. Just—just hear me out."

Vincent leaned against the doorframe, head cocked quizzically. Without a coat to hide his form, his trousers shaped his hips and thighs nicely. The pristine white of his shirt contrasted with his bronze skin, and his black hair glinted in the light. Every iota of desire Henry had felt over those long days at Reyhome Castle came rushing back.

But Vincent wasn't inviting Henry inside. And his expression remained carefully neutral. Was Henry too late? Or had there ever been a chance to start with?

"I've found only one way to keep you from talking," Vincent said. "And as it isn't appropriate for a public hallway, I suppose I'll have to hear you out."

Henry flushed. Was Vincent only goading him, or did the sight of Henry affect him, as he did Henry? "Can we at least step inside?"

Vincent considered for what felt like an eternity. Then he stepped back and beckoned Henry to follow. As soon as Henry was inside, Vincent shut the door and leaned against the wall, blocking him from coming in any further. "We're inside. So talk."

Carelessly heaped clothes and piles of books made the tiny apartment seem even smaller. The scent of cooking food was muted by the walls, replaced by the smell of Vincent's citrusy cologne. A lone door opened off onto what must have been a bedroom, and Henry noticed the large bag of salt sitting on the floor beside it.

"I didn't realize Miss Prandle meant to send the entire prize to me," Henry said. "When it showed up in my bank account, I wired her in protest. She said she had to respect her uncle's wishes."

"Congratulations," Vincent said. "Our prize was to not be reported to the police, on the condition we closed the shop."

"Oh." Damn Miss Prandle. "I'm sorry. I didn't know."

"It was only a place." Vincent shrugged. "No matter what it meant to us…well. Dunne wouldn't have wanted us to sacrifice everything to hold onto it. I'm only sorry it took us this long to realize it. At any rate, Lizzie and I are still in business together. I've even started channeling again."

"Good," Henry said. "I'm proud of you."

Vincent looked surprised. "Oh?"

"Well, yes." Henry shuffled his feet. "I know how much your gifts mean to you. Even I could tell you weren't happy not using them. So yes. I'm proud."

"Thank you." Vincent shifted his weight. "So why did you come? Or did you have other business in the city and decided to visit me in hopes of spending the night?"

"Of course not." Henry wasn't certain if he was more angered or hurt by the words. "I can't speak for you, but our time together meant more to me than that."

Vincent had the grace to look embarrassed. "Forgive me. You said you had a proposition…?"

Now came the hard part. Henry drew in a deep breath. "I want to make an offer to you and Miss Devereaux. I decided to come to you alone, at least to begin with, because frankly I fear what Miss Devereaux might do to me should I dare darken her doorstep."

"Wise man." Vincent's expression eased into a cautious smile. "I don't think she's forgiven you yet. What is this offer of yours?"

"We can split the prize money three ways," Henry said. "No strings attached. Or…or we can pool the money and use it to open a new business. One combining the best of all our talents."

He'd managed to catch Vincent by surprise yet again. "Go into business?" Vincent repeated. "Together? I thought your fondest wish was to replace mediums, not work with them."

Henry shrugged awkwardly, remembering to only use his right shoulder this time. "The events at Reyhome Castle showed me the error of my ways. When we worked separately, we both obtained some results. But when we worked together, science and spiritualism, we were far more effective."

Vincent still stared at Henry as if he thought it some elaborate prank. "But what about your plans to start production on the Electro-Séance? The phantom fence and all the rest of it?"

"I still have hope my inventions can be of use to others. But given our experiences, I think they're best used in tangent with a medium. Someday I—we—might be able to move beyond the prototypes, but as for now, I've given up on the idea of mass production." Henry bit his lip. "So…what do you think? You believe my inventions might have some value, don't you? I understand you and Miss Devereaux may wish to remain in New York—Jo and I can relocate. Or we can all cut ties with the past and start anew somewhere else."

Vincent's lip twitched in a grin. "You've thought all this through, haven't you?"

"Of course." Henry swallowed nervously. "I made mistakes at Reyhome. I was too proud, too quick to assume deliberate injury when I found out about your past. I was a blind fool at times. And if you can't forgive me, I'll happily split the money, and—"

"Yes," Vincent said.

Henry's heart sank. "Of course. I'll have the bank draw up a check tomorrow."

Vincent snorted. "Not yes to the money, you fool. Yes to you. To working together."

"Oh?" Henry couldn't seem to catch his breath. "Do you mean it? And what about Miss Devereaux?"

"Yes, I mean it." Vincent reached out and took Henry's good hand. "If we'd had your ghost grounder last summer, perhaps Dunne wouldn't have died. Without the grounder and your quick thinking atop the tower, I'd certainly be just another spirit trapped in Reyhome Castle."

"You're the one who realized there was more than one spirit in the first place," Henry said, tightening his grip on Vincent's hand. "Or that one of them was dangerous. Your ability to channel, Miss Devereaux's automatic writing, and my instruments—"

"Are a powerful combination we can't achieve separately," Vincent agreed. "As for Lizzie, let me explain things to her. I'm sure she'll come around."

"I'm prepared to grovel," Henry assured him.

"That will help." Vincent's expression turned serious, his dark eyes gazing solemnly down at Henry. "The night on the tower, you could have left the phantom fence up. Stayed safe behind it. Instead, you risked everything to save me."

"You're the one who put me inside the fence and then went out to face the ghosts by yourself," Henry countered. He swallowed thickly. "It was one of the bravest things I've ever seen anyone do."

"Desperate, perhaps."

"Brave," Henry insisted. "Just as it took courage to come there in the first place, to guard Miss Devereaux from what you feared awaited. To remain even when I'd given you every cause to leave me to my fate." He looked down at their joined fingers, a latticework of copper and ivory. "A man like you doesn't come along every day. Even if you hadn't agreed to go into business together, I would have wanted to find some way of-of remaining friends. Lovers, if you'll have me."

Vincent's grin turned wicked. "Hmm...you've convinced me of the business part of your proposition. I think I still need persuading as to the rest." He stepped back in the direction of the bedroom, drawing Henry after. "I think you'll have to make your case again, at least once. Possibly more."

Henry's face felt as if it couldn't contain his smile. "Don't worry," he said. "I'm willing to dedicate all night to the task."

ABOUT THE AUTHOR

JORDAN L. HAWK grew up in North Carolina and forgot to ever leave. Childhood tales of mountain ghosts and mysterious creatures gave her a life-long love of things that go bump in the night. When she isn't writing, she brews her own beer and tries to keep her cats from destroying the house. Her best-selling Whyborne & Griffin series (beginning with *Widdershins*) can be found in print, ebook, and audiobook at Amazon and other online retailers.

If you're interested in receiving Jordan's newsletter and being the first to know when new books are released, plus getting sneak peeks at upcoming novels, please sign up at her website:

http://www.jordanlhawk.com

Made in the USA
San Bernardino, CA
02 June 2017